# GRAND FREEDOM
## Paragraph 175 & How It Affected A Gay Man's Life

# Also by RODION REBENYAR

**BOYS ON PURPOSE**
Poems, Prose and Short Stories with
Decidedly Gay Overtones
(illustrated)

**THE CHOICES WE MADE**
Story of Gay Friendship,
Love and Tragedy

**FELLOW TRAVELLER**
Whimsical Poems, Prose and
Short Stories about a
Gay Man's Adventures

**FIGHTING FOR LUCHO**
A Gay Man's Struggle Begins

**WILLIAM GERHARDT**
A Story Largely Untold

# GRAND FREEDOM

Paragraph 175 & How
It Affected
A Gay Man's Life

by

# RODION REBENYAR

Contains Many Photos and Illustrations

**Fair Haired
Boy Press**

Copyright 2015 by Richard S. Podnar

This book is a work of fiction. References to real people, events, establishments, organizations or locales are intended only to provide a sense of authenticity and are used fictitiously. All other characters, incidents and dialogue are drawn from the author's imagination
and are not to be construed as real.

All rights reserved. This book may not be reproduced in whole or in part without written permission from the publisher in any form except in the case of brief passages used for review, nor may any part of this book be reproduced, stored in a retrieval system or transmitted in any form or by electronic, mechanical, photocopying, recording or other means without written permission from the publisher.

Cover design provided by Createspace.com

All artwork and photos,
including front cover design and frontispiece,
are in public domain.

ISBN-13 978-1502444103
ISBN-10 1502444100
First printing October 2015

Printed in the United States of America

In memory of our "Pink Triangle"
sisters and brothers who perished, and
dedicated to the survivors who could not or
would not speak about the horror and
injustice perpetrated against them.
This is their voice.

**CONTENTS**

Chapter One   AFTER THE FACT   1

Chapter Two   WIEDERSDORF BLUES   5

Chapter Three   DIFFERENT WAVELENGTHS   13

Chapter Four   A FIRST TIME FOR EVERYTHING   20

Chapter Five   FULFILLED AND UNFULFILLED   30

Chapter Six   PROPOSALS AND ENCOUNTERS   35

Chapter Seven   SPRINGING UP ALL OVER   52

Chapter Eight   BAUHAUS vs. SCHAUHAUS   60

Chapter Nine   CINEMA AS A WEAPON   73

IMAGES FROM WEIMAR GERMANY   88

Chapter Ten  SYMPHONY OF A CITY  95

Chapter Eleven  FIGURING IT OUT  104

Chapter Twelve  SOUNDS AMID THE SILENCE  113

Chapter Thirteen  UP TO SNUFF  124

Chapter Fourteen  PAIN IN THE ASS  140

Chapter Fifteen  ENABLE YOU, ENABLE ME  151

Chapter Sixteen  THE PERFECT SERVICE  167

Chapter Seventeen  SECOND TIME AROUND  188

Chapter Eighteen  SURVIVING THE THIRTIES  200

Chapter Nineteen  THE STARS ARE SHINING  220

Chapter Twenty  GRAND FREEDOM NO MORE  245

Epilog  DIFFERENT FROM YOU AND ME  280

**Chapter One   AFTER THE FACT**

"It can't be true," I scream. "It's impossible."

Sitting across from me, staring blankly and not saying a word, is Herr Biedermeyer, my attorney. He shuffles a few sheets of paper absentmindedly, and then begins fidgeting with the buttons on his coat. I have the strange feeling that he must have bribed somebody to obtain his degree in jurisprudence. I cannot get it into my head that this bungling man with the vapid look on his face ever made it through law school.

"What can I do?" I ask in anguish. "Is it possible to file an appeal, *lieber* Herr Biedermeyer?

A small glint of light hits Biedermeyer's eyes. He pulls on one of his coat buttons with such vigor that the thread breaks. He looks down at the loose button cupped in his hand. Total confusion crosses his face. He pops the button into his breast pocket and adjusts himself in the chair.

"Not a snowball's chance in hell," the attorney quips. He surprises me with such a graphic metaphor. "We're not dealing with one of our courts. It is a tribunal from somewhere else." He pauses to catch his breath. "The occupation forces, if you will," he informs me, spitting out the words with contempt.

"Yes, I realize that," I say resignedly. "Anyway, our courts must have improved over what has been taking place during the past twelve years, wouldn't you think? Isn't that a reasonable conclusion?"

Biedermeyer knits his brow, and his eyes really come to life now. "There are many changes underway," he explains. "At least most people on trial are no longer humiliated by the likes of a maniac like Roland Freisler." He coughs, clears his throat loudly and adds, "You know --- assumed guilty until proven innocent, but really with absolutely no hope of doing just that, and having the gallows waiting for you in the end anyway."

I bolt upright in my chair. "But this is no different," I fume, "and I have to suffer not only more prison time, but the possibility of injury and bodily harm at the hands of people who are hostile to this country."

Biedermeyer switches back to his poker face and says, "I regret to inform you that the law stands as is."

Now I am really beside myself. "So you mean to tell me," I screech, "that they drop bombs on our cities, lay our nation to waste, slaughter our children and old people, and now preside over us as judge and jury?"

"Don't include me," the poker face's lips utter. "I'm not on trial."

"Oh, great!" I snap at him. "Some trial! Merely a tribunal to assert its authority over my rights. A process straight out of Franz Kafka." Holding up my right hand with my palm toward the ceiling, I assume a dramatic pose and proclaim, "I have been declared guilty of guilt!"

Biedermeyer's nose wrinkles. "Why do you have to mention that Jew?" he asks in astonishment. "His books have been banned for years in this country."

I lower my arm and slap my palm on the table. "That does it!" I cry in disgust. "I've had it up to here with your kind. *Sieg Heil*!" I break down and start bawling my eyes out. "I can't stand the sight of you anymore," I add, choking on the words between sobs.

The attorney stands up, shoves the sheets of paper into his attaché case, nods curtly and leaves. A guard leads me back to the cell. He has the initials MP stenciled on his sash. I assume it stands for the same thing as in German: *Militärpolizei*.

He is a young blond soldier of medium height and a fairly nice musculature. He has a stern look on his unblemished, finely chiseled face. He doesn't conceal his annoyance at the way I shuffle along. He grabs my arm and forces me to pick up the pace. I feel like I'm being dragged.

Arriving in front of cell number two hundred twenty, he jingles a large set of keys as he fits the appropriate one into the lock. He pushes the door open brusquely and shoves me in. He pulls the door closed instantly. I crawl on the floor and reach the cot. Kneeling there for a second or two, I rub my eyes with the sleeve of my prison garb, trying to dry my tears.

A little hatch in the door has been unlocked by another guard. He peers in at me, starts clicking disapprovingly with his tongue several times, and says in heavily accented German a word somebody probably taught him recently: "*Schweinehund!*"

**Chapter Two   WIEDERSDORF BLUES**

Depression and thoughts of suicide loom large in my mind. I can't shake them and really haven't been able to do so for the past five months since my imprisonment, followed by liberation and then imprisonment anew. When I start feeling too low, I begin recalling years past and what life used to be like.

Invariably I associate certain events in my life with either a song or a movie that came out at the time. The image of Hans Albers, perched on a cannonball in *Münchhausen,* flying toward the audience in the darkened theatre brings to mind the first Allied air raids my neighbors and I experienced. Too horrific to think about. I go back further and start whistling some stupid Ilse Werner tune like *Ich hab' dich und du hast mich* (I've Got You and You've Got Me) or *Die kleine Stadt will schlafen gehen* (The Little Town Wants To Go To Sleep). Songs like hers make me think of afternoons in Potsdam meandering at the Sans Souci Palace. No wonder Frederick the Great dubbed the place "carefree," for I've seldom felt more relaxed in my entire life in a place as I have when I go there.

I propel myself back to the thirties and laugh when I recall how girls and women went crazy for Zarah Leander's new hairstyle. Like a herd of sheep they flocked to their hairdressers and pleaded with the stylists, "Make me look exactly like her in that movie!" Soon we had copycat Gloria Vanes prancing around towns and villages throughout Germany. That was around the time our troops had marched into the Sudetenland, but well before the Gleiwitz radio station incident that plunged us into war with Poland. Why England and France had to suddenly jump in is something I'll never understand. A technical adviser to three different movie studios doesn't pay much attention to politics. I always had my hands full with what they threw my way and barely picked up a newspaper in those days.

The further back I go, the better I start to feel. These gray, fingernail effaced and graffitied walls won't conquer me --- I have victory over them! Prison bars can't hold me when my spirit soars above the clouds! The lesson I learn from all this is to never completely put my trust in anybody, whether it's the Führer or Admiral Dönitz, the Wehrmacht or the Anglo-Americans. At least the Bolsheviks never got to me, although I hear tell that most of those Russkis have enormous dicks and will screw just about anybody or anything.

I see one of the occupiers peer through the peephole for a few seconds (the tiny shift in light lets me know he's there) and soon I'm aware that a platter of food is being shoved through a narrow opening located at the bottom of the door. I uncover the tray and look at some sort of *Ersatz* stew with a few partially peeled potatoes and a half dozen tubercular carrots all chopped up, a hunk of *Kommis-*

*brot*, badly baked, with a pat of margarine and some sort of compote consisting of cling peaches and prunes. Once I determine that this food looks way better and is more plentiful than anything we were ever given in camp and that it probably isn't sprinkled with poison, I dig in and enjoy my first substantial meal in quite a while. "Maybe captivity under these guys won't be so bad after all," I reason to myself.

But as I pop one last peach half in my mouth and gum a little of the remaining potato, I come to the conclusion that I won't be enslaved any longer. The food gives me a burst of energy to soar high above the clouds. Could my imaginary flight be taking me back to Wiedersdorf? I haven't seen the place since I left in the late summer of 1929.

Yes, Spirit of Flight, it really is as far back as I want to travel. Nothing earlier than that, please.

Some of the kids in my class remember their fifth birthday, others the miniature *Lederhosen* their mother and father dressed them in at age three. Waltraud Scholz-Hanfstaengl (the only one of my female classmates whose name I've never been able to rid my brain of because it's so crazy) claims that she knows exactly how the world looked the moment she emerged from her mother's womb.

I, however, must be weird because I can't recall anything before the age of ten.

Do you plan to add that strange attribute to my laundry list of infractions, Mister Prosecutor, sir? Is that type of personality quirk interesting and dangerous enough for you, dear Jailer?

Grandmother told me she was my age when the Danube overflowed and flooded the original village of Wiedersdorf, burying it forever under water. "Our family moved to Himmelsheim," she would tell anyone who was within an earshot, referring to the biggest town in that region along the border region of Baden-Württemberg and Bavaria. Clearly it was no Munich or Stuttgart, but to Grandmother and her family it was too large and intimidating.

We hated every minute we had to stay there," she would complain. "Big towns like that still scare the living daylights out of me." I don't think she'd ever wandered farther than fifteen kilometers from Wiedersdorf in her life, that being the exact distance from Himmelsheim to the present-day reconstructed village.

"They managed to salvage some of the original plans for the City Hall and the layout of the town square," she would proudly announce. Even at age ten I was fascinated by her reminiscences and always listened attentively, though others might wander off from disinterest or sheer boredom. Nobody ever falsely claimed that the citizens of Wiedersdorf were by and large a pack of dullards and halfwits. I can't help having been born in the wrong place with such a brilliant intellect! (Please write that down and retain it for my file, Mister Interrogator, sir!)

The village was transplanted in rebuilt form two

kilometers upstream from the original site. That assured its survival into the new century and a safe, productive life for Granny. Raising a family and making certain that her daughter would grow up, get married and give birth to healthy children was uppermost in her mind. My mom accomplished all those things and provided excellent moral support to my dad.

Father was a victim of circumstance. He returned from battle with a mild injury, losing most of the hearing in his left ear. My mother had gotten hitched to him shortly before he was called up in October 1914 to fight in the Kaiser's war. Since my parents were staunch Catholics and wouldn't even have given so much as a thought about "knowing" each other prior to the marriage commitment, they were certain that I would be born solely within wedlock virtually nine months after that both said «*Ja.*» Dad was already in the infantry, holed up in a trench somewhere in France when Mom plopped me out. They weren't able to get a single letter to one another before Germany was defeated and he was demobilized, so he only learned of my birth a little over two years after the fact.

"There were massive food shortages right before the war ended," Mother would tell me. "Folks from Himmelsheim and beyond came out to our village to scour the surrounding fields for leftover potatoes, carrots, beets, turnips and other root vegetables, not knowing we'd already picked them over ourselves.

Wounded soldiers supervised those forays lest anybody get out of hand. People were desperately hungry and might have even killed a neighbor just for something to eat."

My friends in Berlin had always mentioned how gruesome life was for the German population in the wake of defeat. Street fighting had ensued between warring political parties. Nobody was certain who was fighting against whom and what it was all about. Mostly I'd nod and bemoan the bad memories, but in reality I hadn't the slightest idea what they were talking about. My father returned to his blacksmith shop, my mother continued to cook meals, clean the house, do the washing and play little games with me. Our lives went on, untouched by the designs of city dwellers with their incomprehensible political and social intrigues.

The ghastly inflation of 1923 scarcely affected us either. I only saw photos of women pushing wheelbarrows crammed with worthless banknotes to buy a loaf of bread years after departing from Wiedersdorf. As rightful country bumpkins who lived off the land, raising enough to feed ourselves and barter for things we needed from our neighbors, none of this tragedy ever mattered much to us.

Now that think of it, I could have been content to live my life out completely in Wiedersdorf. But a village in south central Germany is suited for a "normal" person like my father who wants to be a slightly deaf blacksmith and aspires to nothing else.

My mother is also content to be stuck there forever because she listens complacently to fellow villagers who "tried and failed" to make it, even in Himmelsheim with its current population of only seven thousand souls. Such adventurers lost their desire to branch out. They gave up on spreading their wings and flying. And they brought back lurid tales of the dangers and pitfalls of cosmopolitan life.

"Oh, there are beggars, thieves, gamblers, prostitutes, filthy Gypsies, and Negroes selling bananas," claimed a wide-eyed aspirant named Beppo Hainsaecker. He waylaid my mom shortly after returning from a year of trying to make it in Munich. "I couldn't stand being around that riff-raff."

Mom listened to Beppo condescendingly. She was one of those types of people who was convinced that evil existed in the world. Her faith and piety had taught her that she didn't have to look at it dead-on with all its warts and pockmarks. She was content to leave it sight unseen, and she pitied young men like Beppo Hainsaecker who had to see it for themselves, to experience firsthand that the grass was not always greener beyond the village.

The tales Beppo brought back, however, intrigued me, especially the ones about people in such dire straits who would do anything to survive. "I couldn't believe it," he declared to me when I was in my final year of school. "Besides the gals, there were actually boys --- big strapping farm lads, cadets from the military academy, effeminate students from the big university, you name it --- who offered to go with their 'gentlemen callers' and commit unspeakable acts of shame." He slapped the palm of his right hand over his mouth and looked from side to side. "Don't let your mom or anybody else around here find out that I told you," he warned.

The fact that the acts were unspeakable naturally made me curious to find out what they were. I decided to stop spending the little allowance my parents gave me on frivolous trinkets and begin putting it aside for my future plans to work and play in Munich.

**Chapter Three   DIFFERENT WAVELENGTHS**

Radio plays a bigger role in my life than even motion pictures. The fact that I'd never seen a radio receiver until I was well into my teens and far away from Wiedersdorf makes me double, triple and quadruple my love for the medium in order to make up for so much lost time.

*Münchener Neueste Nachrichten* featured some advertisements for wireless consoles and listed the shops where they were available. I counted my extra Reichsmarks and decided to buy one for my little room. I placed it on top of the chest of drawers so that the speaker and dials were eye-level. The sound was fairly good. Broadcast hours were few, but they increased with time. Late at night I could pick up Austrian radio and even heard a Czech station once or twice, but couldn't understand a word of their staccato language. It felt like I had a window on the world right at my fingertips.

I loved hearing news about my favorite movie stars: Greta Garbo, Anny Ondra, Conrad Veidt, Ossi Oswalda, Charlie Chaplin and so many others. Aside from the lengthy classical selections I occasionally heard popular and jazz dance band music like Dájos Béla, the Weintraub Syncopaters, Marek Weber and Peter Kreuder.

Another sound invaded my radio in the early thirties. In fact, his warbling and carrying-on filled many a radio listener's ear in that era. I was used to hearing comic routines by the likes of Antek and Frantek, so it didn't faze me to tune in one weekend and hear the rantings and ravings of someone who sounded like a crazed maniac. «*Donnerwetter,*» I muttered, "who the hell let this guy out of the loony bin?" He spoke with a gravelly voice in an accent with a slight Austrian lilt, but flat and devoid of charm. "No, he can't possibly be a comedian," I mused, concluding that the man must really have an ax to grind.

Somehow the more you tried to ignore that pathetic growl, the more he sucked you in. He was definitely gifted: not the best speaker in the world, and certainly one with the most outrageous pronunciation of German words I've ever heard, but he had an inimitable style and charisma. He made you feel like he was a victim of gross indecencies committed by dyed-in-the-wool enemies of the German Reich: a martyr for the German people. He alone personified Germany in its intense suffering.

«*Ach, Liebchen,*» Aunt Gusti cried, "turn that infernal racket off." I hadn't been allowed to "hit the road" and be on my own until my thirteenth birthday after Mother and Father got wind of my plans. They did, however, agree to let me go to live with Augustina Fischer, a distant aunt on my dad's side. She had also grown up in Wiedersdorf, the rebuilt version which she found, similar to me, too isolated, stifling and backward. She moved to Himmelsheim when she was a mere child of twelve, and then on to

Munich at the ripe old age of sixteen.

"Sorry, Auntie," I answered sheepishly, switching the radio off and pouting. That Hitler character was always good for a few laughs, though I was aware that some people took him dead seriously, swearing he was Germany's savior.

Munich was like a great big candy store to me, full of wonderful things to taste, colorful worlds to explore and new adventures around every corner. Aunt Gusti was delighted that I was delighted, and we delighted one another. She was a tall, lanky but very attractive lady in her mid-forties when she took me in. Her husband had perished during one of the last battles of the Kaiser's war. She was very style-conscious and made certain that she always looked her best. Many male heads turned when she made her way down Leopoldstraße or strolled through the *Englischer Garten*.

The first time she laid eyes on me, she broke out in tears. »*Ach, mein lieber Junge,*« she exclaimed, "how shabbily they dress you." I didn't think I looked that grotesque in my cotton shirt, brown lambskin knee britches with matching suspenders, *Haferlschuhe* Alpine-wear shoes and a green felt Tyrolean hat, but it evidently upset Aunt Gusti. "Come, let's go buy you a complete new wardrobe." She had superb fashion sense, knew what suited an adolescent boy best and kitted me out beautifully. It boosted my self-confidence to be so nattily attired.

Although she lived a rather fast life, stringing

along several beaux at once and drinking with the best of them at the *Bürger-Bräu Keller* or the *Hofbräuhaus,* Aunt Gusti didn't ignore the cultural, literary and social development in the Weimar Republic. She imbued me with a love of literature and an eagerness to read practically anything I could get my hands on. I devoured the works of Rainer Maria Rilke, Franz Kafka and Hermann Hesse, Philosophers like Emmanuel Kant and Friedrich Nietzsche fascinated me, too. (And still do!)

And I went to the picture shows. Unlike village life where everything rolled into darkness the moment the sun went down, Munich came alive in an entirely different way at night. Neon signs glared, car horns tooted, cafés, restaurants, coffee houses, student recreational clubs and dancehalls were crowded with merrymakers. The Odeon-Palast became my second home. I loved seeing the flicker of the movie projector frames on the large screen and a wonderful world of dreams come true unfolding before my eyes.

Although the Palast and the Kinothek still showed the silent films of Emil Jannings, Lil Dagover, Garbo, John Gilbert, Vilma Banky and Chaplin, sound was coming into vogue. Movie theatres throughout Germany were rapidly being equipped for the new medium. We audiences flocked to see and hear Marlene Dietrich tell us how she was designed for love from head to toe (I believe that when she and Jannings filmed a separate English language version of *The Blue Angel*, the lyrics of »*Ich bin von Kopf bis Fuß auf Liebe eingestellt*« were changed to "Falling in Love Again") as well as Peter Lorre cower in fear as a hunted baby killer in the Fritz Lang thriller *M* or kids my age getting into all sorts of crazy fixes in *Emil and the Detectives*.

Walking the streets of Munich I started to notice the letters NSDAP and a weird twisted cross symbol in black, usually planted in a white circle in the middle of a bright red flag. I heard people speak in glowing terms about the guy who sounded like a roaring lion on the radio. Some said that he had taken a flat here, a city where his unruly party members had rabble-roused so blatantly that he and several of his followers were brought before the judge, found guilty and sentenced to prison.

Aunt Gusti laughed it off. "Can you imagine someone like him running for office?" she asked, astonished. "I mean, really! I wouldn't vote for him if he ran for dog catcher."

"I saw a couple of young men wearing armbands with the weird symbol, walking as a group down Sonnenstraße," I piped in. "Their brown shirts are kind of nice."

My aunt looked at me warily. "The way they dress may impress you," she scolded, "but they are very bad boys. Decent people won't have anything to do with them." She had a flat square package wrapped in brown paper in her hand. "Here," she said, holding it out for me to grab, "I went to Kannon-Musik and picked these up for you, *Liebling*."

Excitedly I unwrapped it and found two of my favorite songs on phonograph records: »*Nimm dich in acht vor blonden Frauen*« (Beware of Blonde Women) by Dietrich and »*Kannst du pfeifen, Johanna?*« (Can you whistle, Joanne?) by the Comedian Harmonisten, plus a third surprise offering. "Put that one on the Victrola and see how you like it. Don't look at the label yet!"

I did exactly as I was told and began convulsing with laughter when I heard Leo Monosson's tenor voice sing the words, »*Einen großen Nazi hat sie,*« a comical play on words. "That's too funny, Auntie," I chortled, still doubling up with laughter. "'A great big Nazi has she' --- brilliant!"

Certainly less amusing was the letter I received from my mother a few days later. Aside from her usual complaining about how hard life was in the village and incessantly worrying if I was getting on all right in Munich and behaving myself at Aunt Gusti's, she included a few lines at the end of her missive which I suppose signified cheerful news to her:

*"Herr Fürstenbrenner, the old wheelwright, bought the first radio in town. He lets everybody in Wiedersdorf come to his place most evenings to listen. Sometimes the reception isn't very clear, but we enjoy hearing what the outside world has to say to us.*

*"Last night we heard Herr Hitler for the first time.*

*Hopefully it will not be the last. What a fiery speech! He talks the way we think and says the things we really want to hear. We are very excited about him and his party, and the way they want to change the direction Germany is going to make us a proud nation again."*

**The Comedian Harmonisten**

## Chapter Four    A FIRST TIME FOR EVERYTHING

Aunt Gusti remained one of Munich's most eligible bachelorettes. Her beaux liked her independent, carefree manner. Some of the more enterprising swains admired her for her fashionable address and her grand apartment, most likely coveting the possessions her fallen husband had provided her. I always feared that some sweet-talking cad would sweep Aunt Gusti off her feet and proceed to rifle through her bank account, try to make her crazy, send her away to a nut house, and then take over everything that remained. I need not have feared, however, because she was level-headed and shrewd. Nobody could pull a fast one on her, no matter how hard they tried.

I was startled at how well she handled herself even in the stickiest situations. If one of her paramours became too aggressive, she would dispense with the scoundrel bodily. She had thrown many a bounder out on his behind that way. She possessed Herculean strength and could let loose at a moment's notice. I wished I'd had her moxie.

This rang especially true on the third night in August. I had my first run-in with the Nazis. I had stayed out late to watch the new Willi Fritsch and Lilian Harvey movie, *Die Drei von der Tankstelle,* a second time, confounding the usher who swore up and down that he'd seen me enter the Palast much earlier in the day. Those guys belonged to some sort of contingent and called themselves »*die Sturmabteilung*.« To my fourteen-year-old mind they came off like a bunch of thugs. Those brown shirts of theirs caught my eye and I just couldn't help staring. The tallest of the troopers, a gorgeous Siegfried-type blond demigod, sneered and signaled to his companions to close ranks. They approached me and were about to put up their dukes, but I slipped away quietly, shunting through an alley I remembered that led to the high end of Schumannstraße and a clean shot back to my aunt's place. My heart was racing for five minutes after I came through the door, and I felt like I was hyperventilating.

Aunt Gusti said she wasn't crazy about the fact that these bands of "Storm Troopers" were running around town willy-nilly, setting fires, destroying property and striking fear in the populace. "I want you to stay in after nine every night," she admonished. "The streets of Munich have become too dangerous."

I frowned. "But what about you, Auntie?" I asked in protest. "You run around until all hours, I worry about you, you know."

Grinning, she quipped, "It's not me they're after, *Liebling*. I'm not their type." Desiring to change the subject, she added, "Besides, you're much too young to understand grown-up stuff like that."

She was wrong, of course. Not only did I know exactly what she was referring to, I had already engaged in it myself lots of times and with great enthusiasm, might I say. Hans Stoberbein had seen to that.

"Hey, you wanna come out to the far side of the meadow next to Schmittsteiners?" Hans had asked me one afternoon just after my eleventh birthday. "There's an abandoned hut there. I've got something special I wanna show you." The way he stared at me with his dancing blue eyes and brushed away wisps of his blond hair which fluttered in the breeze like spokes on a wheel made him irresistible. I idolized him and considered being asked to go with him not an invitation as much as a passport to enter a privileged country, closed off to all except a select few. I didn't care what he had to show me as long as I could walk alongside him and enjoy his company.

For a boy Hans Stoberbein had extremely high cheekbones. When he smiled his whole face lit up magnificently. I was glad that he smiled often because at other times he looked so sullen and preoccupied with the cares of the world. He was the type you'd be prompted to ask, "Is anything wrong?" and receive a quick reply of "No, nothing," followed by his precious award-winning smile from ear to ear in an attempt to switch off the gloom.

Frau Stoberbein was the best seamstress in Wiedersdorf and her son's homespun garments had a luster and attractiveness about them unequalled anywhere. His shirts sewn from snow-white cotton clung tenaciously to his body as if they had been molded. I could usually make out the dark beige hue of his nipples through the translucent fabric. It thrilled me to think what it would be like to touch them and feel if they were soft and malleable like clay or solid like molten lava.

Over the white cotton shirt he usually pulled on suede britches with multicolored suspenders, a folk design his mother embroidered into the cloth inserts that ran the length and crisscrossed from behind. At the intersection of the two straps she had woven a bright yellow sunflower pattern, a color that perfectly matched his blond locks. The britches hugged his body and accentuated every curve, every sleek line and every indentation. The pants material guarded his crotch like a fortress, prohibiting the invasion of any and all intruders, while the meticulously stitched sections around his firm buttocks filled out his dorsal regions like a classic sculpture. His legs were strong and the sinews were visible above the knee socks that clung to his sturdy calves.

It was such a shame that his footwear was shoddy, the result of too many long hikes through meadow, forest and the hills which gently rolled down toward the river. Most likely he was very hard on his shoes and didn't bother much about swapping out multiple pairs. *Haferlschuhe* Alpine wear shoes were supposed to be sturdier than that.

Hans beamed with his radiant, toothy smile as we walked the length of the field the Schnittsteiner clan claimed was theirs, but in fact belonged to no one in particular. The hut had been used in the days before Wiedersdorf was transplanted in the great flood. Granny had told me she remembered it from her childhood. A grizzled old hermit had holed up there for ages and resented the "newcomers" as the original Wiedersdorfers were labeled. He had flown the coop, cursing as he went and assuring them he'd be going off somewhere else to die.

I lagged behind as Hans walked with much bigger steps than I through the meadow. He'd glance back every so often and ask, "Can't you keep up?" I nodded feebly, tried to move faster and was soon out of breath. Hans grabbed me by the shoulder, opened the creaky door to the hut and sat me down on a wooden bench inside. Having closed the door we were plunged into near darkness, indeed a stark contrast after being out in the bright sunshine.

In spite of the seemingly pitch black interior, my eyes soon adjusted themselves as I groped around for Hans. I could hear him breathing, but didn't quite place where the sound as coming from. Shortly I had felt a patch of suede material. Instead of the smoothed-out texture fitted to a well-formed body, the fabric was wrinkled and gathered up in a mound. My fingers wandered seamlessly from the crinkly britches to a silky plateau of flesh. From this flat terrain an object poked upward, insinuated itself between my index finger and thumb, throbbing slightly. I traced the length of it with the two digits of my hand and arrived at a conclusion which I voiced loudly enough to pierce the darkened interior: »*Donnerwetter, du bist so furchtbar groß!*«

Hans had moved his hand up the length of my left arm, shoulder and neck. Grasping the back of my head he murmured, "You're damn right it's big. And it's all for you, my little one. Have your way with it!"

His voice was warm and encouraging, but I was scared half to death. "I like it very much," I said with a catch in my voice, "and I like you. But I don't know what to do with it. It's my first time."

Hans sensed my uneasiness, but he was a kind and patient teacher. "Why don't you bend down and put your nose and lips against it?" he asked invitingly. "If you enjoy the smell, you might want to take a taste. Run your tongue up and down on it."

I backed off. "You want me to lick it?" I inquired innocently. I simply had no idea that a boy derived pleasure from having another boy's tongue darting up and down the length of his shaft. "I won't hurt you, I promise."

Hans chuckled in a way that made me think he was having fun at my expense. He calmed my nerves when he finally caught his breath and replied, "I know you won't hurt me, I trust you. Why else would I have brought you out here?" I could see his blue eyes in a muted glow and was able to make out his smile and shadowy face. "I'll like it a lot if you swallow it whole in your mouth when I'm ready to shoot."

I had heard about some sort of strange, sticky goo that came out of boy's penises when they became aroused. At that time I hadn't produced any of my own yet – I was much too young. But I knew I was building up a good supply of it because every time I grasped my own knob and ran my fingers up and down, I felt a pleasurable pumping inside the shaft. What intrigued me was how the feeling subsided. I knew that someday soon I'd be shooting my wad of spunk like a champion, exactly the way Hans did the second I curled my lips around his bulbous cockhead and swallowed his beautiful shaft right down to the base. Warm liquid flowed directly into my throat and I greedily drank it all up.

Hans was selfish, though, and made no attempt to reciprocate. I chalked this up to me being too young to return the favor in mind, but would be in a better position in another year or so to empty my precious cream whenever he would desire: deep in his throat, across his massive chest, a geyser of it bubbling over while he jerked me off with his tight-fisted grip (I'd really want him to fondle my balls with his left hand while trying to "milk the cow" with his right!) or even shooting a line of it the length of his back while straddling the deep groove between his butt cheeks.

Naturally I wouldn't want to stick my little weenie into his hole: that was more like something he should do to me, I had reckoned. As a matter of fact, I longed to be penetrated and to feel his silky emission flood the walls of my anal cavity. I'm sure it would have been heavenly.

Alas, it was not to be. Hans loved to hunt, and the dense woodlands that covered the entire hillside were perfect for him to indulge his favorite pastime. No creature of the forest was safe whenever Hans headed out with a Schmidt & Habermann rifle slung over his shoulder. He supplied his mom with plenty of tasty venison to cook up throughout the long winters as well as loads of game birds in springtime. When he wasn't traipsing through the woods, he'd scour the meadows and dells for rabbits, opossums, grouse and wild piglets. My friends and I watched with glee one afternoon at the beginning of July as Hans raced fleet of foot in pursuit of a medium-size wily hare, catching up with the poor startled animal and grabbing it by the ears. Hans smiled so disarmingly that it diminished the savagery of the procedure. It occurred to me that if he ran that fast normally, it was no wonder that his footwear always fell apart.

About three weeks after the incident with the hare in the meadow, Hans was chasing no less than a wild boar amid the closely planted rows of birch trees that led practically to the shoreline of the river below. Two hunters from a neighboring village who had made their way just shy of Wiedersdorf mistook the rustle of leaves and bushes for the rapid movement of an elk. Firing two shots, their faces fell as they heard an unmistakable yell from a human being in agony.

The normally docile Wiedersdorfers were so enraged, they demanded retribution for the fallen son of Herr and Frau Stoberbein. The bereaved parents begged their fellow villagers to hold back their anger, for they considered it merely the type of accident that could have happened to anybody. Fortunately, cooler heads prevailed among the village elders who comprised a panel of judges. The unfortunate hunters were exonerated. One of them, a prosperous merchant, made a generous monetary donation to the victim's parents as a way to compensate for their loss. No amount of money, however, could alleviate the heartbreak they experienced as they buried their sole offspring.

I'm lost in thought as I recall how they dragged the bloody mess that remained of Hans out of the forest. It was shocking how the bullets from the rifle had cut so deep. I guess that behind the sinewy veneer poor Hans was just a big lump of jelly.

There's pounding on the cell door again. An American MP opens up and stands there with a disgusted look on his face. He speaks no German and I'm not sure what he's babbling about.

"Fuckin' Kraut," he spits out the words as near as I can guess them. "Twah-lett-uh," he adds with a twang so that I understand the word we borrowed from the French for crapper in no uncertain terms. Somehow these Americans are going to make themselves understood by us weary "Krauts."

The MP motions to another officer who's dressed in an entirely different type of uniform: khaki instead of gray. He looks like he just stepped out of the jungles of some South Sea island to come and guard us on our bathroom breaks, and he's not pleased about it. This'll be the final one before lights out, so I'm determined to make it a good one.

On the way back to the cell, "Khaki Man" removes a pack of cigarettes from his shirt pocket, extends one to me and a faint smile plays upon his lips. I refuse and tell him in German that I don't smoke. The smile turns into a frown and he jostles me so that I almost trip.

"It fuckin' figures," he mutters. "Goddamn pansies never smoke. That kinda thing's for real men only." Even if I can't understand his words, his intent comes through loud and clear. The Americans and Germans may have been enemies on the battlefield, but on this particular issue they're kindred spirits, holding hands and gleefully skipping down the road.

## Chapter Five  FULFILLED AND UNFULFILLED

No matter how people around me insisted, I never cared either for smoking or taking any drugs. I drank beer now and then and it reminded me of how piss tastes. I guess I made up for lacking in those vices by doubling and tripling up on the number of men and boys I engaged for sexual relations. Labeling me a whore wouldn't have bothered me in the least.

Bunches of young male Wiedersdorfers loved skinny dipping in one of the numerous ponds in the forest clearing. As a real pup of a kid I hid behind hedges and spied them enviously. I admired them for their sense of freedom, releasing themselves to the beauties of nature. My folks would have freaked out if they ever suspected that I had these feelings for others of my sex.

I missed Hans Stoberbein terribly and tended to project all my fantasties about him on other boys, selecting one attribute or the other to complete the picture. Dieter Moltke's cornflower blue eyes, Heinrich Putzkammer's nose and chin, Werner Schornstein's droopy blond locks, Gerhard Schimmelbrett's sculpted chest, Karl-Heinz Staubenfeger's two large, scrumptious-looking fleshy nipples and Uwe Holzschnitzel's muscular legs gave me a sense of nearness to Hans.

I did, however, feel guilty for not being all that particularly choosy about cock size. Hans trumped the lot of them, but he was gone and I settled for the smalls and mediums among the Wiedersforfer lads.

And I eventually bedded all of them. Maybe "bedded" was not the right term because rarely was an actual bed involved in any of my liaisons except in Heinrich Putzkammer's case. We took advantage of his parents' absence for two days to attend a *Gaufest* in Ulm to hunker down in their double bed. While Mama and Papa Putzkammer were eating *Bratwurst*, dancing the polka and *Schuhplatter* and making merry with participants from surrounding villages, their horny son and I whooped it up between the sheets. His cock tasted divine, he knew how to rim me expertly and he screwed me in style over and over again until I was virtually raw.

"Bedded" in other instances meant thrashing about with Dieter behind a haystack, climbing to Gerhard's favorite hilltop and having him ravage me in a small field of clover (I had a dickens of a time explaining away the green stains on my britches to my mom after those little forays), Karl-Heinz's "secret" ravine near a stream that flowed into the big river alongside which he allowed me to go all over his body with my eager tongue, paying special attention to the sublime texture of those delectable nipples, or swallowing Uwe's bite size cock and tiny testicles in one mouthful as he wrapped his legs around me and squealed with delight. Endless possibilities and variations also existed and I took advantage of every single one.

A horse groomer from Baron von Gelsingeichen's

estate took a liking to me. My feelings about him went far beyond mere affection. Just to have Xaver Scharffbrunner, for that was his name, come into view set my dick roaring with a fury that made me cream inside my underpants. "Oh dear God," I cried out that night in my prayers after first laying eyes on him, "I believe that you exist. I thank you and praise you for making someone even more beautiful than Hans exist in my life."

Xaver Scharffbrunner's complexion was ruddy and had the sheen of finely tanned leather. Set against his yellow-gold bushy hair, thick black eyebrows and piercing emerald eyes, aquiline nose and full red lips resembling the blush of a blooming rose in springtime, he had all the makings of a hero from one of Wagner's operas. A clinging muslin shirt, tight tan riding britches and slick black boots with a gloss in which a face could be mirrored rounded out the appealing picture of freshness and vitality. He made many a young damsel's bosom heave as well as a whole slew of his male admirers' cocks throb lustfully.

Early on I sighed discontentedly and gave up any hope of Xaver having the remotest interest in a freckle-faced, gangly twelve-year-old Wiedersdorfer kid. I devised little excursions along the Danube and long hikes that would just coincidentally land me in Hunnerskragen, the site of the Gelsingeichen estate. I discovered an open meadow that led to the bright white stables with the cherry red tiled roof. All of the

Baron's horses were superior to any in the region. Xaver took pride in grooming them to look their best.

"He looks more like somebody who deserves to inhabit the palace, doesn't he?" I heard a voice behind me interrupt my train of thought. "It's such a shame that the grisly old Baron is not resigned to the dung heap instead." I turned to see a wiry youth with curly brown hair standing by one of the hitching posts. He looked about my age, maybe a little older. He grinned and showed dimpled cheeks.

Shrugging, I replied, "I dunno. You're probably right, but I'm no expert."

The kid looked me up and down. "I'll bet you're pretty knowledgeable about lots of things," he blurted out. Extending his right arm and making a chopping motion at the elbow with the closed fingers of his left hand, he added, "He's huge, you know. And he knows how to use it like a pro."

His remark astounded me and I asked innocently, "What do you mean? I have no idea what you're talking about."

The curly-haired lad chuckled. "Like shit you don't," he said sarcastically. "I saw you practically undressing Xaver with your fucking eyes." Stepping closer and smelling like a combination of chicken broth and chamomile soap, he snarled and added, "If you don't want a broken nose, you'd best hightail it back to wherever the hell it is you came from. He's mine alone to fiddle with. I don't like competition."

I backed up slowly and ambled toward the open

meadow, picking up the pace as fast as my feet would take me. I'd never experienced jealousy and possessiveness like that before. It was then I realized why the inhabitants of one village rarely reached out to their neighboring number. It dawned on me how antiquated and superstitious such attitudes were and only hastened my desire to get out and explore the world beyond our neck of the woods.

Even now as I lie on this bunk in a jail cell that becomes colder and damper by the minute, I think of Xaver Scharffbrunner, the marvelous way he filled out his tan britches and I dream about what might have been.

## Chapter Six   PROPOSALS AND ENCOUNTERS

Something strange was happening between the end of 1931 and the beginning of the New Year. My teenage mind couldn't process it, but I arrived at several conclusions just by observing people and scenes playing out around me. Time was slowing down and taking its toll on Germany. Unrest was in the air.

"There's a huge slump going on in America and Britain ever since the stock market crashed," boomed Lothar Langenschlaff, Aunt Gusti's latest flame. He was speaking at table after one of my aunt's scrumptious Sunday dinners to which he was invariably invited. Suave in manner and meticulous in dress, he cut a dashing figure. His soft chestnut colored eyes exuded a calm, almost dreamy state of mind; just looking into them always made me totally relaxed and carefree. His hair and moustache color were the same auburn hue, his lips were the most sensuous I'd ever seen on a man, and his neck was long and slender. It made his head look curiously detached from the rest of his body.

"The import-export end of my businesses has practically dried up," Langenschlaff complained. "The Americans and British aren't buying our goods in the quantities we've been used to seeing in the recent past. Some orders have stopped altogether and the respective firms have gone out of business."

Aunt Gusti shook her head in disbelief. "Surely,

Lothar darling," she began, "it's only temporary, right? I mean, once it bottoms out, things will improve, won't they?" She looked at her beau lovingly. It was difficult to determine whether she loved him because of his dreamy eyes or his massive wealth and all the corporate influence he possessed. I knew one thing: she was seriously head over heels for him.

"Time alone will tell," he replied. "If what's happening to my companies reverberates around the country, Germany could be in for some rough sledding." Taking a sip of coffee, he continued. "There's a big election coming up, as you know. If business failures and unemployment start rearing their ugly heads, voters are going to look for alternatives. Hindenburg may be out on his duff."

Although I was totally ignorant of politics, I recognized Hindenburg's name because I'd grown up on him and heard him spoken of ever since my tenth birthday. "So if he's not our president, who will be?" I asked, trying to sound like an inquisitive adult. "What other choices do we have?"

Langenschlaff laughed. "Well, *you* don't have any," he quipped, "because you're too young to vote. But there will be lots of parties to turn to, all claiming they can solve Germany's problems. Social Democrats with Otto Wels, National Socialists with Hitler and the Communists with Ernst Thälmann will figure prominently on the next ballot." Emptying his coffee cup, he took out a pack of cigarettes.

Aunt Gusti shuddered just to hear the names and affiliations. "That Hitler character seems like a long shot," she put in. "My nephew and I have had many a good laugh about him, never expecting that he'd come this far. *Ach*, and the Communists frighten me to no end!"

Smiling good-naturedly and trying to be as charitable as possible with simpletons like me and my aunt, Langenschlaff exclaimed, "Voting for the Reds isn't as far-fetched as you may think. They're doing some amazing things in Soviet Russia since the Communists seized power. Their whole political, economic and social system has insulated itself from anything bad happening in the rest of the world. Some Germans are likely to look admirably upon their agricultural and industrial gains, and desire the same thing for this country."

Aunt Gusti surprised both Lothar as well as me when she weighed in on the Soviet Communists based on some exclusive information she acquired. "It won't pan out," she asserted, "I dated a Russian émigré who escaped from the Solovetsky Islands where a huge camp complex exists. What he described to me sounded like the pit of hell."

Removing one of the cigarettes from his pack, Lothar lit it, took a puff and asked, "What was he sent there for? Do you know what crime he committed?"

Gusti threw her head back and replied wistfully, "He claims it was for something his accusers called 'wrecking.' He was charged with sabotaging an entire factory project because, as the foreman, he couldn't persuade the workers to finish it within the time limit set by the central planners."

Shaking his head in dismay, Lothar retorted, "That sounds rather feeble. Personally I'd take that story with a grain of salt. Most likely your boyfriend was a dyed-in-the-wool criminal."

He was willing to let the matter slide, but Gusti slammed her fist on the table. "Not a criminal," she insisted, "but a political prisoner. He informed me that a lot of them suffered at the hands of real criminals: murderers, rapists, thieves, pickpockets and the like. They were mixed in with the regular prison population."

I was taking this all in and became curious about one thing. "Auntie," I interrupted, "you said he was imprisoned on some island. How did he manage to escape to the mainland?"

Gusti's eyes grew bigger and she smiled knowingly. "That's the miracle," she explained. "He was part of a prison contingent that travelled across the channel separating the Karelian coast from Solovki. They were picking up supplies for the massive construction of the White Sea Canal, a hair-brained scheme of Stalin's to celebrate victory in the completion of one of his country's insane five-year plans."

Lothar looked daggers at her. "How dare you criticize the Great Stalin, leader of a respected nation like the Soviet Union," he declared, his voice trembling with emotion as if he were defending the honor of a close family member. "Why, even the superb Russian author, Maxim Gorky, toured the White Sea Canal project and the monastery at Solovki. He wrote about the wonder-working effect of the work on the laborers, many of whom volunteered outright to contribute to the greater glory of the project."

A sweeter smile could not have crossed Aunt Gusti's lips at the moment. "It was more like forced conscription," she said dryly. "My former beau told me that he bailed out of the column of prisoners when the guards had turned their backs momentarily. It was only due to their slip-up that he managed to sneak away by the hairs of his neck. He almost starved to death in the Karelian forest before making his way to Finland. Tell me, Lothar," she asked pointedly, "does that sound like a volunteer to you?"

They went on arguing for five or ten more minutes whether Auntie's ex-boyfriend's escape was justified due to cruel and unusual imprisonment or whether he was a fugitive from justice for having violated the Soviet penal code. I heard the name of Maxim Gorky come up several more times: Lothar Langenschlaff sang his praises while my aunt pooh-poohed him as a "hack writer." It made me want to read some of his books to find out for myself.

"You know," Aunt Gusti wagged a menacing

finger, "the Commies took over here briefly in Bavaria right after the end of the Kaiser's war. There was so much bloodshed when opposition forces came back to throw them out, I can't even tell you."

Langenschlaff merely shrugged. "You don't have to tell me about spilt blood," he declared. "I was in Berlin for the whole Spartacists debacle with Karl Liebknecht and Rosa Luxemburg." More names I've never heard of and events which I knew nothing about. I felt like a dumb cluck and tiptoed away from the table as the grownups continued going at it. I became envious not only of Lothar Langenschlaff's obscene good looks, but also his brilliant intellect. I could easily see why my aunt was so taken with him.

Lothar's stately home in Schwabing made my eyeballs virtually pop out. I thought that the last thing he would have wanted was to have me tag along with Aunt Gusti when she was invited to visit him for the first time, but he wasn't like that at all. He extended every kindness imaginable to me. He even had a fabulous swimming pool at the rear of his property and the three of us frolicked in the unseasonably warm weather, not minding at all the relentless beating of the sun's rays on our waterlogged bodies, such was the extent of our swimming and sunbathing.

"If you don't come out of the water soon," Aunt Gusti warned playfully, "you'll end up looking like a prune. Hurry up and dry off." Handing me a fluffy towel, she added, "Lothar's chef has whipped up a fabulously delectable luncheon for us."

I was even allowed to drink a glass of Mosel wine with the noontime fare as well as two glasses of champagne for dinner. It was a pretty heady experience for a fifteen-year-old, even though my folks often gave me beer as I was growing up in Wiedersdorf. Wine and champagne, however, were so much more sophisticated and made me feel like I'd "arrived." I could easily leave the beer behind.

After a second helping of Rouladen and a third of parsley potatoes, combined with a small goblet of Liebfraumilch that Lothar poured for me himself in spite of Aunt Gusti's protests, I felt sleepy. "Is it all right with you if I take a look at your library before I doze off?" I asked woozily, sounding a bit like an adolescent Hans Moser well into his cups. Nodding in the affirmative, Lothar pointed the way.

"Your aunt and I are going to the shops so that she can pick out a few items," he told me, fingering a billfold groaning with 100 Reichsmark banknotes. "I don't know whether she informed you yet, but I'm taking you both with me for a short jaunt to Berlin next week. I've got a business deal to wrap up with one of the studios there."

I recall my heart definitely skipping a beat. Berlin! Just the mention of Germany's majestic capital city set my heart reeling. And the studios? Did he say what I think he said? I began to wonder if I'd have the chance to meet any movie stars or visit a real live filming. I didn't dare ask at the risk of sounding too pretentious, but curiosity ate away at me like a slug nibbling on a tender leaf, stripping it row by row until every vein was devoured.

"I think a change of scenery will do both of you good," he continued, puffing away on an aromatic "Brésil" and eyeing me intensely almost to the point of scaring me half to death. Was he planning to put us on a train to nowhere in a seated compartment? How could we ever escape his clutches?

"Lothar is of the opinion," my aunt chimes in, "that Munich has become too dangerous, what what Nazi Brown Shirts, insurrectionists and thugs running around in the streets."

"Nerves are frayed over this havoc and it's high time to get away for a while." Making a sweeping gesture with his hand, Lothar added, "I'm closing up this house and relocating to the larger one I have in Dahlem."

I began to wonder how Lothar Langenschlaff remained prosperous while so much unemployment and political instability existed throughout Germany. Aunt Gusti alluded to Lothar's acquisition of many choice properties during the horrendous inflation at the end of 1923.

"Lothar and his then-wife had invested heavily in foreign currency," she explained to me, "more like speculators, hedging their bets. It turned out their hunch paid off." It seemed unfair that Mr. and Mrs. Langenschlaff were able to acquire homes and parcels of land for a song in those hectic times, but such was the nature of the capitalist stranglehold on the Weimar Republic. "The unfortunate woman died of kidney failure about two years ago," she added, "and it broke Lothar up something fierce. But now he has me to fill the enormous void. He tells me he is also very fond of you, dear." She patted me on the shoulder and gave me a little hug.

"Do you think he'll ask you to marry him, Auntie?" I asked with a slight catch in my voice. "Most likely you two won't want me hanging around anymore once you become his wife."

My aunt smiled and drew me closer. "Let's not put the cart before the horse," she admonished. "He hasn't asked me a thing yet except the time of day." We looked at each other and burst out laughing. I loved her so much, and I appreciated Lothar's affection toward her. But I couldn't get my mind off Berlin and all the excitement the capital of the Hohenzollerns generated in my imagination.

In our time remaining at Schwabing, however, I took advantage of raiding Lothar Langenschlaff's library every afternoon following luncheon. Even better than his impressive complete works collections of Goethe, Schiller and Heine was his fabulous selection of phonograph records. I might be skimming the lines of a Bertolt Brecht play and listening to the strains of Austin Egon crooning »*Es sprach der Marabou*« or lightly doze off after staring at the ceiling while Fritzi Massary warbled »*Ich bin eine Frau, die weiß was sie will«* and not think anything of it. Though the sun may have been shining brightly outside, the comfort of Lothar's dark wood paneled "man cave" excited me more and made me feel strangely close to him even when he wasn't physically near. The fact that he was willing to share that most private of all domains and let me have the run of the place spoke volumes about the level of trust and confidence he had in me, a mere snip of an adolescent.

Lothar's extraordinary library was a somber affair. Browns, tans and deep umber dominated the furnishings, among which I loved the huge overstuffed sofa best. Two matching Naugahyde chairs with sturdy oak frames and legs complemented "my" couch and I supposed a gentleman of Lothar's caliber would have preferred to seat himself on one of these with a copy of *Im Westen Nichts Neues* or the latest issue of the Social Democrat newspaper in hand.

I was still basically a kid, so I sprawled out on the sofa and even rubbed my crotch sometimes while immersed in reading. Could it have been that just reading or the art of good dialogue on the printed page of a work of fiction excited me sexually?

»*Mein lieber Gott im Himmel,*« I cried one afternoon after a brief departure from the classics and delving instead into the Wild West stories of Karl May. I became so aroused and my mind was racing. "Does this mean I want to be fucked by a cowboy?" I wondered for the rest of that particular day. The idea tickled my fancy to no end.

Artifacts that Lothar Langenschlaff had accumulated as a result of his worldwide travels also adorned the "man cave." A four-foot-high bejeweled ostrich with gold feathers, a pair of grotesque tribal masks from the deepest, darkest jungles of Africa, an ivory-handled Samurai sword from Japan and a giant defunct Alpine cuckoo clock were the most noteworthy in his collection. Various paintings and posters (one featured Karl Marx, Friedrich Engels, Vladimir Lenin and Leon Trotsky in semi-profile), fine china plates and Majolica pottery, Herend porcelain knickknacks and little silver spoons with the names of German, Austrian and Swiss cities and a representative landmark on each were scattered around the room.

Little busts of Beethoven, Mozart, Liszt, Chopin, Brahms and Wagner were arranged in a semi-circle atop a small upright W. Richter-Hamburg piano. Sometimes I'd plunk out "Chopsticks" or something as innocuous and look intently at Beethoven who seemed to grin at me. Aunt Gusti considered me daft when I admitted it to her one night after I took my bath.

"'Ludwig van' certainly has better things to do than listen to you play so feebly," she scolded me. "Didn't I tell you not to put your fingerprints all over Lothar's things?"

"But he said I could have full run of his library," I

protested. "He has wonderful stuff, even better than yours. You know how jazzed I get about all these charms of the big city."

Gusti smiled and pulled a comb across my damp hair. "Ooh," she cried, "this mop of yours is such a tangled mess." She was always so gentle when she unknotted the unruly strands, unlike my mom who always got so frustrated and began pulling until my follicles started to tingle and hurt like anything. As my aunt smoothed out the last of my tangles she murmured, "I know, sweetie. It's a different world here compared to old, cranky Wiedersdorf. Just promise me you won't break anything." I wondered how much of Lothar's world also dazzled her, even though she already had nice things of her own.

Aunt Gusti went on a group picnic with former colleagues at Blohm & Voss where she had worked when my uncle was still alive. Since it was not a family inclusive event, I stayed at Lothar's place that Saturday afternoon swimming, sunbathing, eating, drinking, reading and relaxing to my heart's content. For some reason my aunt failed to show up at the hour when she was expected at nightfall. I had been reading *The Buddenbrooks* by Thomas Mann. As with most of his egregiously long descriptive passages, I ended up nodding off and slept like a rock.

I'm not sure how much time must have passed when I finally opened my eyes again and drowsily became aware of something strange occurring below my waist. Lothar had unbuttoned my trousers and extracted my erect member, lavishing extraordinary attention upon it unlike any of the fellows back in the village. All sorts of crazy ideas crossed my mind as I leaned to the right on his sofa, forcing the ample volume of Mann to fall on the hardwood floor with a thud. I was remotely cognizant that this was Aunt Gusti's beau who was servicing me so expertly at the moment. It surprised me for the fact that he had never made a move on me prior to this particular time, more than what it was that he was performing so exquisitely. I wondered if he made a habit of ravishing the sons and nephews of relatives, friends and associates.

*Donnerwetter*, how I absolutely loved the way he swallowed my cock whole, all the way down to the base! Was my cockhead tickling his tonsils? Did grownups even have tonsils? When he wasn't chowing down on Old Reliable, he gently sucked on my balls and licked the underside of my crotch, stopping just shy of my poop chute. He eyed me lovingly as he worked between my knees: a hearty, lustful look which turned me on to an even greater extent than I'd ever felt before.

Stretching out, moaning with abandon and letting loose with a huge load of semen which squirted halfway across the room, I was vaguely aware of Lothar's sigh. »*Um Gotteswillen, Junge!*« he scolded playfully. "I wish you could've held off a bit longer. I wanted you to come in my mouth so I could taste your creamy goodness." He sounded a lot like Dieter who used to say something similar to me, although without the emotional aplomb.

Sleepily I smiled and purred, "Maybe next time." I lifted my head off the cushion and blurted out, "Hey, does my aunt know you're doing these kinds of things to me?"

Lothar shook his head. "Not a chance," he exclaimed. "Gusti's very sweet, but she hardly satisfies me sexually. You, however, are another story altogether. I had my eye on you the first time I was invited to dinner. I've waited impatiently for this moment and you, *mein Kind*, didn't disappoint me. You can't even begin to imagine how I've obsessed about you day after day, week upon week."

His words massaged my ego like gangbusters and I felt more like a man than ever before. Lothar was so classy, well-heeled, sophisticated and adept at his craft, whether it was making shrewd investments or hobnobbing with the leading lights of German industry, commerce, banking and show business. He could have his pick of any number of ready, willing and able men or boys who would do his bidding, but he chose me in this place and at this time. It made me feel special, but I still worried about Aunt Gusti's reaction. Was it possible she already knew and just let it slide because Lothar Langenschlaff was such a prize catch?

I bucked up and asked boldly, "Do you like girls as much as you like boys?" Lothar was lightly touching my back with his right hand, slowly working his way down to the slope which led to my buttocks. Inserting a finger into my hole and wiggling it deep inside, he replied breathlessly, "No, I like boys much more. In fact, I love them." Pausing for effect and kissing me tenderly on the neck, he whispered, "And I love you."

I was emboldened to take charge of the situation. I sensed that I had this man in the palm of my hand and could command him to do anything at this point. "I want you to take all of me," I barked, reaching for the buttons of his trousers and getting a good handful of aroused manhood in the bargain. I was hardly able to figure out how confined his rockhard prick must have felt encased in the pants' material. It must have throbbed painfully before I released it to spring to attention in all its glory right before my eyes. "Slap my butt cheeks with it a couple of times," I snapped at him, "and then shove it into me so deep that I'll scream to the top of my lungs!"

Things could not have worked out any better. Aunt Gusti had run into Heinz Lübke, a work colleague and old flame at the Blohm & Voss picnic. Evidently the fire had never gone out, as they say, and they rekindled the flame to a romance that started long ago, but was hindered by both of them being married to other people. She ended up not coming back to Lothar's house in Schwabing that night nor many days afterward as could be expected, although we did sit down to a pleasant "farewell dinner" a few weeks later. By this time I had become Lothar's "special boy" and was spending more time in Schwabing than at Aunt Gusti's.

"I'm engaged," she announced, blushing to the roots of her hair and flashing a sizeable ring, "and we'll be married right after he comes back from a business trip to Lisbon. He's promised me that our honeymoon will be in Venice." I'd never seen her look more radiant. She was clearly baffled why Lothar, her former "main squeeze" was not broken up by it. The fact that he virtually rejoiced and appeared to breathe a sigh of relief put her off completely. Knowing her, she perceived the sudden closeness between him and me and was able to put two and two together.

Or maybe she didn't, owing to one of her parting comments as she exited from "our" house that night. "Promise me, Lothar," she insisted with all seriousness, "that you'll find the right girl and settle down, for Chrissakes."

With just as serious a mien he said, "And you must promise me that you'll vote for Wels and the Social Democrat ticket in the next election, come hell or high water. You know I'd rather you favored Thälmann and the Communists, but I won't press you about it. The SD is the next best choice."

Throwing her head back and laughing, she replied, "Oh you silly goose! You know I'm a Hindenburg girl, body and soul. He'll give Germany stability and keep us out of the economic mess the Brits and Americans are going through."

Lothar waved away her comment. "Yeah, if he lives long enough," he quipped. "The old man looks like he has one foot in the grave." Wringing his hands, he added, "If that happens, we'll be in one fine mess. Please reconsider, *Liebchen*, and tell me you'll vote for Wels."

My aunt smiled benignly and changed the subject at once. Eyeing me lovingly, she said, "Make certain that this child drinks a glass of milk twice a day and doesn't forget to wash behind his ears."

**Munich**

**Chapter Seven    SPRINGING UP ALL OVER**

After that first afternoon in Schwabing and the wild night of lovemaking which followed (we were no longer mindful if my aunt suddenly returned from the picnic, throwing caution foolishly to the wind), I was as good as attached to Lothar Langenschlaff's hip. "You know, *Junge*," he whispered to me after I'd shot a silky load into his waiting mouth early that next morning, "your aunt used to scold me for not fucking her with enough gusto the few times we made love. She'd always say, 'Pretend like you're screwing a fourteen-year-old boy,' and a picture of you would come instantly to mind." Tweaking my nose playfully, he added, "Now I don't have to pretend anymore because you're here in my arms for real."

I had no idea if Lothar had had other boys before me. He seemed like the consummate sugar daddy. That really wasn't my style. He was hurt when I refuse to accept a small gold ring he wanted to gift to me. "I don't wear jewelry," I protested, "it just wasn't a custom back in the village."

Lothar flashed a look of shock. "Why, pray tell?" My guess was that other little boys before me had not only graciously accepted his lavish presents, but also most likely ran with them to the nearest pawnbroker, hocking them for instant cash to go off and blow on a booze-up with their cronies.

"Because my folks and the other villagers equated

those kinds of things with the Gypsies," I replied. "My mother always held that no respectable German would wear finery like that, even though the Gypsy stuff was gaudy."

Lothar seemed to accept my modest explanation. He took the ring, pressed it into my hand and said, "I'd still like you to keep it anyway. You might change your mind sometime in the future."

I laugh now as I think back on how naïve Lothar was in his Social Democrat and Communist mindset. Riding around in a Daimler roadster and not pounding the pavement like the rest of us poor slobs, he missed all of the mayhem of Munich's streets and back alleys in those months leading up to the 1932 election. He wouldn't have been aware of the swarms of unemployed workers gathered in front of factory gates and construction sites, fervently hoping to snatch up the few positions that were open on a daily basis. He didn't see the endless columns of displaced persons who had been evicted from their flats after a visit from the dreaded *Gerichtsvollzieher*, that haughty magistrate of the district court who attended to such distasteful matters with a certain amount of glee. His world of glittering elegance and opulent grace contrasted sharply to the worn-out carpets and seat cushions at the employment exchanges everywhere. The slow, depressed shuffle of tired feet and the restless shifting of sore bottoms became epidemic throughout Germany. The government of the Weimar Republic had really let its people down, but all Lothar cared to do was hum proletarian refrains and read facsimile accounts in his favorite leftist newspapers. He was oblivious to the fights which broke out in households and the level of violence directed at "the other." Strife gripped the population and groups such as the NSDAP's brown-shirted *Sturmabteilung* took advantage of the unrest to mete out their own unique brand of justice, clubbing a few heads along the way.

"Hey, Youngster," Lothar warned me, "take care not to cross paths with those hooligans." This was shortly before I wrapped things up at Aunt Gusti's and had moved into the house in Schwabing amid the raised eyebrows and furtive whispers of the neighbors. "They've been known to back boys your age into a corner and rape them." How he obtained this information was a mystery to me.

I stroked Lothar's cheek gently. "Well, what do you expect them to do?" I asked. "Why, their leader, that Ernst Röhm character, is the biggest poof in Germany. You've got to admit, *Liebling*," I added with a sly grin, "that some of those young Nazis fill out their trousers in a most enchanting way."

Lothar pulled back and looked daggers at me. "The thought of one of those big dicks shoved up your tight little ass both revolts and excites me," he barked. "See to it that you don't put yourself in harm's way." I promised him solemnly that I wouldn't do anything rash.

I do believe that Lothar loved me more than just physically. I think he respected me for not making demands on him like his other slithery denizens had done. The respect was mutual, for Lothar was certainly the fairest and most well-centered individual I'd ever met. He seemed to have a lot of genuine friends and associates. He surrounded himself with positive, forward-thinking people. Maybe there really was something to say about the Social Democrat approach to Germany's ills. Lothar was making a believer out of me!

The trip to Berlin to visit movie studios at Babelsberg and Marienfelde was postponed indefinitely. Lothar wanted to remain close to his interests in Southern Germany. He had qualified people to run operations in the nation's capital, so he wasn't worried about things becoming unraveled as it did for many in the shambles of a depressed economy. He even surprised me with a proposal made completely off-the-cuff while we went strolling one Sunday afternoon in the *Englischer Garten.*

"There's an entry-level mailroom position that'll be coming up soon at the Bavaria Film-Kunst studios," he informed me. "They're ready to toss out the mailroom clerk who's there now for excessive tardiness and insubordination. By rights the job should come up at the employment exchange. I think I can bypass the normal process and wangle it so that you slip right in." He drew me close to him and asked, "Do you want it?"

My heart skipped a beat and I threw my arms around him, hugging him tightly. "If it weren't for the fact that we're out in public," I gushed, "I'd be covering your face and neck with kisses by now. You've made me so happy."

Lothar smiled and led me slowly over to a bench near the lake. "I was so disappointed when you didn't want to accept expensive trinkets from me like the other boys," he said resignedly. "I should clarify: pleased, of course, but disappointed nonetheless because I wanted so much to show my appreciation."

Still in a state of extreme bliss, I chirped, "Oh, you couldn't have done better than this, *Liebling*," I caught my breath and glanced around lest anyone heard my all-too-noisy and open declaration of love. Lowering my voice, I added, "You know how I love everything about the movies."

Lothar grinned. "Well, you know," he remarked, "working as a lowly mailroom clerk is hardly a starring role."

Placing my hand on his shoulder, I retorted, "The only starring role I want to play is in your bedroom between the sheets with you." We both burst out laughing. "Just the fact that it's at Bavaria Film-Kunst makes it more than worthwhile. Who knows where it'll lead?" My exuberance caused him to laugh even more heartily than before.

"Let's celebrate with dinner at "Humpelmayr's" followed by a late showing of *Morocco* at the Odeon-

Palast," he proposed. "It's the new Marlene Dietrich film she made in Hollywood under Sternberg's direction. They've both gone over the pond and it's doubtful if they'll ever return."

"I heard," I put in, "that there's a scene where she dresses in a tuxedo and makes a pass at a woman sitting in a nightclub."

Lothar sniffed. "I believe it's actually one of the passing chorines in the nightclub number. It sounds campy and fun."

I scratched my head and wondered, "If we lose stars like Garbo and Dietrich to Hollywood, who'll remain?"

As usual Lothar is on the cutting edge of everything in the world of show business. "There's a mild reverse wave, you know. Emil Jannings and Pola Negri have already returned to our soil and are cranking out movies. The talkies may have decimated their careers in English, but they and a couple of others are doing quite well speaking from the screen in German."

Walking anywhere in Munich during those days, the pedestrian was struck with the level of anticipation in the air. The depressed economic situation was counterbalanced by a buoyant election campaign. Posters proclaiming the merits of manifold candidates from a plethora of political parties assaulted the eyes of every *Münchener* as he or she passed the ubiquitous round Litfaß-columns on every street corner. Symbols for the Nazis, Social

Democrats, Communists and dozens of other parties abounded. Amusing graffiti adorned some of the posters, scribbled in the haphazard penmanship of the opposition. The faces of Hindenburg, Hitler, Thälmann and Wels loomed large.

The morning that Lothar drove me to Bavaria Film-Kunst for the first time, I noticed a huge gathering of men and women at the main gate. Maneuvering his Daimler through a narrow passage leading to a separate employees' carpark, I asked him, "Who were all those people out there? Do they think this is a movie house and are waiting to get in to see the show?"

Lothar chuckled as the uniformed attendant raised the crossing arm for the car to pass through. "I have it on good authority that they're shooting an epic and need lots of extras for the huge crowd scenes. Our intrepid *Müncheners* have answered the cattle call and will each earn about ten Reichsmarks for their trouble."

"Gee," I said, "I'd like to be in their number." I had no idea what movie it was or the nature of the scenes which required the masses to flood the screen, but I was eager for a chance to appear on film just for a second and even blurred or fleetingly.

Knitting his brow and shaking his head, Lothar scolded me. "Put that notion out of your head, *junger Mann*. You'll earn oodles more than that by working in the mailroom. Besides, many hundreds of those poor souls will be turned away today."

I sighed, but in my heart and mind I was overjoyed. Though negative things like unemployment and unrest as well as the impassioned claims of the presidential candidates and the burgeoning cocks in the trousers of Nazi SA Brown Shirts were springing up all over, I was gainfully employed, well-kept and tenderly loved, so my future seemed extraordinarily bright.

**Brown Shirts in Munich**

## Chapter Eight    BAUHAUS vs. SCHAUHAUS

Because I was born and raised in the countryside and didn't know much about what was going on in German towns and cities during the years of the Weimar Republic, I missed out on whole movements and lifestyle changes. I knew that I didn't fit the mold of an exemplary adolescent due to my predilection for men and boys. At times I felt alone and alienated. If it had not been for people like Lothar Langenschlaff and my whole bevy of hook-ups back home along the Danube, I would have really been an oddball.

As it turned out, postwar Germany was going through an amazing renaissance, reinventing itself as modern culture proliferated. It bolstered new ways of thinking and acting, flaunting the staid conventions of previous decades. The strict code of Prussian militarism gave way to a lackadaisical nonconformity which was revolutionary by any country's standards. The actions of its participants were more likely to be viewed as scandalous rather than admirable, their behavior something to denigrate rather than emulate.

German popular culture was a wheel spinning out of control. Many people tended to draw comparisons between Paris and Berlin. While the enchanting City of Light offered many unbridled pleasures and fostered a golden age in literature, art and music, the grand capital of the Hohenzollerns rivaled it in its own *avant-garde* development and contributions of many piquant elements and personalities.

Lothar took it upon himself to catch me up on as many of the past decade's advances as he could, but would only do so in Munich. Some museums in the Bavarian capital featured the art of the Dadaist and Cubist schools, and Lothar enjoyed explaining to me the significance of some of the pieces. I learned that the artist's eye sees objects in a completely different way than we mere mortals. For them the world was a jumble that needed sorting out --- they were the interpreters who filtered it to us in ways that we could easily recognize.

"Honestly, Lothar," I confessed, "if you hadn't put it in terms I could understand, I would have said it was one big glob of nonsense. You've given me insights about looking at life and creativity in a fresh new way."

We were at an exhibition of paintings, drawings, statuary and woodcuts by Käthe Kollwitz, Otto Dix, Georg Grosz and Oskar Kokoschka. Lothar grabbed my arm, pulled me into a secluded alcove at the far end of the hall and kissed me long and deep. Smacking his lips appreciatively as he allowed us both to come up for air, he cooed, "God only knows how much I love you. I could never get any of the other lads interested in art and culture, much less drag them to a museum. You're so amenable to everything I suggest, and I love you for it."

I adored his spontaneity and the impulsive way

he'd often grab me for no specific reason that I could fathom and shower me with affection. "The manner in which you're so enthusiastic about a piece of artwork, a musical composition, a moving poem or the beauty of nature makes me enthusiastic, too. Your joy is so contagious and I don't mind being bitten by that sort of bug if it makes me more well-rounded and cultured."

Lothar nodded his approval. "And this is merely the tip of the iceberg, my dear," he asserted. "When we get to Berlin, you'll see how all this pales by comparison." Pulling out his pocket watch and glancing at the time, he added hastily, "They close here in half an hour. We'd better grab a bite to eat at a café before going off to the Operetta House."

It had slipped my mind about the theatre date we had planned. "What is it we're seeing again?" I asked timidly.

He unfurled the latest issue of *Münchener Neueste Nachrichten* and pointed to the playbill section: *Schön ist die Welt,* the newest operetta by Franz Lehár. "Hmm...I dunno about the veracity of a piece of musical fluff that boasts about how fair the world is at a time of turmoil like this," I remarked, trying to sound worldly and wise, but coming off more like a penny ante philosopher.

Lothar never ridiculed or demeaned me, fortunately, although he might pull a few fast punches every once in a while. "Of course it's no *Merry Widow*, *Land of Smiles* or *Count Luxemburg*," he retorted, amused by the blank look on my face as he rattled off the names of operettas I was only vaguely aware of, "but it'll do in a pinch. There's so little good theatre on at present. Besides," he added sheepishly, "I heard that ticket sales are not so brisk because everybody has to weigh the cost of eating and paying rent or going out for a night on the town. We'll be doing the theatre owner a favor."

I wanted to show off again and demonstrate how much knowledge I had accumulated. If truth be told, I gained most of my information from eavesdropping on conversations at work. Even though my job as mailroom clerk was a total dead end, I picked up choice tidbits of gossip and not a few scintillating stories. I also wanted to emphasize how the new medium of talking and singing motion pictures had taken Germany by storm, all but pulverizing any hopes for silent movies to reemerge as a viable choice. Charlie Chaplin would be the exception --- *sonst nichts*.

"They just came out with a film version of Kurt Weill's *Three Penny Opera*," I exclaimed, "and it features most of the original theatrical players. I couldn't imagine anybody except Lotte Lenya playing Pirate Jenny. I hope we'll get to see It sometime."

Lothar blanched a little, a pained expression crossing his face as if someone had just stepped on his toes. "Save your money and bypass these substandard German efforts like *Der Kongreß tanzt*, its English language cousin, *Congress Dances*, or the

Weill piece," he advised, "and take a gander at the stuff coming out of Hollywood like *42<sup>nd</sup> Street*, *Broadway Melody* or *The Smiling Lieutenant*. Those zany Marx Brothers are turning out some hilarious comedies, too. You'll find the direction and pacing much different than comparable German offerings."

I was taken aback by how passionately Lothar praised the attributes of American filmmaking. "You've got a point about Busby Berkeley's choreography as compared to the stodgy, clumpy and stilted dancing of some of our stars," I opined. "Even the French productions featuring Mistinguett and Joséphine Baker --- she's an American, by the way, who somehow became the toast of Paris by dancing in a banana costume and walking her pet leopard down the Champs-Élysées --- even they don't hold a candle to the Americans." That was quite a mouthful even for me and I needed to come up for air.

"They even came up with an adaptation of Remarque's *All Quiet on the Western Front*," Lothar quickly put in, "and it isn't half bad either. Of course Hollywood has never taken on themes of social importance like we did in the silent era. They really have nothing comparable to *Anders als die Anderen*, the first major motion picture which tackled the sticky subject of homosexuality." Assessing me, Lothar added, "You're too young to have seen it. It came out right after the end of the Kaiser's war. It wasn't the best, but at least it was something."

For a mere fifteen-year-old I was holding my own with the likes of Lothar Langenschlaff and even amazed myself at the veritable encyclopedic knowledge I was able to draw upon. "I disagree," I protested, daring to contradict a grown-up (my relationship with Lothar went far beyond that of adult and child, I'm pleased to say). "Aunt Gusti and I went to see *Birth of a Nation*, *Greed* and *The Crowd* at the silent pictures. All three films dealt with glaring social issues and the human struggle."

I wearied of defending American cinema too insistently. I was proud to be German and didn't want to sound too unpatriotic. "You do have to admit, though," I said with a big grin, "that we do horror and fantasy movies better than they do. There's nothing that comes close to *Caligari*, *Doktor Mabuse*, *Nosferatu*, *Metropolis* or *The Ring of the Niebelungen*."

Lothar was impressed with my assertion, but shook his head nonetheless. "I've heard tell that Universal Pictures --- *nanu*, that sounds suspiciously like *Universum-Filmgesellschaft* or UFA, *nee*? --- are rolling out a new feature called *Dracula* based on the Bram Stoker classic novel as well as a faintly Germanic-sounding suspense film with the title *Frankenstein*. Both are guaranteed to scare the pants off you."

I grinned and chimed in, "I'd rather you do that, *Liebling*." Besides, I couldn't imagine anything more frightening than *Nosferatu* in a million years.

As exciting as the finished product on celluloid was, the daily routine of a Bavaria Film-Kunst mailroom clerk could not have been more humdrum. I tried to sneak a peek at a few of the sound stages while wandering around during breaks, catching a glimpse of Hans Moser, Theo Lingen, Paul Hörbiger, Paula Wessely or Luis Trenker before some uniformed security man shooed me away.

"No unauthorized personnel allowed on the sets," he said menacingly, pointing to the words »*streng verboten*« on a signboard.

"But I work here," I moaned, trying to jockey into position to look over his shoulder at Leni Riefenstahl on one occasion.

"Doesn't matter," he responded, again with fingers pointed in an unwelcoming gesture. "These sets are 'hot.' Do you know what that means, *Bursche*?" He cheekily used the slang word for "kid" as he eyed me dubiously. Not waiting for an answer, he continued, "It means that everything on this set is ready to go for the crew and actors to shoot the scene. Nothing can be disturbed," he insisted, making a sweeping gesture, "and I mean *no-thing*! The lighting technician has taken a reading of how every single object will look on camera, so if something is pushed even one millimeter askew, two things happen. Do you know what they are?"

Again he watched me shake my head and didn't let me answer. "The scene is ruined," he snapped, "and I lose my job."

Expanding my horizons way beyond the narrow confines of sorting incoming letters and parcels and running them around in a pushcart to various departments, I began to realize how crucial the art of filmmaking could be. From this point onward when I watched a new movie, whether it was Hans Albers in *F.P 1 antwortet nicht*, Elisabeth Bergner in *The Rise of Catherine The Great* (she had flown the coop, too, but went to England instead of Hollywood) or Claudette Colbert and Frederic March in *The Sign of the Cross* (also being vaguely titillated by the scenes with Charles Laughton as Caesar with his slave boy), I looked for specific production values and imagined how the sets had been meticulously styled and perfected. Lothar noticed me scribbling copious notes and I suppose curiosity got the better of him. He broke down and asked me about it one day.

"It's hard to put my finger on," I replied. "Instead of taking that security man's scolding in a negative way, he actually spurred me on to see motion pictures as much more than meets the eye." I stroked Lothar's cheek and added kittenishly, "I guess I have you to thank for exposing me to all this culture. Between your fantastic library and opening up an entire array of art and music, my view of the world around me has become a little greater."

Lothar drew me close and smiled. "I always sensed that you were someone special," he said warmly. "From the moment I met you I perceived that you went beyond being one dimensional like all my other little fuck buddies."

That wasn't exactly the most ideally romantic comeback, but I was getting used to his way of putting me on a pedestal: the Ganymede, the *ephebus* who surpassed all his previous fleshly pursuits. No longer did I frown or pull away when he expressed himself like that; his heart was always in the right place as far as I was concerned.

"I'm beginning to see that your days as mailroom clerk are numbered," he confided. It gave me a start because I knew how hard it was to obtain and keep jobs in Germany these days. He noticed my concern and quickly added, "We'll be wrapping things up here in Munich shortly and shoving off for Berlin sooner than expected."

Even though I was overjoyed to hear the news of our oft-postponed departure, I couldn't help ejecting a bit of sarcasm into the mix. "Gee, Lothar," I moped, "I don't know if I can stand to be away from all the gossip and backbiting that goes on in the mailroom over at 'Bavaria.'"

Kissing me gently on the forehead he retorted, "Oh yeah, I can see how broken up you are about it. At any rate, I've got bigger plans for you."

I dozed off right after he gave me a good shagging. I hated it when Lothar became so aroused that he neglected to either use enough spittle on his cock before inserting it up my butt or failed to lubricate my hole properly. I was positive he was giving me hemorrhoids at this stage of the game, but I kept my trap shut. I just chalked it up to his schlong being so much bigger and meatier than anybody else's. He always made the inside of my ass tingle.

Just as I didn't have any recollection before my tenth birthday, I rarely remembered any of my dreams either. Dreamwork, along with many other metaphysical pursuits, had been all the rage in Weimar Germany. Dream analysis became a specialty adopted by learned scholars as well as a whole slew of charlatans. Most everybody had heard of Dr. Sigmund Freud and how he broke down a patient's dreams in order to form all sorts of conclusions about deep-seated psychological maladies and disorders.

Aunt Gusti got caught up in the frenzy of dreamwork and religiously wrote down everything she could remember from her nighttime journeys into the fourth dimension. She enjoyed reading them back to me on occasion and laughing her head off at some of the zanier ones. "That'll teach me to have a second helping of Bratwurst so close to bedtime," she quipped, practically always equating the weird imagery in her dreams with what she'd had on her dinner plate.

My dreams were largely influenced by what I read, saw in the picture show and newsreels or recalled from phonograph records and the ever increasing popularity of radio. I played a little game with myself, sort of a word comparison and how amusing the difference between two similar sounding words could be. My current obsession was the contrast between *Bauhaus*, the emerging bold architectural style, and *Schauhaus*, a popular slang word for one of those establishments where the world's oldest profession was carried out to the satisfaction of sporting clients. Aunt Gusti had often tried in vain to divert my attention from noticing these ubiquitous houses in many areas of Munich, but to no avail.

Although people of all ages throughout Germany were slowly breaking out of their rigid, disciplined lives and spreading their wings (I along with them, but only to a lesser extent), licentious behavior replaced our staid Teutonic morals. Artists, poets, authors and composers were quick to pick up on this shift and reflected it brilliantly in their works.

Censorship in the cinematic arena prevented filmmakers from venturing too far beyond the required strictures, but little glimpses could still be had on screen. And what Germany didn't see fit to include on celluloid the Americans took up the slack with such torrid offerings as *Red Dust* starring Clark Gable and Jean Harlow, blonder, bustier and dreamier than Dietrich could ever hope to be. I imagined myself in her place being screwed by Gable until the man's brains turned to mush and my asshole was on fire.

My mind was rife with ideas and images. I was constantly bombarded by the seedier side of our existence, no matter how much Aunt Gusti or other well-meaning adults tried to dissuade me. Lothar never bothered. He actually did more to stoke those lascivious thoughts and actions. Who better to benefit from them than he?

"In Hamburg there is a street," he once told me, "completely closed off to everyone except horny men. On Herbertstraße one wanders between crimson lighting shining in the houses on either side where the available girls and women display themselves, discuss prices of their services with prospective customers and engage in snappy dialogue to heighten stimulation." I never forgot his description and often wondered if a similar street existed somewhere with boys and men engaging in the same type of activity. It caused me to fantasize a lot about it and wish that I could find out for myself what it was all about.

As a sixteen-year-old, however, I rolled these types of things around solely in my mind or dreamt about them often. In one particular dream I am sitting in one of those windows which Lothar Langenschlaff had described so vividly. Under his stern watch a tuxedoed Lothar exhibits me to a bevy of admirers. Men and boys of all shapes, sizes and complexions clamor to get a look at me, shout obscenities and tease me with promises of candy and wads of Reichsmarks. Scores of ultramodern Bauhaus structures rise high about the street along with skyscrapers and crystal monoliths that are reminiscent of the Schufftan Process effects used in the Fritz Lang classic, *Metropolis*: a grotesque city of the future. Lotte Lenya, half melodious *chanteuse* and half coarse imitation of herself, belts out a tune from her husband Kurt Weill's newest operetta, *The Rise and Fall of the City of Mahogonny*. Her voice booms over the noisy onlookers, but the lyrics are meant for me alone, and I cower:

> *Meine Herren, meine Mutter prägte*
> *Auf mich einst ein schlimmes Wort:*
> *Ich würde enden im Schauhaus*
> *Oder an einem noch schlimmern Ort.*

> (Dear Gentlemen, my mother once
> Impressed upon me an ominous word:
> I would end up in a brothel
> Or in an even worse place.

I woke up in a cold sweat, panicking for a second or two until I looked to my right and saw Lothar's head on the pillow next to me. He was snoring away contentedly, as usual. His long, slender neck still struck me as curiously feminine. Poking around under the bed covers, I ran my fingers along his stiff member and fondled his ample testicles before nodding off again. I heard his snoring break off abruptly, he made a few crazy slurping sounds with his lips, then turned and breathed normally.

"I probably will end up in a worse place," I mused.

## Chapter Nine    CINEMA AS A WEAPON

I like to read. Thank God one of the American soldiers brings me a German translation of Hemingway's *For Whom The Bell Tolls* and Maugham's *The Razor's Edge* to pass time here in the cell. I enjoy listening to music, but there's no chance of anything like that here. I lack both a phonograph and radio, although I hear one of the privates whistling "Elmer's Tune" which I recognize from Charlie and His Band, alias Lutz Templin. And I adore moving pictures, of course. Scenes from all the old films I've already mentioned plus many more to follow keep reeling through my brain like a never-ending spool on a movie projector. It is the only thing which preserves my sanity in the midst of this incredible twist of events

As a production assistant for the three major German studios plus brief stints at Bavaria Film-Kunst, Barrandov in Bohemia and Moravia (the part of Czechoslovakia that was firmly in the hands of the German Reich) and Cinecittà in Italy, I worked so hard on the actual projects and rarely got to see the finished product. That's the way it was with many actors, too. Not a few of them would intentionally not watch themselves on film for fear of being overly critical of their work.

It surprises me that some have so little self-esteem and are appalled by their own looks. Lisca Malbran was one of the few actresses I did have the pleasure of speaking to at some length toward the end of the war when she was still doing screen tests for director Boleslaw Balogh. A stunning young girl who could make the heart of a (straight) man flutter and certainly charmed a (gay) man like myself, she had zero faith in her ability or talent. Such a shame! I heard tell that Marika Rökk offered to take Lisca under her wing, teach her a few perky dance moves and give her tools to enhance her screen allure, but finally threw up her hands in frustration.

Those old American movies must have made an impression on me because I still vividly recall images which transcend chains, barbed wire, damp, poorly-lit cells and bolted doors. I fondly remember Shirley Temple taping her way up and down a staircase with a tall, charming Negro named Bill "Bojangles" Robinson, Ginger Rogers and Fred Astaire, both dressed to the nines, gliding across a parqueted dance floor (our version at UFA in Babelsberg was polished to look like glass and hosted the terpsichorean talents of La Jana, Johannes Heesters and the indefatigable Rökk) or a massive dance extravaganza with Judy Garland, Mickey Rooney, Ray Bolger or Eleanor Powell, usually choreographed with military precision under the adept direction of Busby Berkeley or Hermes Pan. The musical numbers ring eternally in my mind and call up both good and bad memories of times long past.

Of course when the Americans declared war on Japan right after that nation's deadly bombing of the

Pearl Harbor naval installation in Honolulu, Hawaii, and Germany, in turn, made the huge mistake of declaring war on the United States, all American movies were removed from our theatres, new releases were banned altogether and American stars were suddenly vilified in our press and *Film-Kurier* magazines. "Jewish domination of Hollywood" was the mantra that appeared time and time again where, just a few years earlier, it had never been an issue because the American product stoked the German public's imagination and kept us in a lighthearted mood. After all, who couldn't love Mickey Mouse, Bugs Bunny and Krazy Kat?

I have no way of knowing, but I have my suspicions about the discontinuance of U.S. films in relation to the viewing habits of two of German's biggest movie fans: the Führer himself and Propaganda Minister Goebbels. My guess is that Hitler and select members of his retinue (the SS bodyguards, perhaps?) continued to view every Hollywood release after 1941. It just seems like something that a powerful man like the Führer would do to relax from the exigencies of orchestrating Germany's demise. (Did he really think that the German people no longer deserved to win the war? Wasn't Himmler of the same opinion? And Goebbels? Oh, I won't even bother to ask what he thought!)

As much as Hitler hated the Americans, I am convinced that he absolutely despised the British.

For all his diabolical posturing, old Uncle Adolf was a smart cookie in many ways. He must have been stunned at how easily the rest of the big nations caved into his demands for more *Lebensraum*, more breathing space for us Germans, and always with the promise that it would be his final request, but then pushing his luck even further.

I believe, however, that he felt truly betrayed by Britain when they wouldn't accept his generous offer to ally with Germany in order to beat down the French who were starting to get too big for their britches in Europe. He miscalculated British zeal and iron will, never forgiving them for not aligning themselves to us in the right and proper Anglo-Saxon spirit. Most likely he confused it with sympathy to the concept of Aryan purity and a bulwark of Western European countries against a rising tide of Bolshevism. It must have confounded his entire way of thinking and caused him to make major mistakes in planning and executing the war.

People throughout Germany clamored to see *Jud Süß,* the brilliantly conceived but overly egregious film directed by Veit Harlan and blessed specifically by Dr. Goebbels himself (with some clicking of tongue in disapproval of the sneaky way his commission for this pet project was shunted to the back burner several times during the course of several years chiefly by the stars and other personages who were looking for every way possible to disassociate themselves from the monstrosity).

Leaders of Hitler Youth and German Girls' League brigades encouraged their charges to see the movie for its significant propaganda value. Unsuspecting Jewish citizens whose misfortune it was to be on the streets near movie theatres were randomly attacked by marauding boys and girls in towns all over Germany who emerged from a showing of the film and were inflamed with passion by its anti-Semitic message. Ferdinand Marian and Kristina Söderbaum, the two principal stars of the movie, became overnight sensations.

That was in peacetime, though, and it remains in our memory more so than the release of *Ohm Krüger* in mid-1941 just as the war with the Soviet Union was getting underway. People forget what a sensation that film made the moment it hit screens all over the country right in the midst of war. It boasted a stellar cast headed by Emil Jannings who, in my opinion, is still our most prolific actor and infinitely more watchable than the ponderous Otto Gebühr in his Frederick the Great roles or even a national treasure such as Heinrich George with his classic alliteration.

Jannings has an enormous ego and a vicious temper if accounts of his relationship to other players can be believed. Marlene Dietrich recounts her near brush with death by strangulation when Jannings as Professor Rath in *The Blue Angel* delved into his character a bit too enthusiastically in one of his final scenes with the brash Lola-Lola. He took his

Ferdinand Marian and Kristina Söderbaum in the
Veit Harlan film,
*Jud Süß*

anger out on her because Josef von Sternberg had paired him with an actress whom Jannings considered vastly inferior for such an important role.

*Ohm Krüger*, in comparison, illustrates the struggle of brave Dutch settlers in South Africa whose nationalistic aspirations ran afoul of British colonial designs for the region toward the end of the nineteenth century. The resulting Boer War is the main theme of the film and every attempt is made to paint the humble, patriotic *trekkers* as cruelly oppressed by the British troops.

The discovery of gold in the Transvaal is at the center of the struggle and the overriding interest of both sides to control the mines should have been the real focus of the story. Dr. Goebbels and the Propaganda Ministry, however, had other ideas regarding the ideological content of the film. The war machine cranked at full speed and it was time to fuel it with outrage from the masses. Just as the historical content of *Jud Süß* sparked controversy about the existence of Jewry in modern Europe, so was *Ohm Krüger* a vehicle for stepped-up hatred and revulsion of the British enemy.

In the movie the unmistakable portrayals of Queen Victoria, Cecil Rhodes and Lord Kitchener are easily discernible. By far the most prolific character was the camp commandant, played effectively by Otto Wernicke. His brutal methods of dealing with the wives and children of the Boer insurrectionists leave a definite impression on the moviegoer, especially during the final scenes of the film. The illusion to Winston Churchill is also not lost in Wernicke's depiction of a gruff, burly officer in service to the British Crown: a vile authoritarian and glutton who allows his dog to chow down whole slices of meat while the concentration camp inmates starve and are stricken with typhus. When the hapless camp doctor dares to point out a can of putrid meat and suggests that provisions for the prisoners are lacking, the Churchill-*Doppelgänger* threatens to send him to the front unless he clams up and agrees that conditions in camp are normal.

It makes me wonder how much similar activity went on behind the scenes between officers, guards, doctors and *Kapos* in our own camps prior to Germany's defeat. For those of us who ended up in one of those camps, the analogy suggested by the movie for the precedence of such camps in modern times was certainly not wasted.

Since foreign movie consumption by the German public had been severely restricted after 1941, along with musical numbers like "U-Bahn Fox/Métro-Stomp" by Belgian jazz great Fud Candrix and other records which Dr. Goebbels had designated "Nigger Jazz," I simply have no idea if subtle yet clever productions similar to *Ohm Krüger* existed on American, British or Soviet celluloid. Surely the enemy nations must have had their share of propaganda films to boost morale so that their citizens would continue to fight onward toward

Promotional material for *Ohm Krüger*

victory. We ordinary Germans were vaguely aware of them, but were not in the select group who were privileged to view such offerings.

What I also do not know is that at this very moment the cinema is being employed as a weapon within the very walls of this prison. Well beyond the confinement of these cells, the officers' recreation room has been set up this evening as a makeshift movie theatre. Instead of a Betty Grable musical, some fluffy period piece or a swashbuckling adventure, the projectionist threads eight millimeter film through the spools of his machine and soon the words, "YOUR JOB IN GERMANY" flicker on the rickety portable screen, eliciting audible grunts, groans and sneers from the assembled personnel.

"Geez, Sarge," a wiry private from Cincinnati moans, "do we havta? I'm gettin' sick o' these friggin' War Department flicks. Ain't we savvy enough already 'bout how to treat the Krauts?"

The big moose of a sergeant, a tall redhead from the Texas panhandle flashes him a stern look. "Evidently y'all need more learnin' 'bout them things," he drawls. "The commandant sent me over a whole bunch o' these here moo'in pict-churz fer y'all to watch – one ev'ry night. Whad'ya think o' them apples?"

Another private winces. "Pretty rotten, if ya ask me," he blurts out in his perceptible Brooklyn accent. "If dey'd throw in a bit o' skin – y'know, somethin' along da lines o' Rita Haywoith or even Bogie 'n

Bacall --- it'd be woith watchin'! We're fed up wit' loinin' 'bout how we gotta treat these Joimens!"

Lost completely on both the sergeant as well as his subordinates is the irony that this series of instructional films was put together under the direction of no less than the brilliant Frank Capra. He's come a long way from winning the Academy Award for *It Happened One Night* to churning out propaganda for the benefit of soldiers stationed on what is still considered "enemy territory," if we are to believe the narrators claim.

Capra was probably caught up in patriotic fervor just like many of our prominent countrymen were during the height of the war. Zarah Leander's participation in the *Winterhilfswerke* comes to mind: a mink-clad superstar helping our soldiers collect discarded warm coats and blankets to be donated to the less fortunate in wintertime. Either that, or forced mobilization to contribute talents and efforts "for the cause," since both Axis and Allies attested that God was on their side. I understand from a Russian inmate back in the Rosenholm camp that Stalin even allowed Soviet citizens to bring out the religious icons they'd stored away after the 1917 Revolution, dust them off and pray fervently with the intercession of the holy saints and martyrs for victory against the Fascists.

The film which flickers on the screen before the pie-eyed soldiers is a compilation of archival footage from the NSDAP vaults, footage taken by Allied cameramen of our country in the aftermath of the war, some of it intact but mostly in ruins, and a few pleasant travelogue scenes of striking natural beauty, rolling landscapes, majestic hills and jolly people roaming about in peacetime contentment. *"You're going to see a lot of pretty country,"* the narrator gushes and follows this enthusiasm with the ominous caveat: *"But never lose sight of one thing: you are still on enemy soil, still treading in hostile territory."*

Next is presented a capsulized version of Germany's history from the time of unification under Bismarck, the development of and traditions linked to Prussian militarism, the devastation wrought by the Kaiser's war, the disarray of the postwar era and the harsh terms of the Versailles Treaty. The soldiers will grasp the concept of a Germany so overwhelmingly steeped in militarism that if the Allied occupiers don't do something to promote everlasting peace and stability in the region, these nutty Germans may well become trigger-happy again and start World War III.

Emphasis on the twelve-year existence of Hitler's Third Reich is the next item tackled by the film. The narrator draws particular attention to segments of the German population who may still sympathize with the Führer's platform for a thousand year empire and a New Order in Europe, one that would become the prototype for Germany's rule over the whole of mankind. A song segment clip from *Hitlerjunge Quex* drives this point home:

*»Denn heute gehört uns Deutschland
und morgen die ganze Welt!«*

The narrator explains that these were the lofty aspirations of the Hitler Youth and likeminded Germans who saw themselves as the Master Race. He also warns that young minds are especially susceptible to ideological molding and shaping. *"The embers of Hitlerian zeal still smolder within the hearts and minds of many German boys and girls, so be particularly on your guard,"* he proclaims.

The film's focus shifts several times and attempts to dissect the root causes of why a cultured nation would plunge itself into the depths of barbarism. The dilemma of a country which produces great men like Goethe, Schiller, Beethoven, Wagner and Einstein but also allows the rise of monsters like Göring, Goebbels and Himmler remains unsolved as the narrator's closing remarks and a surge of orchestral brass signal the end of this particular installment of *YOUR JOB IN GERMANY*.

Many more episodes in the series will follow in the coming days and weeks. Topics such as "Being Courteous," "Respecting Cultural Differences and Customs," "Detecting Pockets of Resistance," and the simple imperative, "Be Vigilant!" will be covered. Whether they have any noticeable effect of the way the soldiers carry out their duties remains to be seen.

Aside from desiring a stash of juicier flicks on hand

to watch during these long summer evenings, most of the youthful occupiers have one thing on their minds. "Hey, Kowalski," a tall, good-looking blond with close-cropped hair remarks to a stubby, dark-haired fellow MP who sticks a piece of Juicy Fruit gum in his mouth, "do you reckon we'll get laid before the weekend is up?"

"Hell, I dunno," he grumbles. "Them German broads are pretty cooperative after you buy 'em a few highballs. But I do believe there's some kinda racket goin' on."

The blond looks confused and asks, "Whad'ya mean, Kowalski?"

Older and wiser by a couple of years, Kowalski assumes a serious expression and explains, "Dames like that ain't just sittin' around to warm the seat cushions. They're in cahoots with the bartender to keep lurin' chumps like us into buying more booze. That kinda of things stinks to high heaven."

The blond shakes his head and laughs. "You're prob'ly right, man. But you gotta admit that it's worth it in the end if you have one o' those delicious li'l gals to get frisky with. No wonder some o' them Krauts put up such a fierce fight if one o' them sweeties is what he's fightin' to get home to."

Kowalski chuckles. "You ain't right too often, Jensen," he chimes in, "but you're right on the money with that one, buddy boy." Scratching his head, he adds, "I wonder why the fuck we got so many dozens o' these perverted li'l pussy boys in this lockup. With all the hot lookin' tomatoes in this country, it just don't make sense."

Grinning, Jensen volunteers, "Yeah. There sure does seem to be a mess of 'em. I guess the Nazis didn't care for 'em much either. That's why they sentenced 'em to hard labor in the camps along with all o' them other desirables."

"We oughta do the same back home," Kowalski shoots back with a frown. "Them filthy pansies ain't got no business living among us normal slobs."

Jensen smiles benignly and his normally dull slate eyes begin to sparkle. He thinks back on the young men's choir from a nearby town which came to serenade the soldiers during a concert at the Allied command post last Friday night. Dressed in muslin shirts with simple embroidered folk designs and leather shorts, he would have gladly shoved his dick up any of their asses. He'd been seeing quite a few exceptional lads since arriving for this assignment. He resolves, however, to keep his own kinky fantasies under wraps, lest his comrades-in-arms brand him a "pussy boy," too. (Never mind that he relishes screwing a fellow more than a gal, but in no way, shape or form considers himself queer...)

# IMAGES FROM WEIMAR GERMANY

**Hindenburg Poster during 1932 campaign**

**Social Democrat candidate Otto Wels**

**THE TWO ERNSTS**
Communist Party candidate Ernst Thälmann (left) and SA (Brown Shirts) leader Ernst Röhm

Opening of the first Dada Exhibition, Berlin

Cultural icons of the avant-garde movement
(l. to r.) Kurt Weill, Lotte Lenya & Bertolt Brecht

Images from the classic Fritz Lang film, *Metropolis*, starring Heinrich George and Brigitte Helm

SA recruiting posters accentuating masculinity and the allure of the brown shirt uniform

Promotion for the Dájos Béla Orchestra

Scene from *Der Blaue Engel* (The Blue Angel) with Marlene Dietrich and Rosa Valetti

Willi Fritsch and Lilian Harvey in *Die Drei von der Tankstelle* (The Three from the Filling Station)

Marlene Dietrich in male attire

Transvestites at the Eldorado club - early 1930's

Elisabeth Bergner

Greta Garbo

Members of the German naturist movement

## Chapter Ten    SYMPHONY OF A CITY

Coming to Munich was quite a jolt to my senses after having spent my blur of a childhood in serene little Wiedersdorf. Even the pleasant liaisons I'd had with the few big-dicked strapping country boys wasn't as exhilarating as being in the whirl of a big city where the variety of things to do never seemed to end. At the time, Munich was a sum total of my exposure to big city life and I was more than satisfied to stay there the rest of my born days.

Berlin, though, was much grander than I'd imagined. If truth be told, I was overwhelmed. The big whirl that had been Munich couldn't hold a candle to the gyro top spinning out of control that was Berlin. Just the mere patterns of vehicular traffic frightened me, but only for a short time. It was all very neat and orderly in a typically efficient German way, although we didn't realize how much more organized we were compared to other nationalities. Omnibuses cohabitated nicely with passenger cars, taxis and delivery trucks jockeyed into position on Unter den Linden or the Kurfürstendamm. Pedestrians tended to hurry more here than in Munich. Where they were headed in such a frenzy I could hardly imagine, but the rhythm and tempo was much accelerated, that's for sure.

Nighttime Berlin seemed a magical place. Neon signs glared, vying with the starry sky and each other to advertise the worth of their products and services.

The superiority of the Kaufhaus des Westens signs were weighed against those of Hermann Tietz. The benefits of Dr. Oetker's baking powder and the pain relief from Bayer aspirin products were touted to the passersby. And the bold nocturnal offerings of Café Monbijou over the equally enticing Kleist Kasino were not to be missed. After all, neon signs don't lie, do they?

The names of Berlin's countless districts and boroughs conveyed vivid images which had little, if anything, to do with the terrain or makeup of its streets, alleyways, parks, graceful mansions or noisy, overcrowded tenement housing. They spoke of solidity and unbroken traditions with the past. Lothar pointed out the various highpoints of Kreuzberg, Neukölln, Wilmersdorf, Pankow, Lichtenberg and his own neighborhood in swanky Dahlem. He laughed as I oohed and aahed at the many intriguing aspects of Berlin's fascinating architecture and massive monuments.

"I can't believe how huge the Brandenburg Gate is," I squealed. "Seeing it in photos and on the movie screen is one thing, but to be standing under it is something else. I'll bet it's as big as, or bigger than, the Pyramids of Egypt."

Lothar shook his head, trying to stifle a laugh. "I've been to Giza and have seen the Great Pyramid of Cheops," he bragged. "Believe me, the Brandenburg Gate is puny in comparison. But there's no denying that it's huge nonetheless." He was behind the wheel of his Daimler car as we moved away from the Victory Column and could easily see the Reichstag building not far in the distance. Reaching over, he grabbed my crotch and gave my cock a good tug through the corduroy material of my trousers.

"How can I ever thank you for everything you've done for me?" I asked in amazement. "Sometimes I just want to burst out crying when I think about how lucky a kid I am." What was also on my mind at that moment was how protected I was from the turmoil that engulfed the German nation. There was no denying that we were in the full throes of a worldwide economic depression. As the July elections approached things didn't seem to be improving.

Lothar's elegant villa was tucked away in Dahlem, far from the maddening crowds and violent unrest that cropped up everywhere in Berlin. There were marches of disgruntled former employees who stormed the gates of factories in Tempelhof. Food riots broke out in Friedrichshain, bricks were thrown through plate glass windows and shops looted down to the last stitch of merchandise. Picked pockets and snatched purses increased at an alarming rate. The local constabularies could scarcely keep up with the rash of burglaries, muggings and even more stringent crimes. Bad things seemed to be happening at every turn, and there was no end in sight.

"I've been seriously thinking about hiring a security detail for this place," Lothar explained to me as we sat in his den drinking coffee on a Saturday morning in late June. "Moreover, I want to bring bodyguards on board for you and me, *Schatz*." I stared at him intently and he said nothing further. Of course I'd read historical accounts of the unwashed masses rising up against their well-fed oppressors countless times before. For the life of me I couldn't imagine the proletarian mobs marching across the lawns of the wealthy in Dahlem or Charlottenburg and laying siege to our impregnable fortresses in sheer numbers. Surely those kinds of treacherous times were relegated to the distant past, not designed to happen in modern times. Contemporary man was above all those sorts of tactics. Or was he?

I began to resent Lothar for insisting that I accompany him to Berlin in the first place. It's true, the initial idea excited me because of the adventures I would have, the celebrities I might meet and the change of scenery. Lothar had promised bigger and better things for me in contrast to the dreary job in the mailroom at Bavaria Film-Kunst, but nothing materialized in this regard. Naturally with the tens of thousands of people being laid off in Berlin and the lines at employment exchanges and soup kitchens growing longer day by day, I couldn't expect him to come up with anything for me at the moment. It's just that I was getting a bit restless, antsy to do something --- anything --- to earn my own money.

"But *Schätzlein*," Lothar protested, his mouth curling into a childish pout, "don't you like soaking up all this splendor?" He spread his arms wide, taking in the entire interior of his glorious villa with little scooping motions. "Why, any lad your age would give his right arm to live in the lap of luxury, yet you seem so ungrateful."

I was in the middle of reading a lengthy article in *Illustrierte Film-Kurier* about the new Fritz Lang thriller, *M*, with Peter Lorre. The description of the child molester/murderer and the reactions of the incensed mob set me on edge, especially in light of everything that was occurring off-screen and for real in Berlin. Sniffing disapprovingly, I mumbled, "I don't want to be dependent for my livelihood on you, Lothar. I like making my own money and being self-sufficient. It doesn't mean I love you less. You know that I appreciate everything you do for me."

The iconic photo of Peter Lorre with eyes wide bugging out in fright stared at me from the page and I marveled at his ability to emote. It seemed that all of our actors possessed this unique talent and used it to their advantage in the transition from silent films to talkies. Lothar and I had just seen a Czechoslovak import entitled *Ekstase* which, ostensibly a sound film, contained minimal dialogue and was as effective as anything from the rapidly disappearing silent screen. I would have gladly seen Charlie Chaplin continue to make silent films and couldn't imagine what he'd sound like if his vocal chords ever uttered a peep.

Lothar sought to distract me. "Well, youngster,"

he said patronizingly, "there are lots of things to occupy time and enrich your life. Moping around here all day reading movie magazines doesn't help. There's plenty to do here in Berlin that is a lot healthier."

I was vaguely aware of the bawdy side of Berlin and the tolerance Berliners had for different lifestyles. But I was at too tender an age to be led to Nollendorfplatz or Motzstraße to see the goings-on inside the Eldorado Club. I wasn't old enough to go dancing at Schwanenburg when the normally staid café crowd receded and the place was taken over by the "yoo-hoo boys" who danced, cavorted and screamed their heads off whenever a rumor about a police raid circulated. Curiously enough, the authorities never bothered much about the place or the wild goings-on there.

I often used creased pamphlets and other bits of paper as bookmarks when all else failed. Lots of them were available now since every political party worth its salt was handing them out. I pulled a flyer that I'd folded in half and utilized as sort of a line ruler to help me read small newspaper type. I showed it to Lothar and he looked intrigued.

"Where did you get this?" he asked, smiling.

"A really handsome young blond guy was standing on the corner of Ku-Damm and Uhlandstraße the other day when you went for your fitting at Schiff's and I was wandering around looking at the shop windows. I neglected to mention it to you."

Lothar held up the flyer and pointed to a date and time printed under the photo of a corpulent man with a bristly moustache and an academic air. "I've heard of this man many times before. He is the founder of something called 'The Scientific Humanitarian Committee' which has now blossomed into the more expansive 'Institute for Sexual Research.' He has some fervent revolutionary ideas about folks like you and me."

Puzzled, I asked him, "Like you and me? What's so special about us that this kindly-looking man would take an interest in?"

"He's an advocate for the rights of the 'third sex' and has been campaigning for a long time to have Paragraph 175 repealed."

My brain was in a total muddle. "Third sex?" I asked, trying to imagine what type of conglomeration that would be. "And what's Paragraph 175?"

Lothar winked. "The anti-sodomy law," he replied. "It's been an integral part of the Penal Code in this country for decades. Ever since Bismarck and unification, to be precise. People haven't paid too much attention to it."

Shaking my head, I exclaimed, "I've never heard of such a law. You say it's in the Penal Code?"

"It's there as plain as the nose on your face, *Schatz*," he said, "although I doubt if the little people of your Podunk village even know it exists." I resented his insinuation and name-calling directed at

Wiedersdorf, although deep down I agreed with him. "In Munich people are aware of it, but don't care one way or the other. And in Berlin they openly flaunt it."

Feeling brazen myself, I asked, "So you mean to tell me that there's actually a law on the books which prevents you from shoving your prick up my ass and fucking me? I wouldn't have ever given it a second thought. I always believed people were just repelled by it on moral or religious grounds."

Lothar's eyes brightened and a sly grin played upon his lips. «*Menschenskind,*» he murmured, "I just love it when you talk dirty, *mein Junge.*" He grabbed the magazine and the flyer, threw them aside and swept me off the chair into his arms. "I just can't help myself," he added breathlessly as he carried me to the bedroom for a bit of afternoon delight.

**The Brandenburg Gate**

Two of the hundreds of thousands of unemployed throughout Germany in the early 1930's

Berlin dance club for men only

## Chapter Eleven   FIGURING IT OUT

The unthinkable happened. For reasons that I didn't wrap my head around, Adolf Hitler and the National Socialist Workers' Party gained higher visibility during the months leading up to the elections. I saw Brown Shirts everywhere: marching, distributing flyers while perched aboard campaign buses and makeshift rostrums, and creating a definite presence among the general population. Some people welcomed them and felt they lent an authoritative air to the atmosphere of unruliness which seemed to have Germany in its grip. Some even went so far as to claim that the Storm Troopers could restore order and safety to the streets.

"Our policemen's hands are full and they need all the help they can get," opined a wizened gentleman who often passed by Lothar's house and tried to strike up a conversation out of loneliness. I usually stood there and made no comment when he spouted off. Lothar, on the other hand, was seething about the way the Social Democrats lagged in the polls and ready to counter any statements contrary to his unique *Weltanschauung*.

"What about vigilantism, *mein lieber Herr*?" he asked point blank. "What makes you think they're all honest and upright? Some of them could be dyed-in-the-wool troublemakers. The SA bathes them, throws nice clean brown shirts on them and they banter about with glorious Nazi symbols. But they're basically rotten to the core --- just a bunch of thugs, hooligans and no-counts."

The old warrior was ready for battle, but something that Lothar had mentioned gave him pause to consider. Scratching his head, he spoke slowly and deliberately with rhythmic clicking, for his dentures were ill-fitting. "I don't mind hooligan or no-count so much as I do the rumor that most of them are sweet on each other." Lothar and I exchanged a meaningful glance.

"And what difference does that make?" Lothar asked sarcastically. "Do you believe there are homosexuals within their ranks? They still carry out their work efficiently, don't they?"

The normally stooped old man straightened himself and, despite being short, stood with an air of Prussian arrogance, puffing up his cheeks and throwing his chest out. He waved away Lothar's concerns and exclaimed, "I don't have to remind you that it's common knowledge that their leader, Ernst Röhm, is the biggest whoopsie in all Germany." I was taken aback by the elderly man's brashness and didn't know which way to face in order to hide my embarrassment. "If he's taking sexual liberties with any of those boys, then the Führer needs to be informed so that appropriate measures can be taken."

Fortunately Lothar had been following the campaign minutely and heard the candidates' speeches and read about them down to the last detail in all the newspapers. Although he always listened more attentively to those running on the Social Democrat ticket, he kept abreast of what the opposition was saying and had answers at his fingertips as well as snappy comebacks to every argument.

"The 'Führer,' as you so lovingly refer to him, has already done something," hisses Lothar. "He claims that the Storm Troopers cannot be likened to a young ladies' finishing school, but it is a training corps for fighters. He insists that whatever extracurricular activities they are engaged in should not be subject to public scrutiny. Furthermore, he asserts that the party apparatus is not interested in any of their internal struggles just so long as they remain loyal to him and defend the honor of the German people."

The wrinkled old man looked crestfallen and his whole body and stance became more shriveled than ever. "If the Führer says it," he conceded, "then I take him at his word. Still, just the idea of those fornicators indulging in unspeakable acts with one another repulses good, upstanding Germans like myself." Eager to change the subject, he proudly pointed to his lapel and boasted, "Did you notice my Adolf Hitler campaign button? It's coated with something that glows in the dark!"

Lothar looked aghast, leaned toward me and *sotto voce* said, "That's all we need: Hitler's face shining bright and guiding our way through the dark night."

We bid the old man *adieu* and he grunted. "It just goes to show you how the uneducated voter in this country is swayed by every little gimmick."

Thinking back on the way the old man's button looked, I chimed in, "It is pretty clever, you've got to admit. Who knows? Those'll probably be worth something someday."

Lothar's face turned sour and he retorted, "The only thing those buttons'll be are faded souvenirs of a failed candidacy. He won't even be a footnote in the history books once Wels and the Social Democrats wipe the floor with him and his renegade Nazis. "

I wasn't remotely interested in politics, but even a casual observer couldn't help but notice the excitement that Hitler stirred up. I always heard Lothar wax enthusiastic about Otto Wels. For the life of me I failed to see anything but lackluster in the darling of the Social Democrats. Even though I was far too young to vote, I think I'd prefer my favorite candidates to possess at least some charisma. Love him, hate him or feel indifferent about him, Hitler fit the bill.

I'll be the last to admit that I had ever taken him seriously. I cringed when my mom had written how impressed she and all the Wiedersdorfers had been after first hearing him over the radio. I was tempted to reply, "*Jawohl, Mutti*, he's the funniest comic with the most bizarre sounding delivery I've ever heard," but knew such barbs would only anger or confuse her. She had been against me relocating to "that big, bawdy city, Munich," anyway, and would have probably chalked up my sarcasm as just another vicious habit I'd picked up to corrupt me further.

In my quest for truth and beauty in life, though, I considered all things and was shaped in my thinking by many different points of view. Although I disliked Hitler, I was curious to find out how I could be in the minority. I discussed it with Lothar, but he was too much of a cheerleader for the Social Democrats that I could never get an objective analysis from him.

Help in figuring it out came from an unexpected but familiar source: Aunt Gusti. She insinuated herself into our lives again after things with her former coworker, Heinz Lübke, didn't pan out. It turned out that her fiancé never returned from Portugal, but instead fell for a dark-eyed beauty with olive skin in Funchal. Gusti broke off the engagement and made her way to Berlin. Although she didn't have Lothar's address and just vaguely remembered him mentioning Dahlem, her resourcefulness paid off and she found the place.

"It quite simple, *Liebling*," she said, "but whatever you do, please don't let Lothar know I spoke to you about Hitler. He's such a fuddy-duddy Social Democrat bordering on full-fledged Commie that he's liable to have a hissy fit." I nodded and promised it was "mum's the word."

Pointing at me, she continued, "You like the movies, so you already know that he's pure theatrics.

He has all the right moves, makes all the appropriate gestures and takes the entire weight of Germany's problems on his shoulders. Modern-day martyrdom, pure and simple."

"But where do the theatrics come in?" I asked and Gusti noticed the puzzled look on my face.

"Oh, come on now, *mein junger Mann*," she replied in a sing-song voice, "have you seen him in the *Wochenschau* newsreels or only heard him on the radio?" Without waiting for an answer, she plodded on. "No matter. Here it is in a nutshell. He always starts out his speeches in a calm, collected manner. As he begins to identify what he thinks is wrong with the country and who the enemies are, his voice grows louder. When he rails against the Versailles Treaty, the causes of the economic depression, the predominance of Jews or the shoddy way ordinary Germans have been treated, he embodies everything that one feels in the gut: pain, degradation and defeat. Rising to a crescendo, he places himself on the altar of sacrifice and pledges to make all things right again even if he himself dies."

Gusti looked out of breath and totally spent. Her explanation was quite a performance in itself. There was a strange gleam in her eye, exactly like the one I'd seen in published photos of Hitler's followers gathered round him while he spoke. "You sound as if you admire him, Auntie," I hazarded to say.

Staring at me with the unmistakable gleam frozen on the whites of her eyes, she chimed in dreamily. "I dunno. You all know that I've been a Hindenburg supporter for ages, but the Old Soldier doesn't look so hot nowadays. If he's elected, I fear he may die in office."

"But I thought we once agreed that the clown in the Charlies Chaplin moustache didn't have a snowball's chance in hell."

Gusti gave me a little jab in the ribs and exclaimed, "In case you haven't been paying attention, he's posted tremendous gains in the latest polls. That's what you get from keeping your nose shoved in all those movie magazines."

"Yeah, I know," I shrugged. "Lothar harps at me about the same thing. I'm just not charged up by politics. The stars are so much more glamorous."

Gusti grabbed me by the arm, pulled me over to the window of her little room in a Moabit boarding house and pointed to some posters affixed to a Litfaß-column on the opposite side of the street. The man's shadowy portrait in brown and black, a group of huddled, miserable-looking creatures and the words, »*Unsere letzte Hoffnung,*« (Our Last Hope) and the huge capital letters H I T L E R caught my eye. "There's your next big star, *Liebchen*," she declared, and there was an eerie finality about her words.

Two campaign poster from the 1932 election

Charlie Chaplin as a Hitleresque character in *The Great Dictator*

**Typical Berlin street scene in the early 1930's complete with a Litfaß-column where advertising, bills and campaign posters could be viewed**

## Chapter Twelve  SOUNDS AMID THE SILENCE

Every morning after breakfast my prison cell is unlocked by the guard. I am escorted to the enclosed yard and given a chance to walk around for about half an hour. Day before yesterday the normally blue sky clouded up and it started to rain heavily, so the time was cut back my ten minutes. That patch of blue sky is the only real color I see above the gray walls and black iron grates of this four storey prison.

I've been locked up here for a month while the occupation forces along with the German courts try to sort out my case. I have little if any idea of what is going on under that blue sky. Is our country laid to waste? With the stepped-up bombing raids during the last six months of the war it is certainly possible. How much rubble is there to clear away? How are the people coping? What about children without parents, husbands separated from wives, the elderly and infirm? Are our women and girls safe in the hands of the Allied occupiers or has every last one been defiled by the conquerors?

I also wonder how many millions of people are roaming around Europe, not knowing where to go, possibly searching for lost family members or loved ones. How desperate is the plight of former concentration camp inmates and survivors of the slave labor brigades at places like the Krupp Works, I.G. Farben and the weapon building sites? After all, Hitler and Goebbels kept bragging to us about the new "miracle weapons" which would be unleashed on the enemy, so I have to assume that extraordinary measures must have been taken to develop and test such horrific devices. That normally involves "expendables."

My thoughts sail four flights up, float over the roof and soar into the clear blue sky, beckoning to my countrymen: "You are out there, walking around free. I am here, a captive. No matter what you're going through, the desperation you feel or the brokenness you suffer, be thankful that you are free. I am a prisoner and I will gladly trade places with you!" I realize that my words go nowhere, but it's fun to contemplate if I can register my thoughts telepathically with people on the outside. Then the sobering reality: how will they reach me in this impenetrable fortress? Oh well, it was nice while it lasted.

I join a group of fifteen or twenty other prisoners, all in the same ill-fitting garb and with identical shaven heads. None of us look particularly well-fed, although a few have gained some weight since being thrown in here. We eye each other warily as we walk in a circle in the middle of the yard, guarded by six soldiers with weapons and probably observed by somebody sitting behind one of those metal grates. It seems like overkill since there is no perceptible way out of this space. They really could save themselves a lot of trouble. I guess their intention is to make certain that we prisoners learn how to walk slowly in a perfect circle. And why wouldn't we? We are Germans and always do exactly as we are told!

No talking is allowed during this half hour of exercise. Prisoners are prevented from passing notes to one another. Last Monday I became alarmed when an older man with huge liquid black eyes embedded in his ashen face managed to waylay me when the exercise period was nearly over and the guards were ostensibly distracted. He brushed close to me and whispered, "You're cute, dearie. If we ever get out of this shithole, I'll take you with me to Ingolstadt and show you a good time." I have no idea how many of us are incarcerated for Paragraph 175 offenses, but I am clearly the youngest of the lot. The average age of the inmates being clearly fifty years and over, I am indeed a little chick among a bunch of old hens. Or perhaps a choice bit of chicken in the midst of a bevy of hungry chicken hawks. I'd like to tell him not to get his hopes up for me, but I just stare and say nothing.

Since silence tends to pervade the cells at almost all times, I hear snatches of dialogue between the guards. I go strictly on voice inflections and little, if any, on actual comprehension because I really don't speak or understand English. Aside from what I've heard in movies (Ginger Rogers proclaiming the end of the depression with "We're in the Money" from *The Goldiggers of 1933* or Hans Albers's brief, threatening stream of expletives directed at Mohamed Husen in the biopic, *Carl Peters*), I try to catch a word here and there and piece them together in a crazy quilt sort of way. I notice that Americans are much more voluble than their British counterparts. Visions of the New York skyline, Southern plantations with magnolia trees, the Wild West with covered wagons and stagecoaches flood my mind as I listen to two MP's chatting practically outside my door this morning. The words go in one ear and out the other, so I can only play it back verbatim and allow you to draw your own conclusions since it is really out of my hands.

"Did ya get a load of that hayseed who's livin' in the White House these days?" a bass voice asks. "Man, what friggin' turnip truck did he fall off?"

His fellow MP, younger sounding and definitely higher pitched, cries, "Whadya talkin' about? That's the man from Missouri. Independence, Missouri, to be exact. There's more to him than meets the eye."

"How the hell do ya figure?"

"I don't figure, Lieutenant," the young voice rings with confidence. "I know for sure. He was the junior senator from my home state before FDR pigeonholed him for the position of Veep. He's got a truckload of common sense."

A third individual materializes in the corridor. His well-modulated, pleasant-sounding voice echoes as he passes through this wing of the building. "I heard tell that he was widely known in Kansas City as Boss Tom Pendergast's stooge. That distinction evidently followed him all the way to the halls of the Senate."

Hans Albers and Mohamed Husen in *Carl Peters*, a biopic about German colonial rule which Propaganda Minister Goebbels used to emphasize Aryan superiority over the Askari tribesmen

"Oh, yeah?" the high-pitched defender responds. "Well, I'm tellin' ya that ol' Harry Truman is his own boss. Why, before we even entered the war, he'd made a tour of all the military camps and installations around the country, using his own transportation and paying all his own expenses. He uncovered millions of dollars of waste and saved the taxpayers a bundle."

I hear the rustle of cigarette packs and matches being struck. After a drag or two the bass-voiced lieutenant opines, "You can't imagine how I cried like a baby when ol' Franklin Roosevelt kicked it. We all sorta knew he wasn't gonna make it through a fourth term. I saw the newsreel where they showed him at the inauguration and the poor guy looked like death warmed over. Still, it was such a shock when he really did up and die. We felt like a flock o' lost sheep."

"Some o' my family back in Virginia turned out to see the train as it made its way up from Warm Springs to D.C.," the young voice brags. "My cousin wrote me how moving it was. There wasn't a dry eye in the pack and people were so choked up, they couldn't speak."

I hear a collective sigh and about thirty seconds of sniffing and grunting. The only thing I understand is Roosevelt's name and I surmise that they are mourning the loss of their great leader, a man who was vilified by the German press. I still remember the *UFA-Tonwoche* newsreel of the Führer's speech to the Reichstag, mocking the communique he'd received from the American President asking for assurances that the sovereignty of European nations would be respected in the wake of Germany's territorial claims and quest for *Lebensraum*. The wolf-like laughter ringing through the venerable chamber was captured by the newsreel camera and still makes me chuckle. At times Hitler was able to tap into our sense of the ridiculous, even though he was far from being a humorist. He related to ordinary Germans' frustrations at gut level, never seeming bland or indifferent. I wonder if Americans feel the same way about their beloved Franklin Delano Roosevelt. I conclude from the sounds in the corridor that they do.

"I was too damn young to remember Coolidge or Hoover," the well-modulated voice complains. "To me, FDR was the man for the ages, the only president I ever knew while growing up in Wichita. I miss him, just like everybody else, and I'm afraid Harry Truman's got some pretty big shoes to fill."

I sense that "Bass-Voice" is seething with anger every time the name of the new American president is mentioned. I suppose he pales in comparison to the one who died a couple of months back. I only learned of the man's passing after our camp was liberated because we had been denied access to newspapers and radio in captivity. When one of the prisoners cornered an SS guard and asked point blank about the camp rule allowing inmates to subscribe to and read National Socialist publications, he was beaten with the butt of a rifle. Little snipets of news leaked to us about battles being fought, cities being gutted by aerial bombing and troops advancing in certain areas, but I learned to treat it all as unsubstantiated rumors. I reasoned that knowing too much about one's fate in camp was a bad thing and could drive you crazy with worry in the long run. At this moment I still think the same way; the less I know, the better off I will be, especially as it relates to my case.

"They showed us one o' them *Movietone* flicks before I was shipped here," Bass-Voice snorts. "Do you know what that sonofabitch Truman is fixin' to do?" Dragging long and defiantly on his cigarette, he blurts out, "Desegregate the damn military, that's what!"

Silence falls upon the assembled soldiers once more. I hear nervous shuffling of feet, a cough and the clearing of throats as well as a couple of sniffs. A cigarette stub hits the concrete floor with a butterfly-wing trickle and is stamped underfoot. Although I cannot see him, I guess that Bass-Voice's face contorts into a grotesque sneer. "I'll resign my commission before they force me to serve alongside any o' them fuckin' coons."

"Hey, Lieutenant," the squeaky voice pipes up, "I saw that same newsreel in Mainz. Truman says that he's appalled to learn that a lot of Negro servicemen served faithfully overseas, dodgin' bullets and doin' a bang-up job of defendin' our country, yet are being beaten up when they arrive at the Greyhound stations in their hometowns all across America. It's inexcusable."

"Wasn't that the press conference where half the reporters got disgusted and walked out?" the man from Wichita puts in. "Most of 'em are from the South and can't fathom the idea of whites and colored people mixin' like that."

"Ain't nothing wrong with that, moron," Bass-Voice says emphatically. "Do ya think I wanna eat in the mess hall off the same plates and drink from the same glasses that a bunch of niggers've been slobberin' on before me? And I sure as hell ain't gonna step into the same shower room where some burrhead stands next to me splashin' and soapin' up his big fat black ass."

More nervous shuffling of feet echoes through the corridor. "Personally I have nothin' against colored people or anybody else, for that matter. In Wichita and Kansas City we always keep to ourselves and the races don't mingle. But when it comes to servin' the country and fightin' for the good ol' USA, I think we oughta make an exception. After all, we're all on the same side, aren't we?"

A brisk stamp of a soldier's boot against the concrete floor startles the assembly and me. "Watch yerself, Buster Brown," Bass-Voice scolds. "Talk like that can get ya into trouble. I was out on the Coast when they rounded up all them Japs and sent 'em to the desert. A buddy o' mine who was on that detail told me all about it. It was for their fuckin' protection because the rest o' the population was getting' all riled up about 'em once we got into the war. But would ya believe some namby-pamby bleedin' hearts protested 'em bein' taken away?"

"Of course it was the thing to lock 'em away," the young squeaky voice reflects. "They're all a bunch of saboteurs and probably sympathetic to ol' Hirohito anyhow. I'd personally strangle every one of 'em to avenge my poor brother's death at Wake Island." His voice cracks with emotion as he utters these final words and sounds like he wants to burst out crying.

"I'm certain that Truman'll come to his senses," the soldier from Wichita says calmly," and the idea of desegregating the armed forces'll go right outta his head. He's got a whole slew of advisers who'll set him straight. I mean, what the fuck? If they allow that sort o' thing to happen, the next thing you'll see is all the limp-wristed powder puff boys invading our hallowed ranks."

Audible grunts, gnashing of teeth and tongue-clicking greets his suggestion. "Just let 'em try," the pathetic boy soprano booms, dispelling any doubt that he is all-man, although slight snickers from his comrades-in-arms greet this declaration. "I'll beat the pulp outta any o' them quicker than all o' the Germans I've ever fought against – combined!" With that, the assembly breaks up and they resume their normal duties.

I'm certain that whatever they were talking about wasn't complimentary. I ponder what it could possibly have been until the lunch tray is pushed through the hatch at the base of my cell door, shattering the usual nerve-wracking silence.

*(above)* **German lessons for GI's**
*(below)* **GI's give candy to German kids**

## Chapter Thirteen   UP TO SNUFF

I never pretended to understand the political process of that era, nor did I bother to glance at any news beyond the chatty stuff I'd read in *Illustrierte Film-Kurier*, *Filmpost* or *Das Programm von Heute*, my favorite movie magazines. The whole business of majority seats in the Reichstag and coalitions set up by the winning parties in an election alluded me. Things were, however, definitely on the move in Germany and everyone hoped it was for the better.

Not surprisingly, Hindenburg was reelected President. Gusti reconfirmed her enthusiasm for the grand old warrior in the wake of his election triumph, even though I knew she had some level of admiration for Hitler and the NSDAP. Her "Hindenburg girl" act wasn't as convincing anymore. I also noticed that she tried to get back into Lothar's good graces, but he soft-pedaled the idea of welcoming her into his arms again and acting as if nothing had happened. I was Lothar's love interest anyway, though we always carried on as the picture of propriety.

Nevertheless, Lothar had regular social obligations which forced him to pair up with suitable female company. Gusti fit the bill perfectly and with a tinge of jealousy I watched them dress to the nines and climb into the Daimler coupe to go off to some evening bash. Lothar always looked so good in his tuxedo and white tie that I could have attacked him on the spot. It goes without saying that Gusti dolled herself up likewise and was the modicum of good fashion sense.

"There will be plenty of motion pictures and plays we can attend together," Lothar assured me when I became glum about all the attention he lavished on Gusti. "This stuff is just society and business folderol I have to put up with. Don't forget that we promised each other that we were going to pay a visit to that 'Hirschfeld Institute' before summer's end. I'll get away soon --- you'll see."

Thousands more people were being thrown out of work and the unemployed wandered the streets of Berlin in greater numbers than ever. Even I realized that strong leadership was necessary and President Hindenburg just wasn't delivering the goods. For reasons I didn't understand, Adolf Hitler was being considered for an appointment to Chancellor of Germany. Continuing to speak over radio and in the newsreels, he started making lots of sense to a hurting nation. When Germans lose their sense of pride, the healing process can be long and drawn out. Hitler's words became a much-needed instant balm to soothe worried minds and cure all of Germany's ills. The Nazi party was gaining acceptance and winning hearts.

Hitler's juxtaposition to the Hindenburg administration put Lothar in a foul mood. He carped over the fact that Otto Wels and the Social Democrats had less of a chance to win any type of plurality in the Reichstag. For Ernst Thälmann and the Communists hope of regaining any political steam all but fizzled. Word of evil things happening in the Soviet Union under Stalin's iron fist were filtering through to the German public, fueling hatred and fear of Bolshevism. The idea of something ten times worse than imprisonment on Solovki and forced labor on the White Sea Canal project soured perspective supporters and converts alike.

I got fed up with waiting for Lothar to fulfill his promise of taking me over to the "Institute for Sexual Research," not to mention the plays and movies which continued to be performed and shown practically nonstop. With the little allowance he gave me on a weekly basis I began striking out on my own. Berlin was still the apex of cultural and social life for the entire planet, at least in my mind. No matter how desperate the financial situation, the indomitable »*Berliner Luft*« continued unabated: the wonderful "air" which enveloped the entire atmosphere and rhythm of the city. Berliners handled any circumstance »*mit Schnauze und Humor,*« a combination of British stiff upper lip, common sense and the ability to laugh at oneself as well as at life in its rawest, most pockmarked form. The inhabitants of Berlin were always »*auf dem Kien*« (up to snuff) --- their best attribute.

Getting to know my way around town better and always looking for bargains, I managed to score a cheap ticket to a Bertolt Brecht play as well as a last

**Clark Gable & Jean Harlow**     **Cary Grant**

**Gary Cooper**

minute cancellation at a reduced price to a fluffy new operetta by Eduard Künneke. My real heart, though, was in motion pictures. I nipped out to the UFA-Palast in Charlottenburg or the Kinothek in Wilmersdorf to see all the latest releases from Hollywood, Gaumont and Pathé as well as our homegrown entries from Babelsberg.

I fell in love with Cary Grant, Clark Gable and Gary Cooper. Josephine Baker delighted me as she danced and sang her way through all sorts of zany adventures with an exotic frenzy. (I only found out later that she was really an American who had landed in France, learned French and became the toast of all Paris. I relished the stories about her banana dance, numerous paramours and her pet leopard.) I wished I could be as dapper as Willi Fritsch (usually in the arms of Lilian Harvey as Germany's answer to Nelson Eddy and Jeanette McDonald), as daring as Hans Albers, as snappy as Heinz Rühmann or as frightening as Peter Lorre. What actors, what movies --- what fun!

My one visit to Dr. Magnus Hirschfeld's "Institute for Sexual Research" was a little less enchanting. The preponderance of effeminate, swishy men and boys who loitered in the hallways outside the main auditorium, gushing effusively over Dr. Hirschfeld's work and acting out in all sorts of bizarre ways, put me off totally. Dr. Hirschfeld, a huge walrus of a man with a giant moustache that resembled a push broom, spoke about human rights, the "third sex," inferred that homosexuals throughout Germany should be treated as handicapped because of society's restrictions and receive benefits on par with the disabled in our country. He and another speaker touched on several other topics which went way over my head.

I did manage to obtain some fairly good written information on the proposed repeal of Paragraph 175 of the Penal Code as well as tips for prevention of venereal diseases. The fact that I was cruised by three-quarters of the guys in the place and "accidentally" brushed up against several times as well as blatantly groped once by a tall, skinny, grotesque-looking queen with plucked eyebrows made my skin crawl.

**Germany's favorite couple**

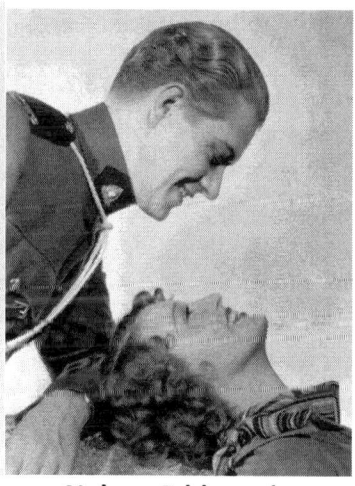

**Nelson Eddy and Jeanette McDonald**

Josephine Baker.

I rushed back to Dahlem and soaked in a hot tub for over an hour because the experience of being around urban homosexuals made me feel dirty. "That'll teach you to go places on your own without me protecting you," Lothar scolded me, but he alternated between frowns and chuckles. "You're probably the hottest-looking number who ever walked through Hirschfeld's doors. You must have had those ditzy queens salivating to get into your pants." I didn't see the humor in his remarks and I resented him having a good laugh at my expense.

"It's all your fucking fault," I pouted. "You promise things to me and never follow through. I finally gave up waiting and decided to see for myself what the joint was all about. I never imagined to be half-eaten alive!"

Lothar shot me a glance, grinned and said, "That's what you get for being so damn sexy." Pulling me out

out of the bath water and drying my back, he reached around and jerked me off while planting kisses up and down my neck and tickling my balls.

Both he and Gusti got concerned about me being alone on the streets of Berlin in light of increased unrest as well as the visibility of Ernst Röhm's Brown Shirt thugs. Ostensibly patrolling the back alleyways and maintaining order in places where the regular police force normally did not venture, the Storm Troopers usually roamed in packs of four or five, unsmiling and taking their jobs far too seriously. I rarely, however, saw a Brown Shirt who was not a total hunk: muscular, good-looking and desirable in every sense of the word.

Unwittingly I discovered how tantalizing (and somewhat frightening) closer contact with one of these groups of marauders could be. I stayed at the Kinothek for a late showing of *Million Dollar Legs*, a crazy American comedy which poked fun at the Olympic Games that had been held in Los Angeles the previous summer. (Wasn't Hollywood somewhere near there, too? I wondered...) Berliners were enthusiastic about the film, even in its subtitled version, because "our" city was slated to host the next round of Olympic competitions in four years' time.

Realizing it was way past ten when the movie let out, I figured that Lothar was panicking and calling Gusti or half a dozen other people to find out if anybody knew my whereabouts. I thought about

It's Insane - It's Joyous
MILLION DOLLAR LEGS
WITH
JACK OAKIE
W.C. FIELDS
BEN TURPIN
LYDA ROBERTI
GEORGE BARBIER
ANDY CLYDE
HANK MANN
HA HA
HA HA
HA HA
HA HA
a Paramount Picture

finding a phone myself, but I had run out of small change and didn't have the heart to ask any passersby to lend me a couple of *pfennigs*. Besides, so much begging was going on in the streets of Berlin these days, so I didn't want to appear like another of the pathetic urchins who were constantly being ignored, turned down or ridiculed.

I decided to step up the pace and try a shortcut back to Dahlem. I was treading on unfamiliar territory and going more astray with each street I passed and every intersection I crossed. The streets themselves were looking meaner: low class tenement housing, gated and shuttered store fronts and nary a policeman in sight.

»*Donnerwetter*,« I muttered. "I'm hitting one dead end after another. Isn't there any way out of this maze?" I had just stumbled into my ninth or tenth cul-de-sac when I heard footsteps echo in the alleyway. I peered into the dark and expected to see the gleam of metal from a cop's helmet. The grinning faces of five Brown Shirts came into focus instead.

"Hey, Fritzchen," the tallest and blondest of the quintet quipped to his shorter, darker-haired companion who looked at the Teutonic leader in total awe, "get an eyeful of what we have here! *Gott im Himmel*, doesn't he look like a delicious little morsel, the kind you just wanna grab onto and never let go?"

»*Ja, und wie!*« Fritzchen interrupted, licking his lips. "Those sweet little buns of his are just crying out to be plowed....and hard!"

Three other Brown Shirts flanked the rear. All were nearly the same height, had equally clear complexions (except the redhead in the middle with freckles covering his cheeks and the base of his nose), steely blue eyes and stupid grins. Nodding in agreement, they slapped each other on the back.

"So what are we waiting for?" the leader asked as he looked me up and down. I moved away, not aware that I was backing into a concrete wall. "Fritzchen, stand by the street entrance and make sure that nobody disturbs our special little operation here." Pointing to two of the goons in the rear, he barked, "Turn our juicy little friend around and pin him to the wall, each taking an arm and leg."

He stepped forward and tugged at my belt which loosened quite easily in his massive hands. He pulled my pants down with a rapid jerk and my underwear went with them. He made them cling to my kneecaps in such a way that I remained entirely immobile.

I felt him insert a calloused finger into my quivering hole and wiggle it around roughly a few times. Leaning forward with his lips against my right ear, he whispered, "Where the hell have you been keeping yourself for so long, tender one?" Drawing back and hearing the unmistakable sound of his own trousers being unbuttoned, he shouted loud enough for his voice to resonate through the cul-de-sac, "I'm first, *Jungs*, but don't fret --- you'll all get a turn. There's plenty to go around."

Being fucked dry by five horny Brown Shirts who didn't even bother to remove their kepis from their heads as they each had a "go" had always been beyond my wildest imagination. Aunt Gusti had feared that I might have a violent confrontation with them when we still lived in Munich. The fact that I'd be warned about it and it never happened caused me to grow complacent and unsuspecting. I took the easygoing, nonchalant attitude of Berliners too much for granted and never conceived that such insidious acts could be perpetrated here. These were, however, treacherous times and people acted in extraordinary ways.

Each Brown Shirt rammed his eager member into me with gusto. My asshole was raw and on fire, although I attributed this more to the ringleader's ample cock more than his four cohorts who seemed not to be as well endowed. The young men flooded my chute with so much warm jism that the silky liquid acted virtually as a lubricant, making each new insertion a bit easier to bear.

The night was full of more surprises. Instead of leaving me to rot in the alleyway, the group's leader who finally introduced himself as Hartmut asked, "Why is a good-looking Aryan boy like you wandering the streets like some two-bit male prostitute?" Explaining my predicament, he said cheerily, "If you don't mind remaining in our company a bit longer, we'd like to make certain that you reach Dahlem in one piece. What do you say?"

Shrugging, I replied, "Sure, why not? After all, we know each other in the most personal way possible." I looked at all five and added with a grin, "I place my life in your hands." There was a brief silence, followed by peals of laughter.

"Have you ever thought of joining us in the SA?" Fritzchen inquired. "Naturally you'll have to wait until you're a bit older, but there's a young folk organization that we can recommend. They'll start you out there." I smiled but said nothing. Cheeky fellows, I thought: fucking my brains out one minute, then inviting me to become one of their number the next. I switched gears quickly and we chit-chatted on a number of topics as we walked along.

Germany was getting more insane as 1932 drew to a close. A runoff election had consolidated Nazi power, Hitler was appointed Chancellor and shared the limelight with Hindenburg in a way that completely confounded me. The younger man outshone the old warrior and was clearly the leader of the country. His party members had been referring to him as »*Führer*« for ages, and now the title welled up in the throats and proceeded from the lips of ordinary Germans.

Unrest and petty crime grew exponentially. Even ever watchful Lothar and overly cautious Gusti did not escape the vicious cycle. The former's pocket was picked during a visit to the Pergamon Museum as he stopped to ogle the reconstruction of the Temple of Isis with its unusually beautiful stones. The latter's purse was snatched during a shopping trip to Kaufhaus des Westens, the thief making it out the Tauentzienstraße exit before store security could nab him.

In a way I felt safer while walking with my "benevolent rapists" from the SA than I had the entire evening since leaving the Kinothek. They stopped short of entering Dahlem. "The rich people won't appreciate a bunch of us roaming amid their fancy houses," Fritzchen chimed in. "You can make it safely the rest of the way by yourself, *Bengel*." He slapped me on the back.

"Think about what I said about joining up with us," Hartmut repeated as we approached the area around Thielallee. "We're on the cutting edge of what's happening in Germany, plus we have a lot of interesting extracurricular activity." Making fists and pounding them together several times, he added, "You get my drift, *nicht wahr*?"

Answering his question while my butthole was still smarting from the fiery intrusion of one gargantuan hammer followed by a quartet of medium size dicks was silly at best. I nodded vaguely and came forth with a halfhearted, "Who knows?"

Before the group turned to leave, the redhead scratched his head and asked, "Ain't there a lot of filthy Jews livin' in these fuckin' mansions?" The others stared at me and watched my reaction to such a provocative inquiry.

"Gee, I dunno," I replied, shrugging. "I really don't

hobnob with the neighbors here. We know one old man who's an enthusiastic supporter of the Führer. Otherwise, I don't know who's Jewish or who isn't."

"Who's 'we?'" Hartmut's tone was menacing, not at all a casual question, but more like the interrogation under blinding hot lights that I'd seen in numerous detective and suspense movies. If these strapping guys expected me to cower and sweat like the tragic-comic Peter Lorre, they were very much mistaken.

"Lothar," I answered sheepishly. "He's a friend of my aunt, Augustina Fischer. I've been dividing my time between them since I left my folks' place in the village. He and my aunt were going to be married. She ran off to get engaged to somebody else, but it didn't work out and now she's back."

The redhead still frowned and asked, "And that Lothar character ain't no Jew, huh?" The level of doltishness among these SA brutes was astounding, but I treated them with kid gloves and shook my head.

"It was good running into you, *Kleiner*," Hartmut exclaimed. "Usually we only find male hookers and scared Jewish boys roaming around at night. We've fuck up a whole mess of 'em."

I grasped that he meant much more than just bending them over and making them take it up the ass. I'd seen young men walking around Berlin with black eyes, big gashes on their faces and bruises on arms and legs which we Germans have the habit of calling »*grün und blau*« (green and blue). I knew that physical assaults were a part of the general crime spree that gripped most larger cities throughout Germany. Now I had an inkling as to who some of the perpetrators were.

Fritzchen laughed. "It's just the tip of the iceberg, *mein Junge*," he asserted. "If the Führer and Commander Röhm have anything to do with it, all the Jews, homos and other mongrels are in for rough sledding ahead."

**Peter Lorre in Fritz Lang's *M***

**Chapter Fourteen     PAIN IN THE ASS**

In addition to a crazy time, it was also a confusing time in Germany. I am free to think back on those final months of '32 and the whole of January '33 now that I am securely behind bars and guarded twenty-four hours a day, seven days a week. The last vestiges of freedom in the Weimar Republic were to be enjoyed at all times prior to the night of January 30th. Hitler stood on a balcony, flashing a big smile and waving to the crowd below. Illuminated by torchlight, his followers and admirers congratulated him on his official ascendance to the Chancellery position and the further consolidation of Nazi power. What followed in the days and weeks ahead sounded a death knell to all personal liberty and human rights throughout Germany. As the rest of Europe and the world would soon learn, a carbon copy of these events occurred anywhere and everywhere »*Großdeutschland*« extended its tentacles.

My thoughts keep going back to the aftermath of the encounter with my "benevolent rapists" because the same physical repercussions are involved. Corporal Heintzel, the sadistic SS man who headed the penalty brigade in Rosenholm singled me out for a gruesome punishment a few weeks before our camp was liberated. His abiding hatred for us "pink triangles" reached the boiling point when I dared to mouth off to him and refused to doff my cap, a requirement of all prisoners when an officer of any rank came into our presence. I was fed up with the entire system of protocol and defied my captors' authority as much as possible when it became apparent that they were running scared in the shadow of the Allied advance.

Grabbing a broom handle from the carpenter's shop, he assumed an academic air, all the while eyeing me with a sinister leer. "Let us conduct an interesting experiment," he began, addressing a group of hollow-eyed onlookers. Some of the inmates flashed me looks of sympathy and pity, others were full of contempt and revulsion. "It is an operation which should produce a great deal of amusement for everyone involved. If it is successful, I shall repeat it many more times in the future with this scum or anyone else who dares to step out of line with our authority."

Without further explanation he shoved me against a sawhorse and pushed me down. A *Kapo* dutifully pulled my arms parallel to the wooden legs and locked my wrists in the manacles. Heintzel tugged violently at the bottoms of my prison garb and they fell noiselessly. I have no idea many times he rammed the broomstick inside me or how far it went before I lost consciousness.

Every once in a while my anus feels the pain from those unwanted thrusts all over again. The doctor here examined me and pronounced extensive tearing of the membranes up and down the inner wall of my chute. He warned me that complete healing might never take place. It is a similar diagnosis as the one pronounced by Lothar's family physician, Dr. Steifwang, thirteen years ago in Berlin.

I concealed the reason for my late arrival back in Dahlem on the night of my ordeal, and Lothar didn't press me about it. I was pleasantly shocked that he accepted my feeble excuse about taking a shortcut and getting lost in two different districts. I went to soak in a hot tub because I wasn't in the mood to hear Lothar being overly solicitous about my plight. I noticed a few streaks of blood in the bath water before I pulled out the stopper. I also vigorously scrubbed a large red spot off my underwear.

My hole still burned red hot for days afterward. I was fearful of defecating because I felt like my entire anal cavity was being set aflame. I developed a severe case of gas and, try as I might, could scarcely hide my embarrassing flatulence from Lothar, Gusti or members of the household staff (the villa in Dahlem was run by a majordomo and a half dozen servants). More blood appeared in my underwear and the toilet water.

"It's high time you saw the doctor," Lothar insisted. The poor man could not have been more sympathetic to my dilemma. I felt guilty that he blamed himself for my condition. "I know I've been going a little too rough on you since we arrived in Berlin," he said practically with tears in his eyes, "but I honestly can't help myself when you're near. You bring out the animal in me and I go wild."

**Paul Hindenburg and Adolf Hitler**

I merely smiled, let Lothar know that he was a wonderful man and a most excellent lover. I took the scalding sitzbaths that Dr. Steifwang recommended, applied the ointments and suppositories he prescribed and regulated my bowel movements, even wearing diapers designed for incontinent patients and procured from the local hospital. Wetting and messing in a cloth diaper was kinky, to say the least, and I imagined how much fun it would be to hurl steamy hot feces at my enemies, beginning with Hartmut, Fritzchen and the rest of the Brown Shirts. Hell, I might even have included Ernst Röhm and Adolf Hitler in their number.

In my restless, roaming mind, the only truly free entity I enjoy in the midst of this confinement, I reflect on the words that Fritzchen said that night before the quintet departed: "All the Jews, homos and other mongrels are in for rough sledding ahead." Wasn't it well-known that the SA was rife with "homos" at the time? Why did he and the others consider themselves any less "homo?"

True, they were full-fledged rapists and thugs. Surely I felt offended to be classified as that type of "homo" and evidently the Führer and the Nazi leadership leaned the same way, for they finished off Röhm and his SA renegades in a well-publicized event which eventually became known (in whispers) as "The Night of Long Knives." I have wondered off and on for years whether Hartmut, Fritzchen, the freckled redhead and the others were in attendance on the fateful night in Bad Wiessee. Even though I had mixed feelings about them, I shudder to think of how they might have ended.

I realize that places like Dr. Hirschfeld's "Institute for Sexual Research" attempted to delineate the meanings of "homo" in comparison to the unique word we Germans adapted to explain the genre: »*schwul*«. The term transcends all limitations of time and space. It is on par with the French expression *gai*, the designator "third sex," and often defined as "different from the others."

That was how the suppressed 1919 landmark film, *Anders als die Anderen*, got its name. Lothar was one of the few moviegoers who saw the film and became familiar with the Institute and its campaign to repeal Paragraph 175. Dr. Hirschfeld himself appeared in the film, discussing sexual ambivalence with the protagonist, Conrad Veidt.

"Despite the naturist movement, the loosening of morals and the high visibility of »*die Schwulengemeinschaft*« in places like Hamburg and Berlin," Lothar explained to me one bleak winter day over steaming cups of cocoa, "Germany as a nation is not ready to embrace the concept wholeheartedly.

Without blowing the gaff about my source of information, I asked, "What about people of certain political persuasions who talk about finishing off the 'homos' when they themselves belong in the same class?"

Lothar did a double take and look puzzled. "Wow,

"Institute for Sexual Research" display

Scenes from *Anders als die Anderen* with Conrad Veidt and Dr. Magnus Hirschfeld

*Junge,*" he responded, "you certainly do ask some probing questions which are reflective of the current situation. It is precisely their confusion over the terms 'homosexual' and '*schwul,*' that is baffling. But not one of them is too bright anyway."

This time I was the one who was puzzled. "So what exactly is the difference between the two?" I asked.

I knew that Lothar loved to expound on the subject. "The homosexual is the man or woman who enjoys having sexual relations with someone of the same gender. In the case of the male, some men and boys seek after it passionately and cannot help themselves. They do it as a passing fancy and are so obsessed with the physical act that they have no sense of kinship or community. People who are *schwul,* on the other hand, immerse themselves in the lifestyle, mainly the performing and expressive arts and most certainly the counterculture. You've already seen some working in the motion picture industry. 'Community' is in the loosest sense of the word because there are no precise geographic points I could show you which are exclusively *schwul* at this time, although it can change in the future."

Rubbing my chin, I inquire, "Do you actually think it will happen in Germany?" I had Dr. Hirschfeld's campaign against Paragraph 175 in mind.

Lothar winked and exclaimed, "The fact that that the Storm Trooper wing of the NSDAP government is thick with cocksuckers and headed by a big fat fudge-packing commander who's one of Adolf Hitler's old warriors is a good indicator that some influence will be exerted to change the existing law or at least modify it."

None of what he explained seemed to jibe with my assessment of "rough sledding" for "Jews, homos and other mongrels" which reverberates in my head to this day. And I was confused that Lothar hadn't discounted Hitler like I was used to hearing him do for ages. Were he and Gusti gradually becoming admirers of *Der Führer*?

Evidently Lothar anticipated my next question and delved right in without waiting for me to ask. "As somewhere in the middle politically between Social Democrats and the Reds, naturally I can't stand the Nazis. Hitler and his party, however, are sitting pretty in the Reichstag and pushing for policy changes to get this country moving again. We can only hope that the best policies of the present Weimar Republic will merge with reasonable changes proposed by the NSDAP to pull the country out of the doldrums. Lukewarm posturing is too tame, and strong-arm tactics are much too bold. Middle of the road is best and will get us on our feet again. We Germans are too levelheaded to settle for anything less."

I wanted so desperately to believe Lothar's outline for our country's future course. Although I never bothered to read *Mein Kampf* (and knew lots of others who hadn't either), it was enough to know that Adolf Hitler spewed a great deal of hate as the premise of his book. In his speeches he always came off as a leader who pulled no punches and spoke about his vision for Germany. That vision seemed to be more exclusive than inclusive, and I couldn't figure out why Lothar discounted the obvious biases of the newly-appointed German Chancellor. Did he believe that Hitler made grandiose claims and had no way of accomplishing what he set out to do?

Nobody knew then how the Führer was going to stick it to us. High hopes for recovery came with a price tag, a sum measured not so much in Reichsmarks as in shed blood and untold misery. I still shudder when I think of how many of us took it up the ass, literally as well as figuratively. Hitler was a diabolical fiend, to be sure, but at the beginning of the so-called Thousand Year Reich he and his followers looked so good to us all.

Kindly Dr. Steifwang never asked for, nor did I volunteer any details about why my anal cavity was bruised so badly. I am sure that he had his suspicions. Similarly, the unsmiling American doctor assigned by the occupation forces to examine former camp inmates draws more conclusions based on his own supposed understanding of such matters than he cares to ask me through a translator. The cold stainless steel probe he introduces into the sore cavity exacerbates the burning sensation in my rectum so much that I am ready to hit the ceiling.

"Relax and breathe normally, please," is the examiner's translated admonition. Through the translator I also learn that the doctor is curious about the wood slivers and other microscopic debris he finds as deep as ten inches inside the cavity. The measurement is incomprehensible to me until the translator converts it into metric and calculates roughly twenty-five centimeters.

"They cannot be removed without major tearing of the membrane," he explains. "They will work themselves loose in time with normal bowel movements." With the stainless steel probe still lodged inside me and the spring lock engaged for one final look, the poker face added, "A pity. A real shame." He says these words in a tone of voice that confounds me: does he think it's a shame that Heintzel stuck the broom handle in me in the first place, or a pity that he only went twenty-five centimeters deep?

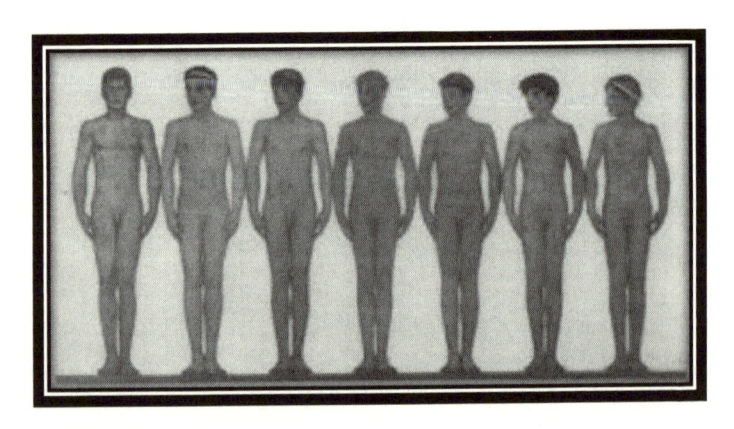

**Sascha Alexander Schneider – «*Gymnasion*»**

## Chapter Fifteen     ENABLE YOU, ENABLE ME

Fast and furious characterized the way Germany moved during those first few months. Hitler, Röhm and Reichsmarshall Göring weren't satisfied with keeping things at a slow, even keel in the nation's recovery. Events occurred one after the other and in the shortest time possible. It was radical surgery, and it was astounding.

I was never much of a newspaper reader, but even a cursory glance at the front page of the *Berliner Morgenpost* or the *Deutsche Allgemeine Zeitung* during the period stopped me dead in my tracks. Huge headlines praising the majority votes in the Reichstag for this, that or the other proposal virtually screamed at the casual observer. Lengthy columns of text accompanied each banner headline and spoke glowingly of a new dawn ushering in the Third Reich, an empire which would last a thousand years.

"If so much is crammed in at the beginning," I reasoned, "the remaining nine hundred ninety-nine years are going to be incredibly dull." Nobody, least of all I, knew what Hitler and the Nazi leadership held in store for Germany.

Other headlines churned up hate and revulsion for the nation's supposed enemies: "The Jews Are Our Misfortune," "Menacing, Ominous Destruction by Bolshevik Conspirators," "Vicious Plot Hatched by Jewish Bankers and Insidious Plutocrats Leads to Financial Chaos," and the like. Everything from the crushing demands of the Versailles Treaty to Germany's humiliation at the hands of nations who stole our former colonies as spoils of war was blamed for the country's ills. Similarly, press reports confirmed that only the NSDAP was capable of effecting real and lasting change.

"Expect the unexpected," said Gerd Eichenbaum, a friend of Lothar's. His family lived a few doors down from us in Dahlem and visited often. "I don't put anything past Hitler and his henchmen. Those SA boys are a particularly nasty lot." I smiled benignly and kept my own opinions locked away. My fucking asshole still burned even at the mention of their name.

"But Herr Eichenbaum," Aunt Gusti protested, "the various organizations associated with the National Socialists are mobilized to keep order and assure everyone's safety. You've got to admit that something needs to be done to stem the rash of petty crime and assaults on unsuspecting Berliners," she sniffed, adding, "Both Lothar and I have been victims of the prevailing lawlessness. I wish somebody like them had been around to help."

Eichenbaum shook his head in dismay. "Really, Frau Fischer," he scolded, "those overgrown perverted Boy Scouts don't have yours or my interests in mind at all. They've turned into a bunch of deviant thugs in cahoots with the police."

Gusti stepped to the forefront again. For having claimed allegiance to Hindenburg years on end, one

Newspaper headline announcing
Reichstag passage of the "Enabling Law"

could swear that she was performing full-blown public relations for the Nazis as well as damage control. "You're mistaken, Herr Eichenbaum," she responded in a friendly but firm way. "Our police force operates quite independently from the organs of state."

A harsh frown crossed Gerd Eichenbaum's face. "You might think that, Frau Fischer," he asserted, "but I've had more firsthand experience with them. I protested when the SA vandals showed up with paintbrushes and started covering my shop windows with five-point stars and the word '*JUDE.*' Not only did the police stand to one side watching it all happen, but I was also labeled 'a filthy old Jewish fool' by the precinct captain. He also warned me to never lodge another complaint again or I'd regret it."

I didn't doubt Eichenbaum's words. I had seen plenty of businesses around Berlin where Storm Troopers stood around preventing customers from entering. Equipped with sandwich boards which read "GERMANS! DEFEND YOURSELVES AGAINST JEWISH ATROCITY PROPAGANDA! BUY ONLY AT GERMAN STORES!" they were usually accompanied by a cameraman who photographed every citizen who dared to cross the picket line. To my mind, it didn't matter if I bought 10 Pfennigs worth of candy from a Jewish confectioner or a Gentile one. I just didn't understand the difference, but I stayed away from the stores with the SA guys out front for reasons of personal safety.

Since I was still too young to be concerned about Berlin nightlife, the sudden closing of several prominent dancehalls and gathering palaces for the "fringe" element of Berlin's merrymakers didn't faze me. Small box inserts planted within the columns of the city's dailies touted the cries of "immorality and indecency" that such places fostered. Among the closures were all of the meetings places for »*die Schwulengemeinschaft*«. The most glaring example of Nazi aplomb was the shuttering of the Motzstraße's premiere nightspot for transvestites, "Eldorado." The chief of police issued a decree in which he spelled out the "moral indignation" of Berlin's citizenry for such "lewd, unseemly forms of diversion."

"I don't know what he's bitching about," complained Lothar as he crumpled the morning paper in disgust. "Most Berliners are either totally indifferent to the existence of the clubs or they embrace them wholeheartedly. There's practically no in-between. What makes him think that he speaks for all the inhabitants of our fair city?"

Gusti was just finishing her breakfast and was buttering an extra slice of bread as Lothar spoke. I perceived that my aunt was puzzled as to why he was making such a big deal out of some queer nightclubs closing down. None of us made eye contact.

"If you'll excuse me," she chimed in, arising from the table and taking one last sip from her coffee cup,

## Nachtlokale geschlossen
### Einschränkende Bestimmungen für Tanzlokale und Bars

Der Polizeipräsident hatte vor einigen Tagen scharfe Maßnahmen gegen Gast- und Schankwirtschaften angedroht, gegen die in sittlicher Beziehung Beanstandungen erhoben wurden. Auf Grund des § 22 des Gaststättengesetzes sind daher mit sofortiger Wirkung folgende Betriebe geschlossen worden: Luisen-Kasino, Alte Jakobstrasse 64, Zauberflöte, Kommandantenstrasse 72; Dorian Gray, Bülowstrasse 57; Kleist-Kasino, Kleiststrasse 15; Nürnberger Diele, Nürnberger Strasse 6; Internationale Diele, Passauer Strasse 27/28; Monokel-Bar, Budapester Strasse 14; Geisha, Augsburger Strasse 72; Mali und Igel, Lutherstrasse 16; Boral, genannt Moses, Uhlandstrasse 14; Kaffee Hohenzollern, Bülowstrasse 101; Silhouette, Geisbergstrasse 24; Mikado, Puttkamerstrasse 15; und Hollandais, in der Bülowstrasse 69. Außerdem ist bei drei weiteren Lokalen die Polizeistunde herabgesetzt worden.

Auch für die Tanzlokale und Bars sind wichtige Bestimmungen erlassen worden. Tanzdamen dürfen nicht mehr in Balltoilette in den Lokalen erscheinen und mit den dort beschäftigten Bardamen die Gäste zum Trinken animieren oder sich zum Trinken einladen lassen.

**Small article about the closing of dancehalls and nightspots of "questionable character"**

**"Eldorado" closed by the authorities, February 1933**

"I've got to bolt. 'DEHOMAG' likes us to arrive half an hour early each morning for a briefing before work begins." She waved and threw us both kisses as she raced out the front door.

"What's DEE-HOHM-AHGG?" I asked. "I didn't know Auntie got a new job. She barely talks to me now that she's together with you again."

Lothar came around to my side of the table and massaged my shoulders. "Jealous, huh?" he quipped. "Don't give it a second thought, *Junge*. You're still Number One, no matter what happens."

I reached up to stroke his cheek. "I know that," I said in a throwaway manner. "But frankly, Lothar, I'm scared. All this talk about Jews and parasites, the closing of those clubs, the boycotts, the harassment and intimidation by the police who are now in league with the Brown Shirts – all of it has me on edge."

Lothar's smile evaporated and he knitted his brow. "Yeah, I know. I passed by 'Eldorado' a couple of days ago and glanced over without stopping. SA men were thick as molasses around the perimeter. Posters for the upcoming round of Reichstag elections and swastika symbols were plastered over all the doors and windows. You could barely see the name of the place or the *'Hier ist's richtig'* slogan amid all the stuff they've slapped on."

Without betraying my own bad experience with the Brown Shirts, I volunteered, "You did well by not sticking around and staring. The less contact with those brutes, the better off you are." Desiring to change the subject as quickly as possible, I went back to my original question. "So what's that weird name Gusti was talking about?"

"Ah!" Lothar exclaimed. "You mean 'DEHOMAG.' It's an electronics and technology firm, one of the leading ones in Germany. They're trying to develop some sort of computation device that will figure things out faster and better than hundreds of human beings put together. I've invested heavily in it and expect to get a nice return on my money."

"Machines to replace people?" I cried in astonishment. "That's even scarier than what's been going on out in the streets of Berlin."

Grinning, Lothar explained calmly, "Not to *replace* people, *liebes Kind*, but to *help* them. Help *us*. And don't forget that machines break down, so there's always the need for real human beings to be on hand to fix them."

I scratched my head and asked, "So what does Auntie do in a company like that?"

Lothar opened a drawer and pulled out a medium size flyer. "She's involved with the development of a punch card system for the upcoming census. It'll help the analysts sort out data about different segments of the German population."

I nodded and remarked, "That's nifty." In the back of my mind, however, I thought of how easy it would be for the authorities to collect and organize information on different groups of people to either help or harm them. With a system like that there was no telling what horrendous things could happen next. I didn't want to even think about it after everything else we discussed, and I let it slide.

For all its boasting and posturing, the NSDAP was not the Alpha and the Omega, the cure-all and end-all of German malaise. The Reichstag fire surprised everyone and gave more ground for Hitler and his supporters to ramp up the campaign of harassment, intimidation and fear. "Unity and Loyalty" were the watchwords, but the intent was to coordinate all sectors and subject them to a rigorous makeover to conform to the dictates of National Socialism.

The introduction of a proposal to address Germany's emergency needs resulted in the passage of "The Enabling Act." For the greater good of the German people and a speedier recovery of law and order as the embers of the Reichstag fire smoldered, civil rights were essentially invalidated. The NSDAP was poised to destroy the principles of the Weimar Constitution by decreeing and enforcing retroactive laws and effectively abolishing the separation of powers. The Führer, Chancellor Adolf Hitler, was now "chief justice," and the agonizing death of a constitutional state was imminent.

President Hindenburg, old and infirm, passively looked on as political opponents were arrested, interrogated, beaten and sent to newly established concentration camps where many of them languished for months without the benefit of a fair trial or legal representation. The fact that many prominent Communist party members and other "asocial" elements were involved in the Reichstag fire was the Nazi authorities' justification for the increased number of people charged and detained. The testimonies of Martinius van der Lubbe, Georgi Dimitroff and Ernst Torgler were broadcast over the radio and held the attention of Germany's listeners for weeks. It was better than any soap opera, a story of intrigue with real characters and vicious crimes perpetrated against an entire nation.

What complicated things even more was the curious silence on the part of religious and human rights organizations. It was bad enough that the

**A distraught Martinius van der Lubbe at the Reichstag Fire show trial in Leipzig**

feeble President Hindenburg signed the decrees without questioning his chancellor or those in the ranks of the NSDAP. Worse still was the way the Roman Catholic church in Germany was bought off by the signing of a *Reichskonkordat*. The NSDAP would hence respect the sovereignty of the Catholic Church, while the denomination would raise no objection to Nazi policies such as "The Enabling Law" or interfere with any dictates of the state.

Lothar nudged me one Sunday afternoon as we strolled in the Tiergarten. Gusti had broken away to buy ice cream and was certain to be gone a few minutes. "Don't glance over and attract too much attention," he warned, "but isn't it odd that Hirschfeld's place is allowed to stay open in spite of what's been happening?" The Institute's entrance was about fifty meters from where we stood.

"Didn't you say that you thought it wouldn't make much difference because the Brown Shirts were all a bunch of cocksuckers anyway?" I looked at him and tried to stifle a laugh. "Half of the prissy queens who hang out at the Institute probably service the SA boys, if you know what I mean. They need each other, right?" I gestured with a limp wrist.

Lothar signaled for me to lower my voice and tone down the campiness. "I daresay, some of those fairy princesses are getting a bloody lip thrown into the bargain," he whispered. "You'll recall what I told you about the difference between »*schwul*« and "homo." He clammed up and we both smiled as Aunt Gusti approached and handed each of us a luscious sherbet cone.

Going to the flickers was changing, too. Theatres showed fewer and fewer foreign movies and concentrated on our own homegrown offerings from UFA, Tobis, Terra and my old stomping grounds, the Bavaria Film-Kunst studios. Even a feature or two from Wien-Film made it to our screens, and the Viennese humor was a delightful offset to our glum attitude about daily affairs.

During the intermissions I used to enjoy watching short films about faraway places, new developments in science and technology, funny cartoons or the comedic exploits of Antek and Frantek. Now, however, we were bombarded with newly produced, thought-provoking pieces with titles like "Parasites in our Midst" (a treatise about how despicable it was for mentally ill patients to be housed in luxurious villas with plenty of fresh air and space to move around freely while healthy, hardworking German families had to endure the squalor of crowded tenement housing) or "The Jewish-Bolshevik World Conspiracy" (a pageant of overfed, cigar-chomping oligarchs grinned evilly at the thought of plundering the nations of Europe and laying them to waste in the wake of their greed and conquest). Speeches not only by Hitler, but also Hermann Göring, Rudolf Hess, Dr. Josef Goebbels, Heinrich Himmler, the vile Julius Streicher and Reich Labor Service head, Dr. Robert Ley (whose talk, oddly enough, made sense to me) filled our screens with unparalleled rantings against any policy which did not conform to NSDAP principles. It dampened enjoyment of the films for me, but just like everything else, I gritted my teeth and got used to it. Something you expected to see and hear evolved into a humdrum existence.

At the beginning of May the Institute for Sexual Research was raided by the Berlin School of Physical Education, a Nazi think tank. The premises we had casually viewed during our stroll not more than a month before were looted and destroyed. All the helpful literature about human reproduction, marital problems, issues of "the third sex," venereal diseases, lifestyle choices and abortion was confiscated. Those numerous pamphlets, flyers, research files, meticulously prepared projects and even a bust of Magnus Hirschfeld (who was blessedly out of the country and was forced into exile as a result of being tipped off about the raid) found their way into the bonfires which were set up on the Opernplatz beginning the night of May 10$^{th}$.

Book burnings took place all over Germany in the ensuing weeks and months. The literary and musical works of "Jews, traitors, subversives and degenerates" were hurled into the flames as crowds of Hitler Youth, Brown Shirts and ordinary German citizens stood by and often howled with delight. Those who found this activity repulsive dared not raise their voices in protest.

Since I liked books and enjoyed music, the loss of

some of our great authors from the bookshelves and composers from performances in concert halls and on phonograph records was palpable to me. I supposed, however, that I could live without the benefit of "degenerate literature." And I'd memorized enough of Mendelssohn's compositions, patter songs by Kurt Weill and arias by Richard Tauber and Josef Schmidt that I could whistle any of them at a moment's notice.

"They can burn all the books they like," Lothar explained to me and Gerd Eichenbaum over tea. "They can refuse to play a single note of any composer or prohibit you from listening to a record by any singer they've crossed off the official list. But they can't burn ideas or set hope ablaze. History has proven that since time immemorial."

A huge smile crossed Eichenbaum's face. He started whistling the *allegro vivace* from Mendelssohn's Symphony Number Four, but Lothar quickly put a finger to his lips and begged him to stop, even though we weren't within an earshot of any neighbors. "Still and all," he scolded gently, "one cannot be too careful."

Behind the scenes, Ernst Röhm and his Brown Shirts remained in the Führer's and NSDAP leadership's good graces. Concern was setting in, however, among members of Heinrich Himmler's *Schutzstaffeln*, commonly known by its acronym "SS," elite protection units which had been formed.

They resented the flexing of SA vigilante muscle. With the closing of Hirschfeld's institute, the widening persecution of homosexual men and lesbians (»*die Schwulengeminschaft*«) and the alarm raised by several Nazi bigwigs, most notably Dr. Goebbels and Himmler, about overt homosexual behavior within the SA ranks and its tolerance by Commander Röhm, Hitler became convinced that the Old Guard needed to be purged in the most expedient way possible.

In conjunction with a huge conclave of SA men (along with their boyfriends) from all parts of the German Reich scheduled to take place for several days at Bad Wiessee in late June of 1934, Röhm invited the Führer to speak on the final night. He was certain that an appearance by Hitler would quell rumors of ill will and opposition by organs of state who may have been mistakenly hostile and misguided in their assumptions.

"The Night of Long Knives," as it became known in a whisper campaign throughout Germany, was a bloodbath orchestrated by Ernst Röhm's trusted friend, Adolf Hitler, to weaken the power of the *Sturmabteilung*. The surviving leadership was reorganized and marched henceforth solely to the beat of the Nazi hierarchy's drum. Needless to say, the "homo" element within the Brown Shirt ranks was vanquished forever.

This pivotal event, coupled with the broadening of Paragraph 175 of the Penal Code to include the mere implication of homosexual contact, caused panic within »*die Schwulengemeinschaft.*« Cases of suicide rose sharply. Same-sex couples split up. Others went underground, stayed out of public life or fled the country altogether as the routes to emigration were decreasing and the gates to escape were slamming shut. The Gestapo created a special department for the observation of suspected homosexual behavior among German citizens. Many men and women were raked in via denunciations to the agency and given jail sentences or terms in concentration camps, again without due process of law.

Still others devised more creative solutions to the dilemma. "I'm so happy," Aunt Gusti announced giddily. "Lothar has proposed to me and wants us to elope." I was stunned for a few seconds, but not surprised. I wouldn't have been shocked to learn that many homosexual men and lesbian women had chosen to marry each other, if only to save their hides. Nothing that happened in Germany surprised me anymore.

**Aftermath of the raid and closure of Dr. Magnus Hirschfeld's "Institute for Sexual Research"**

## Chapter Sixteen     THE PERFECT SERVICE

Under normal circumstance a jilted lover acts in many ways. Different paths are available to him: fits of rage, violent confrontations, striking back with retributive acts or sinking into deep depression. Life in the New Germany took care of all those outdated alternatives. As civil liberties were denied and freedom of the press and speech were quashed, so were human initiative and emotional expression sapped. Compared to other nationalities (one always thinks of Spaniards and Italians in this regard), we Germans have never been adept at outwardly showing our feelings. As we observed what was happening around us --- the arrests, humiliation and harassment, the long arm of Nazi ideology spreading out under the watchful eye of the Gestapo --- we retreated even farther into our impenetrable cocoons.

"The only thing people really get revved up about anymore in this country is any appearance of the Führer himself," Lothar opined a day before he and Gusti announced their engagement. Even though they had intended to elope, they felt it was more expedient to let it be known widely since marrying and producing offspring for the Fatherland was suddenly in vogue. "Just look at the way he makes women and girls swoon. Men and boys throw out their chests and stand at stiff attention. Old warriors break down in tears at the mere sound of his voice.

He's got us Germans in the palm of his hand."

I was seething with anger, but I held it in. I could have made a scene, but what was the use? Lothar was going to marry Gusti, and that was that. "Hey, don't be glum," he piped up encouragingly, putting his hand on my shoulder. "After the honeymoon when things settle down, you and I will go off somewhere together. We'll always be together, come hell or high water, and err on the side of extreme caution."

I shook my head. "You're living in a fantasy world if you think something like that is going to happen. Not in good ol' Germany, and not as long as the Nazis have their way."

Lothar shrugged. "Why deny it?" he grumbled. "The pressure has been on me long before the joker with the moustache came to power. You and I could never appear as a couple in a social setting, despite all the sophistication that is our beloved Berlin. We've come farther than the rest of the country, but still have a long way to go."

As much as I wasn't impressed with Magnus Hirschfeld or his institute when it existed, I longed for it as a place to run to. "I know how lethal they've made Paragraph 175," I put in. "Just you and I walking here like this could be construed as an illegal liaison. The fucking Nazis want breeders. I don't blame you for wanting to fix yourself up with my aunt in a sham marriage."

Lothar slammed his fist on the table. "But I really

do love Gusti in my own way," he insisted. "As a matter of fact, *Junge*, you should consider dating some broads and maybe settling down with one yourself, if only for self-preservation.

The anger was bubbling inside me, and it reached the boiling point. "Lothar, *du böser Wicht*," I began shouting, then abruptly toned my voice down to a whisper, "I've never been with a girl in my life, just guys. I wouldn't know what to do if a woman stuck her cooz in my face. The thought of it sickens me."

I watched Lothar rise from his chair and pace the room. "I admire your honesty," he said, "and the way you stick up for the truth. I hope to God it doesn't land your ass in a concentration camp. In addition to beefing up Paragraph 175 and terrorizing the male population of Germany with agents from the special anti-homosexual operations division of the Gestapo, you've got the Reich Office of Race and Hygiene and all those crazy new Nuremberg Laws to contend with." He placed a hand on his forehead as if mimicking a headache. "Did you ever imagine it would be nonsensical like this, dividing people up and categorizing them by race, ethnicity and, in the case of the poor godforsaken Jews, religion?

I nodded knowingly. "Tell me all about it," I quipped. "My mom wrote me about how they had a helluva time getting birth records and verifiable documents going back that far. The original village of Wiedersdorf was washed away in the flood, so those records floated down the Danube, probably all the way to the Black Sea."

"Hmmpf," Lothar grunted. "At least you and Gusti are Nordic-looking enough to dispel all doubt about your Aryan origins. I went through hell and back with the examiners. They checked everything: hair and eye color, measured my head and neck --- everything short of cupping my goddamn nuts in their prying hands." Chuckling nervously, he added, "I slipped by with the dubious classification of 'Eastern Dinaric,' whatever the hell *that* is."

I squinted and put my face close to his, but he shoved me back playfully. "You know, it's all my aunt's fault that this race and hygiene stuff is so invasive. If she hadn't been instrumental in helping to design those Hollerith punch cards for the census a while back, the Nazis wouldn't be able to keep track of people as closely as they do nowadays." I folded my arms and shuddered. "It's kind of scary when you think about it."

Pointing at me, Lothar exclaimed, "Don't think about it then. Just take care of your own affairs and save your own skin. Everybody else is. You've got nowhere to turn. Try making it over the border to France, *Liebling*. There they treat *your* kind with gentle warmth."

I sat there and looked at him thunderstruck. "My French is very rusty, so France is out." Suppressing the urge to punch him in the nose, I added, "And what's this '*your* kind' jazz? When did you become Mister Straight Arrow?"

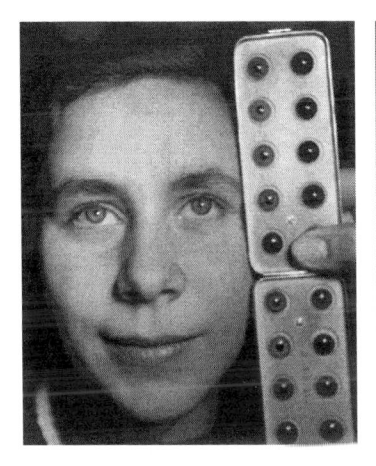

**(left) Race and Hygiene examiner checks eye color
(right) Hollerith punch cards by DEHOMAG**

Lothar spread his arms as if taking in the entire room. "Oh, you know me," he said magnanimously. "I've always swung both ways."

"*Ja, gewiß*," I snapped, "but with a decided preference, I daresay!"

"Well, at least I'm doing all I can to ward off the sniffer dogs from the Race and Hygiene Office as well as the Gestapo. If you're unwilling to make it with girls, maybe joining up with some masculine outfit like the Hitler Youth will do the trick. The Nazis tend to keep the gals from the German Girls' League separated from the boys anyway."

"For Chrissakes, no!" I blurted out. "I've seen what torture they put those kids through. I don't want to end up committing suicide due to their bullying."

Rubbing his chin, Lothar said, "I'd suggest the SA, but the cocksucking Brown Shirts have all bitten the bullet. The surviving membership won't tolerate a little bugger like you in their ranks, although you're more butch than most of 'em."

I frowned. "Why are you suddenly putting me down so much? You used to be so loving. Now that your tying the knot with my aunt, you've taken a hundred and eighty degree turn." Sinking into a chair, I sulked. "I can't figure you out, but then I can't seem to reach out to anybody in Berlin anymore. Everybody's suspicious of one another."

"*Und wie!*" he cried. "It's as if spying and intrigue has replaced *Schnauze und Humor* in the Berliners' lexicon. The only escape is the movies, save for the upcoming Olympics that everyone's abuzz about."

I smiled from ear to ear and broke into laughter. "Have you seen some of the artwork they've placed around the new Olympic Stadium? *Gott im Himmel*, the plumbing on some of the statues of the male athletes reminds me of the big dicks of the farm boys who used to screw me way back when."

Lothar grinned and volunteered, "Yeah, you've told me about the big dicks already, and I've seen the statues. As they say in France, 'ou là là!' I wonder if that's another way they've devised for Gestapo agents to rake in more of us?" I'm pleased to hear him include himself among our ranks this time. "You know: stare too long at a sculpture, end up in a concentration camp? It would be just like Himmler and Goebbels to pull something like that out of their hat."

I stood up and began pacing the floor, too. "That doesn't solve my problem, though," I carped. "I've gotta find some outfit other than the barbarism of the Hitler Youth." I knew that military service was an option. In spite the strict provisions of the Treaty of Versailles which demilitarized Germany, our army, navy and air forces were all slowly being built up anew. Our soldiers reoccupied the Rhineland, and the Saar had been won back by a plebiscite which also necessitated our troops' immediate presence. I had an aversion toward guns and weaponry of any kind, save for a pearl-handled hunting knife my dad had given me (it had belonged to his father and been passed down for several generations). And I didn't relish hearing somebody bark orders at me day and night.

Ignoring most of the speeches of Party officials when they took to the airwaves, I was curiously drawn to some of the things Dr. Robert Ley said in promoting the Reich Labor Service. If truth be told, it appealed to me greatly. And when I watched a short feature about it at the UFA-Palast am Zoo and saw the shirtless men wielding shovels and working up a sweat, my groin swelled embarrassingly and I shifted nervously in my seat.

"It's the perfect fit for you in lots of ways," Lothar gushed. I had the feeling he envied the fact that I'd be surrounded by all those suntanned bodies and rippling muscles. "You know that two years in the Labor Service count toward time that would normally be served in the military. It'll also look good on your record that you signed on voluntarily rather than being drafted. Enlistment in that sort of thing is always preferable."

The whole registration process was fairly streamlined as compared to other agencies where red tape bogged down the speed at which the wheels of state turned. I was issued a dozen shirts with the Labor Service emblem (RAD) emblazoned across the chest as well as work trousers and a sturdy cap. Everything was about half a size too small for me, but fit like a glove. I liked the way my nipples stuck out and showed through the material. Lothar whispered to me that it turned him on so much, he was ready to cream in his underwear.

"The shirts are mainly for show," said the young blond, blue-eyed recruiter while practically staring holes through me. "You'll wear them whenever you go marching to and from the worksite or if some of the *Bonzen* show up to inspect. Otherwise, the guys from the press and other curiosity seekers with cameras can photograph you stripped down to the waist if they want." He grinned in such a sinister way that made me want to shrivel up and melt into the floor.

I waited a few more days until the postman delivered a welcome letter signed by Dr. Ley and a separate sheet with instructions of where and when

*Reichsarbeitsdienst* (The Reich Labor Service)

Labor Service workers building the *Autobahn*

to report for my first assignment. The envelope also contained informational material about how members of RAD were eligible to avail themselves of services and opportunities offered by the KdF organization.

»*Kraft durch Freude*« was the "Strength Through Joy" association I'd heard lots of Germans chatter about, but had no idea what the big deal was. What grabbed my attention the most was the array of trips they sponsored around Germany, Austria, Switzerland and places beyond. It might provide a kid like me with an affordable way to see the world. Lothar had often promised that we'd get to travel together since he often combined pleasure with business. The Nazis came to power and that changed things. He and Gusti were to marry, and Lothar would be expected to sire a hearty bunch of brats, so travelling around with me was out.

My first couple of assignments were close enough to Berlin --- Potsdam, Brandenburg, Zossen that I could have easily bussed myself back each night to Dahlem. I balked at the idea for two reasons: I couldn't imagine strolling back to Lothar's villa in such a tony neighborhood looking like a working class bumpkin; and the allure of staying in the dorm with a bunch of guys from all over Germany with whom I felt a camaraderie was too good to pass up. Even if nothing physical came out of it (and it was a fairly dangerous proposition to even think that way), just working alongside other young men, sharing our meals in the canteen, showering together, sleeping in close quarters and joking around, playing pranks on one another and laughing uproariously at each other's foibles were all like a soothing tonic to calm my nerves and put my mind at ease after so much Nazi Party bullshit.

And we were building stuff to make Germany a better, more prosperous nation for everyone. I could look at a stretch of Autobahn between Hamburg and Sachsenwald and boast, "I helped build that!" which usually prompted all sorts of questions about the Labor Service and my involvement in it. Since my two years with them took me as far west as Aachen and as far east as Königsberg, not to mention from Flensburg to Friedrichshafen and points in between, I felt a certain pride in being one of the scores of able-bodied young men who weren't afraid to expend a little sweat and slog through the mud and slime in order to rebuild the Fatherland.

The Labor Service and the Strength Through Joy people always made certain that we were provided with the best of everything: well-insulated dormitory facilities to ward off the extreme cold or unbearable heat of the changing seasons; clean, sanitized bathtubs and shower stalls plus frequent replenishment of simple supplies like toothbrushes, combs, underwear and socks; and hearty, delicious fare in every canteen. In East Prussia we once lacked the proper indoor facility to lay our heads down, so sturdy tents and the ultimate in camping equipment was brought in and made our time there seem more like a summer vacation than the backbreaking work of felling trees and clearing away loose branches and debris.

At first I hesitated eating all the heavy food they served us: Sauerbraten, Rouladen, Königsberger Klops, huge saddles of pork and lamb with mounds of pickled cabbage and cucumbers plus rich cakes and puddings for dessert. "Don't miss out," one of the cadets exclaimed, sizing me up. "You'll need that bulk to give you more energy." He was right, of course, and I found that I burned up practically as many calories as I took in. From wielding shovels and spades to swinging a pickax day after day for weeks on end I developed an even better physique than what the Almighty had already blessed me with.

And I was not alone in this. Working mostly outdoors, sweating profusely and soaking up the beneficial rays of the sun made us all look like bronze gods. Photographers frequently came to our sites and snapped rolls of film for some magazine article or feature in one of the propaganda newspapers. We looked more handsome and were physically in better shape than all of the leading male stars in German cinema combined.

"My girl tells me she wets her damn panties every time Albers, Fritsch or Birgel appear on the screen," my bunkmate, Roland Biehl, chirped as a bunch of us were sitting around waiting for the projectionist to thread his machine so that we could settle into a KDF

## MATINEE IDOLS OF GERMAN CINEMA

**Willy Birgel**

**Heinz Rühmann**

**Axel von Ambesser**

**Hans Albers**

subsidized "Movie Night." Lifting his right arm and flexing his scorched-red muscles he bragged, "I'd like to see one of 'em match this," winking at me in a disarming way.

A lot of homoerotic teasing went on, but nothing ever came of it. Even in this highly charged atmosphere of manly sweat and the heady aroma of piss, no one would dare end up getting arrested and thrown into a concentration camp.

Even though everyone chalked up Biehl's claim as bragging, there was a certain amount of truth in it. Although all fine actors, our so-called matinee idols didn't hold a candle to the likes of Gable, Cooper or Bogart. On the evenings when the lights in our recreation hall were dimmed and the magic flicker of moving pictures filled the ample screen which the KdF people had provided for us, we guys loved to ogle the glamorous female stars of the day: Renate Müller, Ilse Werner, Jenny Jugo, Lil Dagover, and that most exotic of all creatures, the dancer who called herself La Jana.

"We've gotten a few old clunkers mixed in with the newer releases," complained the projectionist, Kai Fleischner. "Would you believe they tried to sneak in *Emil and the Detectives*? Did you ever? *Menschenskind*, that's as old as the hills!"

"It sure is," I put in. "If they'd stuck in *Berlin: die Symphonie der Großstadt*, *Battleship Potemkin* or *Wings*, at least we'd be treated to some wholesome classics instead of pig's swill.

Kai's face lit up. "Ah! I see I've come across a real movie buff." He showed me a reel enclosed in a sleeve with a photograph of a lovely actress stapled on the front. "She's German, but evidently she's very popular in France, too. Her name is Dita Parlo."

I perked up. "I saw her in *L'Atalante* and was bowled over," I practically squealed, then suddenly remembered where I was and took it down a few octaves. "She is so beautiful, and Michel Simon as the old sailor was brilliant. That director, Jean Vigo, seemed to take a lot of his cues from Eisenstein. The quality of the photography is so lush and I'm sure he was inspired by the great Sergey."

The projectionist set down the reel and stared holes through me. "I don't think I've been this astonished since I won ten Reichsmarks on the lottery," he proclaimed and added with a chuckle, "And believe me, that was some time ago. It's one thing for me to have the privilege of showing films and delighting audiences, but quite another to discuss them intelligently with someone."

His pale green eyes began to sparkle like emeralds. I figured him to be about thirty-five, the same age or a little younger than Lothar. He wasn't a bad looking man, but nothing about him really stood out except for his nominally pale green eyes. They seemed to draw attention away from the mousey brown crewcut, his angular nose, thin lips and weak chin, all encased in a weird, virtually whitewashed complexion. If he had not been so lively and upbeat,

## LEADING LADIES OF GERMAN CINEMA

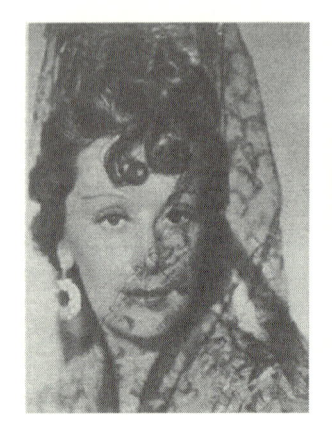

Lil Dagover

Renate Müller

Jenny Jugo

Ilse Werner

*The Indian Tomb* featuring Kitty Jantzen, Philip Dorn and exotic dancer La Jana

his appearance would have suggested a down-in-the-dumps sad sack. His clothes were unbecoming, obviously not properly cleaned or pressed. Having lived with and around Lothar with his penchant for meticulous dress and grooming (and inspiring me to do likewise), I found this civilian projectionist shabby at best.

Having taken all those physical pitfalls into account, his voice was soothing, much like that of a narrator of a children's story, but without the saccharine goo. Since he was not appealing to the eye, he made up for it by sharpening his wit, broadening his intellect and infusing the subjects we found interesting with a love and nurturing I hadn't seen for quite a while, certainly not since the NSDAP had seized power.

"I'm probably no different from most people in this country who go to the movies," I said modestly. "But I tend to notice things about blocking, lighting, the placement of items for effect on a particular set, close-ups of the various actors, crowd scenes and aerial shots --- you know, all the little touches that make motion pictures a treasure trove."

Kai continued chatting with me while he was threading film through the complicated series of spools and pistons. I was always amazed at the ease with which he accomplished this task while carrying on a fluent conversation. He'd come here a few times while we were working on construction projects for the Olympic Village and outbuildings in the surrounding area, but we'd only made small talk, really inconsequential. Suddenly I discovered a kindred spirit and wondered how closely he was connected to film production and distribution.

"You won't believe this," he responded sheepishly, "but I volunteered for two years in this same outfit." He extended his arm and made a sweeping motion of the premises. "Of course, that was a million years ago before the political landscape of our country changed. You guys are involved in a lot more projects than our group ever was." He looked me over and added, "If anything, the new Reich Labor Service is building better, stronger, more fit bodies than our generation ever had." He smiled faintly and the emerald glint in his eyes was even more apparent.

"After the service," he continued as I sat spellbound, "I apprenticed as a movie house projectionist in Kreuzberg. I had the chance to see every release in Germany plus a whole slew of foreign films. I studied all those things you enumerated, made a few connections and landed a job at UFA in Babelsberg, starting off in the mailroom and working my way up the department ladder."

I was floored. "Why, I got my first job in the mailroom at Bavaria Film-Kunst when I was still living in Munich with my aunt," I exclaimed, "though I didn't stay there long. I have a friend who's been promising me another gig with the studios or something similar. With the financial slump of the past few years and a whole bunch of other complications, it never panned out. Now he's engaged to my aunt and no longer has any time to worry about my future."

Kain finished his intricate work with the projector, slammed the cover shut and asked, "Is your friend associated with the studios?"

I shrugged. "To be honest, he's into so many different areas of trade, commerce and business, it's difficult to pin down. His name is Lothar Langenschlaff. Have you heard of him?"

Looking as if he'd been struck by lightning, Kai replied, "Yes, I have." There was a quiver in his voice that I hadn't heard before. The color drained out of his face and he looked like he was choking. Cupping his hand over his mouth and leaning slightly toward me, he whispered, "You and I had better not be seen talking too much to one another. It might arouse unnecessary suspicion. I'll explain more another time. KdF is sending me back here next week and we can talk again."

He glanced around the room as guys from the squad, all clad in the uniform shirts with the RAD emblem, filed into the assembly hall. »*Um Gotteswillen*,« he implored, "go and join the others right now!" He turned and pretended not to see how my face fell. I was saddened by the abruptness of his order. I stared at a new photo tacked to the wall. It showed a girl athlete standing next to one of the well-endowed statues by Arno Breker, depicting a nicely endowed sportsman. My eyes filled with tears, but I wiped them away before any of the other fellows noticed.

## Chapter Seventeen     SECOND TIME AROUND

Nearly a decade has passed since I laid eyes on that Olympic statue photo. I never got the chance to see any of the events because our Labor Service assignments took us to Mecklenburg and Hessen during those fabulous weeks. I managed to see Leni Riefenstahl's monumental documentary after the fact and was thrilled with the presentation.

Well beyond my narrow field of vision in one of a cluster of guest cottages situated about two hundred meters from the prison gate, a young man shuffles a few files around on a dining room table. "Gee, it would be nice if I had a desk for this jumbled mess," he mutters. "And this lighting is just atrocious," he adds as the fluorescent bulb sputters like a taut rubber band being plucked over and over.

"Hmm, that's a new one," he thinks out loud as he fingers a half dozen sheets in a file with my name on it (I am tucked away in my cell at this late hour, so I don't have the advantage of knowing any of his actions firsthand). Scratching his head, he skims a few lines of the original arrest and confinement order. Although he reads, writes and speaks fluent French, German and Russian, the documents have been translated into stilted English. "I wonder why he's firing his lawyer. Doesn't the poor devil know it's suicidal to defend oneself, especially in cases like this?" Shaking his head and clicking his tongue in disapproval, he adds, "Downright degrading."

This was not Lucas Feyerabend's first time in Germany. And, unlike me, he was able to get here and watch as many of the Olympic competitions as he and his group of scholars and erstwhile sports enthusiasts could get their fill of. Many of his Stanford classmates signed on for the junket to Berlin. Most were curious to see what the New Germany was like. Rumors galore had been circulated about bloody revolts, repressive measures, racial and hygiene laws and certain groups being singled out for particularly harsh treatment. Some wanted to see if the magnetism attributed to Adolf Hitler was fact or fiction. A few of them discredited the claim, although they grudgingly admitted that his charisma was above reproach. The way he filled stadiums and sports grounds with tens of thousands of supporters was nothing short of spectacular.

Lucas leans back and reminisces about that second day of Olympic events. A large group of Americans from San Francisco and other Northern Californian cities made their way past the *SS-Leibstandarte* and clamored up to the grandstand where the German Chancellor and Führer was seated with other members of the government. The staid leader displayed no outward emotion, so it wasn't discernible if he was flattered or annoyed by the impromptu attention. He may well have been shocked that a group of pushy American youth had made it this close to him without being detained. He signed no programs or other slips of paper that were held out to him, but he did shake a few hands and was civil enough in his bearing and etiquette.

Lucas smiles at the thought of being one of those fortunate enough to have shaken the Führer's hand. He recalls the limp, spongy grip of the leader who had garnered the admiration and reverence as well as fear and revulsion from two-thirds of Europe's population by the time the war had drawn to a close. He remembers nothing in the man's lackluster gaze, stoic expression or body language that cries out, "I was the Führer and Supreme Commander of all Germany, the Chief Justice of the land and the one for whom millions of Germans swore to fight even unto death." In Lucas's opinion, there is something transcendent about the man, even though it is pretty much agreed that he died either a hero's or a coward's death in Berlin, depending upon the point of view one has.

What amuses Lucas most when he looks back is the naïveté of the Stanford crowd. Not only had the Nazis done a bang-up job of wiping away all traces of anti-Semitism in and around Berlin. There was also a concentrated effort to present the nation as a peace-loving, completely demilitarized and benign entity, fully compliant with the dictates of the Versailles Treaty like a loyal dog who rolls over and plays dead.

Lucas laughs at the way fellow students as well as other visiting Americans he encountered raved about the spectacular progress Germany achieved in industry, agriculture and commerce while still maintaining rigid order and discipline. "It's nothing short of miraculous," a coed gushed, "and even more when you consider that not a single shot has been fired nor a single hair harmed on anyone's head in the process."

Of course it was easy to think that way, Lucas reflects. When a couple of »*Nachtlokale*« that were shuttered back in February 1933 suddenly reopened (albeit with NSDAP personnel to monitor all activity and movement of foreign guests while discreetly shooing away ordinary Germans) and the likes of Greta Keller belting out jazzy blues numbers or Claire Waldoff singing in comical Berlin dialect and rendering songs barely critical of the Nazi regime, you returned to your home country and praised the New Germany to the skies.

Happy German faces greeted the visitor and nary a grumble of protest was heard unless it was something innocuous like, "*Ach*, the cucumber salad they served with the pork loin at Such-and-Such Restaurant was not seasoned correctly." The managers of public swimming pools, parks and amusement venues took down all the FOR ARYANS ONLY and JEWS NOT WELCOME signs, and the foreigner heard and saw nothing of the enforcement of the ferocious Nuremberg Laws, promulgated just one year before Germany threw open her gates to welcome athletes from all over the globe in the spirit of fraternity and good sportsmanship.

The slightest hint of discontent had been silenced

by such a regime long before the foreigners arrived in droves. The original detention facility at Dachau mushroomed into a network of expertly-run, well-oiled concentration camps which locked away any asocial dissenters. Lucas hardly believes ordinary Germans' claims that they knew nothing about the existence of those camps. For several years a troop of SS men travelled through Germany with the blessing of the Ministry of Propaganda and Enlightenment and showed citizens how "only a stubborn mule ends up in a concentration camp," having at their disposal a donkey standing behind barbed wire to prove it!

A Stanford senior majoring in social studies and

**Where "only a stubborn mule ends up..."**

Articles about concentration camp prisoners and «*Erbkranken*» (persons who suffered birth defects and mental illness) were published in mainstream German magazines during the Nazi regime

Hitler and Goebbels visit UFA film studios

anthropology remarked upon the closing of the Olympic Games, "What a fantastically healthy population German has. You don't see infirm, handicapped or mentally retarded folks anywhere." Lucas shudders at the lack of awareness that even a supposedly learned colleague reveals. There have been revelations about the insidious race and hygiene measures, including forced sterilization and, in many cases, euthanasia. Gruesome "mercy killings" performed at the notorious Hadamar sanatorium have come to light to confound the naysayers. It is inconceivable that the nation who produces geniuses such as Goethe, Beethoven and Nietzsche also commits atrocities on a level not witnessed in modern history.

Indeed, a long road existed for Lucas after his return to Stanford to finish his studies and earn a law degree. His excellent work as a trial lawyer, then a special arbitrator for Armed Forces-related cases, and now his tireless efforts to review these pesky repatriation files has not gone unnoticed or unrewarded. Lucas Feyerabend is barely thirty years old and already feels as if the world is his oyster.

Off the beaten path in this normally quiet corner of occupied Germany, he is glad to be serving his country in this capacity. Sorting out the colossal mess of displaced persons wandering around Europe in the aftermath of the devastation is a daunting task. Most of the cases are fairly cut-and-dried while others prove to be more complicated due to the unique eccentricities of German law and the Penal Code. Great sympathy and pledges of support materialize from various sectors such as the Jewish Relief Organization, the Council of Churches and benevolent societies worldwide. It makes Lucas's work of finding suitable placement easier and fulfilling.

He is troubled, however, by one small group which is being unnecessarily demonized. Rereading the provisions of Paragraph 175 under the flickering fluorescent light in these comfortable digs just outside the prison walls astounds him as much as when he first looked into it as a student of international law in San Francisco prior to entering Stanford. Personal feelings as well as his own natural instincts and proclivities weigh into his view of the efficient way German jurisprudence addresses the issue of the "despised ones."

Lucas Feyerabend knows how differently he is wired from most red-blooded American males. He thanks his lucky stars that he was born and raised in a city like San Francisco where one feels as free to pursue certain alternative lifestyles as in New York, or so he hears. Overt public displays by persons of the same sex do not surface, but the undercurrent of homosexuals in the arts, music, culinary, fashion and cultural scenes is apparent and, to some extent, nurtured encouragingly by all and sundry, with the possible exception of law enforcement.

Hardly dashing or exceptional in looks, Lucas still

gets his share of male admirers. He even goes out on an occasional date. He is the epitome of discretion and insists on the same from his partners who readily comply anyway. Especially now that he works as a liaison to the armed forces and is subject to all military regulations, a slipup in that regard can land him in the stockade, not to mention the black mark which is retained on the books in perpetuity. He has expended too much to achieve success in life and risks nothing to jeopardize it. It goes without saying that his conspirators are likeminded.

Visiting Germany the first time for pleasure made him think about all the injustice in the United States. Righteous indignation over acts of discrimination, repression and prejudice seem ill-founded when the finger points back at you for similar homegrown infractions. He discusses his concerns during this second time on German soil in an academic vein with Dylan Sinclair, an associate from the arbitration board.

"Doesn't it strike you as odd that we're also just as guilty of treating some of our folks like second-class citizens?" Lucas asks him over a cup of nice filter-brewed coffee. It's the sort that differs markedly from the *Ersatz* stuff the beleaguered German population has doled out to them in rations nowadays as they clear away the rubble of what was home and hearth. "You have to admit that we still have some fairly horrendous forms of discrimination right in our own backyard."

Smacking appreciative lips not only over the excellent coffee but even more over a delectable slice of *Apfelkuchen*, Sinclair, replies, "Oh, you mean like the WASP-y attitude towards Jews? The PERSONS OF THE HEBREW FAITH NOT DESIRED warning on all the swank country club applications and presentation cards? Yeah, it's not that much different than the ways Jews have been treated by the Nazis, except for herding them into camps to waste away."

Lucas casts a wistful look toward the window. The screech of jeep tires outside punctures the normal silence around the quaint cottages. "You're right there," he mutters, "although you forget that we reserved our 'internment centers' for the Japanese. Those are just glorified concentration camps, except they're out in the desert where tumbleweeds blow in the dust storms. And the sad thing is that the majority of internees are U.S. citizens who have no ties to Japan whatsoever. Why, they're as American as mom, apple pie and the stars'n'stripes."

The associate produces a pack of Lucky Strikes from his coat pocket and offers one to Lucas. After lighting up and taking a puff, he puts in, "I needn't mention the way our colored boys are shoved around. I heard that President Truman's toying with the idea of desegregating the armed forces. He's probably going to rankle a lot of stalwart, non-progressive Southerners with a forward-thinking idea like that."

Always taking the side of the downtrodden and disenfranchised, Lucas shakes his head in disgust. "I've heard about the WHITE and COLORED ONLY entrances and separate facilities as well as the Jim Crow laws. I've never been down South, but my parents did drive us to Arizona to visit my aunt and uncle one spring. We stopped in this little Podunk town to buy some bottles of soda pop. Next to the grocer's I remember seeing a saloon with a big sign on the door: NO DOGS OR MEXICANS ALLOWED." Taking a long drag from his cigarette, he feels the anger churning inside him much like he did as a ten-year-old boy. "I've never been able to shake the memory of those fucking words."

"I'm gonna go out on a limb," Sinclair remarks, "but I do believe that the hierarchy of leadership in various large nations points to an interesting parallel. There exists a cult of personality and an iconic reverence to giants like Hitler, Mussolini, ol' Joe Stalin and even our own FDR. That's why folks became hysterical with grief when he died so suddenly month before last, even though he looked like he had one foot in the grave anyway." The younger man snuffs out his cigarette and adds, "For me personally, Roosevelt is the only president who's been around since I was a kid."

Lucas grins. "I've been alive since Hoover and Coolidge," he chuckles, "and I vaguely recall Harding, though Wilson not at all. Oddly enough, I understand what you're saying, even though a lot of our fellow

Americans might take offense to comparing our dearly departed president to the likes of those vile dictators. The 'cult of personality' thing, though, is spot-on. I cringe every time I watch *Yankee Doodle Dandy* when the huge simulated portrait of him appears over the stage."

Laughing, the associate volunteers, "In that flick and many others, you'll see that display of super-patriotism. Some people even say that the kindly old government worker who helps the Okies get resettled in *Grapes of Wrath* is a thinly disguised replica of FDR."

Lucas is impressed with Dylan Sinclair's keen observations and admires his knowledge of symbolism in the movies. If he only knew how open the young man was on certain subjects, he'd be more than happy to discuss the illusions of behavior, lifestyles and taboos depicted in movies like *Design For Living, Wonder Bar* and *The Man Who Came To Dinner*. But it is best to let go of that topic for fear of betrayal or ostracism by his colleagues. He can never be too sure of who "is" and "isn't." And prosecuting cases like the one for the man who fired his lawyer is ironic for Lucas because he is forced to be impartial.

## Chapter Eighteen     SURVIVING THE THIRTIES

Elderly people were in the habit of coming up to me all the time and warning, "You're young now, but believe me, when you get old you'll see the years just fly by." I didn't have the heart to tell them that I felt exactly that way now that my twentieth birthday was approaching. It only seemed like yesterday that I had joined RAD, then suddenly it was all over. I traded my shovel, hammer and pickax for a typewriter, stationery and carbon paper. I frantically typed up a flurry of resumes and sent them to firms throughout Berlin and the surrounding region. I boasted about my time with the Labor Service, but even that stellar achievement didn't elicit much response from prospective employers.

Sitting at the desk in Aunt Gusti's flat in Moabit, I sulked and wondered what the future would hold for me. She and Lothar went on a second honeymoon skiing in Kitzbühl while I finished off the remainder of her binding lease on the place. Having to eventually leave here threw me into a panic and a cold sweat. Where would I live without money and no prospects of gainful employment? I hardly knew anybody because people weren't so terribly trusting of one another in Germany these days. Tales of "friends" betraying "friends" to the Gestapo were rife. I had this "thing" I could not and would not shake, no matter how hard I tried. I didn't want to call unnecessary attention to myself by having any close associations with guys in my age group. I'd been thrown together with a bevy of muscular, very fit young men and we always lived in close quarters. It was all I could do to fight the urge to jerk off every night in my bed. As a matter of fact, I'd denied myself any physical pleasure for so long that I was convinced I'd regain my virginity somehow!

Germany was coming into its own and regaining its status among the leading nations of Europe. The Rhineland was occupied and the Saar plebiscite had successfully returned that disputed area to the German Reich. The Führer set his sights on his native Austria where the push for annexation was gaining ground. Ties between our country and Mussolini's Italy were strengthened from year to year, along with our friendly overtures to Imperial Japan. A formidable axis of power and influence over entire continents became the focal point of *Realpolitik* during the decade. Il Duce's troops had already occupied Ethiopia, Eritrea, Somalia and Equatorial Africa, indicating a push for colonial domination by European strongmen. Could the Third Reich possibly regain the losses she incurred in Africa and the South Seas as a result of the Kaiser's war? Speculation ran wild, and I'm certain that Hitler toyed with the idea.

The Potemkim village that had sprung up in Berlin and a couple of other places to dazzle the world during the recent Olympics was slowly stripped away. Life in Germany returned to normal. This meant ramping up military production. The quaint ruse of benign factories churning out harmless vacuum cleaners and non-controversial kitchen appliances gave way to munitions, heavy artillery, rocket launchers and other long range weaponry. There was no denying that a war of some magnitude was in the cards. Luftwaffe aircraft had assisted Generalissimo Francisco Franco's Loyalist army crush the Republican opposition during the civil war in Spain, the first instance of aerial bombardments on civilian populations.

Imperial Japan had invaded Manchuria and began licking its chops over other choice regions in China which were ripe for conquest. In his search for natural resources and raw materials to bolster a robust economy and build a formidable war machine, the Japanese Emperor, with the cooperation of his generals and the Cabinet, spared nothing to achieve ultimate victory. Classified reports about the Axis nations building up their respective military-industrial complexes both alarmed and emboldened smaller countries to strengthen their own armies and do a little sabre rattling themselves. France, Poland and Czechoslovakia all justified their own defense.

Whether it was the Maginot Line or the Siegfried Line, Europe was gearing up for a fight while the rest of the world was so consumed in its own policy of neutrality and isolation (which even a laughable League of Nations could not hinder) that it barely heard the rustle of the continent's wings. I felt parti-

"Radio everywhere" throughout Germany

cularly sorry for poor Mother Russia. Through massive purges and show trials instigated by Stalin's own paranoia and lunacy, the Bolsheviks' best and brightest minds were being thrown into the execution pits to rot, leaving her vulnerable to attack from without. Her answer was to increase pressure on her wary neighbors: the Baltic countries of Estonia, Latvia and Lithuania as well as hardy, stalwart Finland. The stage was being set for a massive blowup.

For us ordinary Germans, the upswing in military production signaled a shift in the output and availability of other commodities. At the beginning of 1937 state-regulated consumption of butter, margarine and lard was set in motion. Within two years' time many other food items would be added to the list: meat, fresh fruit, dairy products, bread, coffee and sugar. "As one's stomach rumbles, the human being grumbles" didn't seem to fit our Aryan mentality. NSDAP indoctrination ran deep, quelling any dissatisfaction with the situation or dissent against the authorities. Free distribution of wireless receivers, the ubiquitous »*Volksempfänger*«, insured that every German household had access to a variety of radio offerings including selected news, classical music, light entertainment, and the endless speeches by the Führer and other members of the Third Reich's government, Dr. Goebbels being the most frequently heard whenever the Führer ran out of steam (which was not often).

I still took advantage of "Strength Through Joy" and all of its benefits. Whenever I could get away, I joined a KdF group and boarded a motor coach for scenic excursions to the Harz Mountains, Lake Constance, the Baltic Sea beaches, a Rhine River cruise or wine tasting in Mosel. By far my two favorite trips were the grand tour of the two former imperial capitals, Vienna and Budapest (the spicy flavor of real Hungarian *Gulasch* still lingered on my tongue long after I arrived back home) and an expedition to Egypt. Lothar informed me that I was privileged to join the tour to see the Pyramids of Giza as well as sail up and down the Nile and poke around in ancient Karnak and the Valley of the Kings. Those lush outings to places like Portugal, the Canary Islands, Venice and ports along the Adriatic, trekking in the Swiss Alps or skiing in Norway were normally reserved for Nazi Party bigwigs and derisively called »*Bonzenfahrten*«.

"Somebody is watching out for you," Gusti assured me. "Heinrich Schliemann himself couldn't have had a trip like that just drop into his lap, even though he was the intrepid Egyptian explorer and researcher that we all know and love. You must have somebody in high places pulling strings for you."

I shook my head. "I can't think of anybody because I don't have any close friends or admirers that I'm aware of." I threw my head back, and Lothar shot me a worried glance. My aunt still didn't know about my preferences, to say nothing of her dear husband's bisexuality. She also couldn't have known how I'd denied my urges for so long.

Most Germans spent a good deal of energy denying bitter facts of life in the glorious new and improved Third Reich. One would have had to be comatose not to notice the worsening lot for Jews. The group was singled out for exclusion from Germany's economic, cultural and community life, and the orders came from high places. Aryanization of Jewish businesses and expropriation of their property (often at price levels far below the prevailing market value) hastened the mass exodus of a segment of the German population which had contributed so much to the well-being of our country. Who did not know and genuinely trust a Jewish doctor, lawyer, banker or businessman? Didn't Jewish shopkeepers always offer the choicest wares at reasonable prices? In spite of this, Jews were defamed, marked for ostracism and eventual extinction by the Nazi hierarchy.

*"The Rabinowitzes left their flat and never came back,"* *"the Cohen family went away on some sort of extended vacation,"* and *"we haven't seen Herr and Frau Katz for a while and don't know what happened to them"* became common ways for Aryan neighbors to justify the disappearance of Jewish neighbors, acquaintances and professionals with whom they had dealt and been on friendly terms for years. Even though it was whispered about in every town, village

and out-of-the-way place throughout the country, practically everyone knew somebody who had been thrown into "protective custody," a euphemism which evolved into "detention center" and not long after into "concentration camp." Even at the end of the decade people still thought of "KZ" as a temporary detainment and carried out in individual cases. Some Aryans believed the lie that the camps were used as a waystation prior to the "resettlement of Jewish and asocial vermin" in order to protect the German people. Little did anyone suspect that the system would proliferate and affect the freedom of those shunned by the Nazi regime numbering into hundreds of thousands and, eventually, millions of unfortunate souls.

**A Jewish-owned rubber goods shop which has been "Aryanzied" (names of both owners are shown)**

"Hey, *Bengel*," Lothar said to me out of the blue during one of our numerous walks on a Sunday afternoon in Berlin's Tiergarten. Aunt Gusti was on assignment with DEHOMAG in Breslau. The census for Pomerania and East Prussia began early because ethnic Germans, the so-called »*Volksdeutschen*« were swarming in from those regions in another of the Third Reich's ambitious resettlement programs. The only difference was that a better fate awaited them than the Jews.

"*Hallo*, what can I do for you?" I quipped.

"Some guy named Kai Fleischner contacted me through UFA," Lothar confided. "Why does that name ring a bell?" he asked, stroking his chin while looking down at the ducks and geese swimming in one of the ponds.

"He's the projectionist who showed us films on 'Movie Nights' in the Labor Service," I replied. "I mentioned your name to him once and he reacted strangely, I must say." As I chuckled I noticed that a look of horror came over Lothar and the color drained from his face. It was similar to Fleischner's abrupt change of mood and pale complexion that day several months prior in the RAD recreation hall. "All right, what gives, Lothar? You look like you've seen a ghost."

He gulped audibly and slowly regained his normally rosy cheeks. "I knew Kai back in the days of *Café Megalomania*, Rosa Valetti's place. She played hostess to greats and near-greats of Berlin's literary, social and political scene, and there was always an eclectic mix of people, serious and poseurs alike. Kai was a young, slender morsel whom half of the city's eligible men and boys had bedded at one time or another." Pausing for effect, he added, "I was together with him for a brief fling which ran hot and cold 'between engagements,' as the expression goes. Those were wild, glorious times and they've all but disappeared since certain people have come to power." He placed his index finger under his nose and raised his arm slightly in a *Heil Hitler!* salute when we'd turned a corner and were out of view for a few seconds.

I became intrigued as much as I was amused. "It can't be the same person," I volunteered. "The Kai Fleischner I met is kinda dumpy-looking with a sagging face and dark circles under his eyes."

Lothar nodded knowingly. "I don't doubt it," he declared. "He was like a spitfire in his heyday, you see, somebody who literally as well as figuratively burned up the road behind him as he jumped from bed to bed. The ravages of syphilis, gonorrhea and the devil-only-knows-what-else must have taken their toll on him. He fell out of favor quickly when he began going downhill."

I stopped in my tracks and stared at Lothar. "He never infected you, did he?" I asked with urgency. "You put yourself at risk if you spent any amount of time with him doing…you know what!"

Instead of looking concerned, Lothar just grinned

unexpectedly. "I thought of that," he put in, "so I went to see a doctor right away after the first couple of times we 'did it,' and have continued to visit him on a regular basis for more than a decade now. I'm proud to report that I have a clean bill of health." Rubbing his knuckles against his lapel, he added, "It's too bad about Kai. He was really something special, a feast for the eyes and a delight to the senses. He had his share of getting roughed up, too. The Brown Shirt boys attacked him one night and it left him traumatized. And since the present regime has been up and running, there's no place to turn to for help in that regard, as you and I both know so well."

The bad memory of my own encounter with the big dicks of the SA flooded my mind, and my asshole began to pucker involuntarily. Not changing my deadpan expression or reacting one way or the other, I murmured, "So sad, especially if he was as gorgeous as you claim."

Lothar suddenly had a faraway look in his eye. "Kai always had his fair share of being roughed up. He could really piss people off if he set his mind to it. But he was great sex, hands down, perhaps the greatest ever." He looked me up and down like so many times in the past. "Not all of us age as gracefully," he blurted out sarcastically. "I'll wager that Kai took in quite an eyeful of you and your hunky buddies in the Labor Service. He probably would have eaten you alive if given half the chance. He was always oversexed – a male nymphomaniac."

Playfully (without being too showy, for people strolling through the Tiergarten made eye contact frequently and acknowledged one another) I quipped, "Yeah, well, he ain't skinny no more and his face is pockmarked and disfigured. Like the old saying goes, 'I wouldn't do it with yours, let alone mine!'"

Lothar gave me a friendly punch in the arm. "You're heartless," he said ruefully. "Stop judging a book by its cover. Truth be told, I was going to tell you that I received a memo signed by him late Friday afternoon. He wants to get in contact with you and didn't know how. He has a job offer for you, but we kept going on about what a good lay he used to be and how he's deteriorated. I didn't have a chance to tell you."

I perked up. "Really? A job offer?" I asked. "I wonder what it is…"

"I think I can guess," Lothar responded, and I winced. "No, I'm serious – don't be like that. Two members of the studio focus group have dropped off the radar screen. They need to fill those spots. Kai mentioned briefly in the memo that he admired your knowledge of film and attention to production details."

I smiled and was anxious to know more. "That really sounds like a good gig," I chimed in, "and something that doesn't require swinging a pickax. *Gott in Himmel*, my poor arms are so worn out from the Labor Service."

"I can imagine." Lothar made a fist and flexed his arm. "You know, if you don't keep working out, all that muscle will turn to flab --- just like other people we've been talking about."

My face fell. "You're kidding!" Walking along the edge of the pond for a second or two with my head down, I added, "I'd better start on an exercise regimen tomorrow and stick to it. Now that I've got a possible job offer, I feel a little less depressed."

"That's the spirit, my friend." The fact that Lothar no longer referred to me as *Liebling* or other cutesy names disturbed me, but I understood how it was a reflection of the times and the bizarre country we were living in. "I have the feeling that you'll relish the opportunity and give them lots of good input."

Something troubled me about the whole thing. "If the job is so choice, why did they lose two people?"

Lothar hesitated, and I could see that it was uncomfortable for him to speak about such matters. "The ever-loving *Prüfstelle*, the censorship and rating board, discovered that two of the participants were either Jewish or had Jewish spouses. They were dismissed immediately." Throwing up his hands, he added, "It was bound to happen sooner or later. Things are becoming harder with each passing day even for the Jews who still own property in Dahlem and Wilmersdorf. It's only a matter of time when it'll all be swept out from under them and they'll have to depart."

I was thunderstruck. "Depart? For where?" I knew

what he was aiming at, but I was ready to play devil's advocate. "You don't mean to tell me that you believe all that hogwash about Palestine, do you? Even Gerd Eichenbaum admitted that such nonsense was just a pipedream, designed to give the Jewish community a sense of relief and make them complacent." I knew that Gerd was already in the throes of getting his family together, taking as many of his possessions as possible and heading over the French border.

Lothar shrugged his shoulders and didn't have an answer. Instead, he pulled me aside and warned with the shake of his finger, "Don't raise your voice about certain subjects when we're out in public. Gestapo agents are everywhere, and where there are no agents, there are plenty of loyal citizens who eavesdrop on two men strolling along in public. They enjoy spilling their guts to the police."

Even though news about what went on in Germany as well as the rest of Europe swirled around me, I still rarely picked up a newspaper. Our neighbors in Dahlem as well as the families who were squeezed together in flats throughout Moabit were bombarded by current events and propaganda towing the official line day and night, thanks to the »*Volksempfänger*« radio contraptions. I usually tuned out the "talking" programs and focused on the music and variety shows, particularly movie and show business gossip.

I turned into one of those citizens who was vaguely aware of what was going on. I knew the «*Anschluß*» in Austria was successful and that the Führer received a triumphant welcome in Vienna. I found out that the Munich Conference concluded with an agreement by four countries (and the mysterious exclusion of the Czech government) to allow German annexation of the Sudeten territory, supposedly in order to ensure peace and security in Central Europe. I and my fellow Germans delighted in the Führer's brilliant maneuver in coaxing the Czechoslovak President, Dr. Hacha, to sign a paper which handed over Bohemia and Moravia as a protectorate of the Third Reich.

"German's territorial claims are satisfied," the press heralded, "and not a drop of blood has been shed on the European continent in this quest." These were developments that I should have hailed as victories for Greater Germany, but I could have not cared less. Those places and situations were way out of my grasp of understanding.

One incident which did hit me right between the eyes (and which my fellow Germans would have been hard-pressed to ignore) was the "public outcry" that reared its ugly head throughout our country on the night of November 9th until early on the 10th of that year prior to the kickoff of the war. Herschel Grynszpan, a troubled young Polish man who lived in France took matters into his own hands after learning about his parents' deportation and their abandonment at the Polish-German border. Marching into the German legation in Paris, he confronted a low level secretary named Ernst Eduard vom Rath and shot him point-blank. The "retaliatory measures" seemed a bit too synchronized to have been spontaneous. The sound of breaking glass on house windows, shattered store fronts, the looting and burning of synagogues and individual residences as well as the mock parades and shouts of "The Jews are our misfortune" and "Exodus of the Jews who are not wanted here" were all too obvious to ignore. The whispered euphemism to describe this horrendous night of broken glass, »*Kristallnacht*«, reverberated throughout German cities and towns. Once again, few dared to raise their voices. And certainly no one protested the ludicrous penalty of one billion Reichsmarks slapped on Germany's Jewish community to compensate for the insurance claims to the damaged property.

**Herschel Grynszpan after his arrest in Paris**

Wearers of the yellow star inscribed with the word **JUDE** were seen less and less on our streets. I learned that orders were issued by the *SiPo* (an acronym for *Sicherheitspolizei* = security police) to practically exclude them from all public life. There were restrictions on the days and hours when they could use public transit or visit the shops. They were prohibited from holding professional jobs. Any violations of the edicts resulted in arrest, severe punishment and, in most cases, deportation. The machinery of the concentration camp network was still not well-oiled enough to receive the hundreds of thousands of detainees who would be flooding in once the war began. That too, however, would change in time.

"My old school chum, Nathan's house was ransacked and set on fire on that awful night," Kai Fleischner confided to me. I had managed to get the job with the *Prüfstelle* through him and was now bouncing between focus groups and meetings not only at UFA in Babelsberg, but also Tobis and Terra in Marienfelde and an occasional "gig" for my old stomping grounds, Bavaria Film-Kunst. "To add insult to injury," he continued, "the scoundrels found Nathan's violin among the stuff they were carrying out. 'Hey,' shouted one of the vandals, 'which one of you filthy kikes plays this thing?' Nathan sheepishly raised his hand into which the thug shoved the violin and bow. 'Play something light and airy for us, Jew scum!' he barked."

Symbol of "Justice" in a mock hanging with amused Nazi officials looking on (mid 1930's)

"Exodus of the Jews" after *Kristallnacht* (November 9-10, 1938) in a forced march supervised by NSDAP stalwarts

**Aftermath of «*Kristallnacht*»**

**The Führer's reception in Vienna**

»*Um Gotteswillen,*« I cried, "did he do it? What could he possibly have summoned the courage to play at a time like that?"

"Would you believe '*Wochenende und Sonnenschein,*' that stupid ditty by the Comedian Harmonisten?"

I shuddered and hung my head. What tragic irony to think that Nazi bandits were stripping everything a family owned right out from under them and burning the rest while their son was forced to play the wretched song to which the Americans gave the title, "Happy Days Are Here Again." In spite of the family's misfortune, I had to ask the question that was eating away at me.

"I suppose the bastards smashed the violin before they left, huh?"

"Nuh-uh," Kai replied. "Funny thing. One of the assholes produced Nathan's violin case and gently, mind you, placed it in there and told him to lock it. They took the violin with the rest of the stuff, but it wasn't damaged as far as I know."

Changing the subject completely and knowing that I could exchange racy gossip with Kai because he'd become my best pal, I put in, "Did you hear the rumor going around about one of the Comedian Harmonists riding on the same train recently as the Führer himself? He started ranting about how corrupt the Nazis were. Somebody told me he ended up in France after somebody tipped him off about stoolpigeons who'd already notified the Gestapo."

## Chapter Nineteen     THE STARS ARE SHINING

Kai Fleischner bragged to people around UFA, Terra and Tobis that I'd worked my way up from lowly mailroom clerk at Bavaria Film-Kunst to technical adviser on the *Prüfstelle*. I felt like I had to correct him, even though I was flattered by all the attention. "It's not quite the way you're making it out to be," I insisted. "I left the mailroom job and didn't have a gig for years. I filled in all the time by joining the Labor Service, as you well know."

"Ah ha!" Kai exclaimed, not letting on that we knew each other from my days in RAD. He placated a throng of onlookers by adding, "So it's you we have to thank for the fact that we can now speed along the *Autobahn* between Berlin and Hamburg at a reasonable clip."

Chuckling, I played along by responding, "Yeah, me and a whole bunch of great guys who pitched in to make it happen." Our coworkers were none the wiser for not knowing that Kai was responsible for landing me this position: a dream job for someone who is a movie buff in the first place. Now I and a select group of individuals enjoyed the rare opportunity of watching every movie that came out of German and Austrian studios as well as a few foreign-made films which the censors had approved for screening in cinema houses throughout the territory of the Third Reich.

I joined the *Prüfstelle* at a time when a great shift

was occurring in the composition of films as well as the array of participants in their production. Granted, cinematic giants such as Albers, Rühmann and Jannings still lit up the screen, and the risqué gyrations of the exotic dancer named La Jana sizzled on celluloid before bewildered German moviegoers. I recall one old biddy who shook her head in dismay after the closing frame of *Das indische Grabmal* appeared on the screen at the Germania-Palast. She muttered, "Why do our leaders allow such filth to pollute films nowadays? Why, that woman had no clothes on while she wiggled to that jungle music!" Out of respect, her fellow audience members smiled benevolently and kept their snickering to a minimum.

No, in spite of Hans Albers's intrepid spirit, Heinz Rühmann's comedic timing or Heinrich George's adventuresome dip into meatier dramatic roles, a new energy flooded the German movie industry in the image of the foreigner. Incongruous to a country and society which emphasized Aryan purity, the foreigners came in all shapes, sizes and colors. It was widely known that Joachim von Ribbentrop, Foreign Minister of the Third Reich, had attempted to lure Marlene Dietrich back to Germany with grandiose promises. She didn't fall for any of it, so von Ribbentrop, Dr. Goebbels and even the Führer himself (Germany's number one movie fan) set their sights on other possibilities.

Around this time a beautiful Swedish actress and

singer named Zarah Leander was making quite a name for herself in Germany and Austria. Soon she was elevated to "Queen of the Reich Cinema" and hailed by our movie critics as "the new Garbo." The combination of her sultry voice, crisp delivery of German language dialogue and commanding screen presence guaranteed her and UFA Studios hit after hit at the box office.

"Do you realize that ever since *Zu neuen Ufern* came out," Kai gushed to me, "that every woman and girl throughout Greater Germany wants her hairdresser to duplicate the Gloria Vane look? The damn curling irons in the salons haven't had a chance to cool down!"

Musical offerings in German motion pictures improved greatly, thanks to the multifaceted talents of Marika Rökk, the Hungarian spitfire who warbled and danced her way into the hearts of the German-speaking public. Johannes Heesters, Dutch-born vocalist and romantic lead, delighted audiences with his exuberance. Pola Negri, the stunning Polish diva, great silent film star and one of Rudolph Valentino's paramours, pumped new life into her career which had somewhat faded. Her popularity sagged when her heavily-accented English was heard with disdain by American and British moviegoers who clamored for the new medium of talking pictures. Her shortcoming, however, proved electrifying when transmitted in German. Both *Mazurka* and *Tango Notturno* were even shown to an admiring Hitler and

Promotional material for the Zarah Leander film, *Zu neuen Ufern* (To New Shores), with the oft-copied hairstyle that drove female moviegoers crazy

**Marika Rökk**         **Heinrich George**

**Marika Rökk, doing what she did best**

his staff in the Reichskammer. Olga Tschechowa and Lida Baarova, two other Slavic imports, won over the hearts and minds of a nation whose racial policymakers had declared such ethnicity to be subhuman. Why the exception?

"It does boggle the mind, doesn't it?" Kai asked me over some *Apfelstrudel* in the commissary at Terra right after I'd taken part in an extensive review of *Es leuchten die Sterne* (The Stars Are Shining), the new musical with set decorations, dance numbers and acting ability which rivaled the best of Hollywood's Busby Berkeley extravaganzas. "They make such a big deal about Aryan purity, and yet they promote bewitching imports like the Lecuona Cuban Boys, George Boulanger, Viktor Staal, Laura Solari and Lil Adina."

I nodded and chimed in, "Don't leave out Mohamed Husen either. Even though he's largely been an extra, he's racked up quite a few films where he's played the obedient lackey or colonial stooge brilliantly. He's also one of the few actors I've actually met face to face. He's delightful to chat with. His German accent sounds cute, just the way you'd expect a black person to talk."

An even brighter star was about to shine as 1938 dragged on. Maria Esther Aldunate del Campo was a ravishing South American chanteuse and had already shone with brilliance in Paris and Lisbon. German talent scouts approached her after one of her performances, luring her with a lucrative contract to play in Berlin. Rechristened "Rosita Serrano," she took the capital of the Third Reich by storm, even garnering admirers in Vienna, Budapest, Prague and Warsaw through film, radio and songs written especially for her by composers like Michael Jary, Franz Grothe and Theo Mackeben.

I was thrilled when Lothar was able to score some tickets for us to see her premiere at The Wintergarten. "Her German pronunciation is atrocious," he remarked, "but her presence onstage is a *tour de force*. And when she sings 'La Paloma' to the accompaniment of her own expert guitar strumming and charming whistle, you can't help but fall in love with her. She transports you to new, exotic worlds."

He was right about that. I was never so fascinated by a star before. I could listen to her Telefunken recordings of »*Roter Mohn*«, »*Der Onkel Johnathan*«, »*Bei dir war es simmer so schön*«, or the even more sultry "*Mambo Negro*" until the grooves on the shellac practically wore down. She was so radically different from the image of womanhood presented in Germany since the NSDAP takeover. She smoked cigarettes in public, she drove her own car with the top down all over Berlin (or anywhere else she travelled) and seemed to enjoy life with reckless abandon.

"Rosita comes off like somebody who thinks life is one big farce, a comedy in which she is the center of attention," I raved to Kai. "I wonder how that kind of

Zarah Leander and Viktor Staal in the classic, *Die große Liebe* (The Great Love), one of UFA's biggest grossing wartime film

Mohamed Husen, the most prolific «*Statist*» (cinematic extra) in 1930's German films

Marika Rökk and Johannes Heesters, two regularly paired stars of Nazi-era films

Rosita Serrano

Hans Brausewetter

thing squares off with the bigshots at the studios or the leaders of our government."

Kai nodded knowingly whenever I brought up topics like this. He was my first and only likeminded friend, a great guy to hang around and talk about everything under the sun. "You know, *Das Programm von Heute* and *Lockende Leinwand* present one side of the picture, but there's a lot more going on underneath the surface." We always went on the studio lot to walk between sound stages when our chats became too juicy. Spies and informants lurked everywhere on the studio property, trying to eavesdrop on conversations and watching for improper behavior. Kai and I always carried clipboards and pretended we were comparing notes on *Prüfstelle* projects while furtively chatting.

"The two most scintillating pieces of gossip I have," he began, "are about Renate Müller and Lida Baarova." I already knew about Müller's sudden death and speculations about a possible suicide, although no concrete evidence substantiated such a claim.

"Give me number two," I whispered to him in a tone which suggested indifference to the fate of Renate Müller. She was, however, yesterday's news. I wanted some fresh dirt. "She's the Czech actress, right? The one who starred in *Verräter* (Traitors)..."

Kai mumbled, "I have it on good authority that the 'Club Foot' has been seeing her privately ever since he dumped Jenny Jugo."

As shocked and incensed as I felt, I didn't let on that I knew anything about Jenny Jugo or any of Dr. Goebbels assorted dalliances. To my mind he was supposed to be a paragon of virtue. "I guess when you're a bigwig and have the reins of power, you can command anything from anybody," I remarked smugly. "And you'll always get it, regardless. Does anybody know how the Führer views his extracurricular activity?"

Kai waved away my question with a flick of his wrist. "He's already taken care of it. The Führer is apparently very fond of Magda and the Reich Minister's children. He wants to hold up the solid marriages of his inner circle as an example to the German people."

I grunted and said, "Yeah, marriage. They place such a big emphasis on it. And producing offspring for the Fatherland is uppermost in their minds. Lothar married my Aunt Gusti, but they don't have any kids."

Kai broke into a sardonic smile. "What Lothar went and did is a sham. In more sophisticated circles they call it a 'lavender marriage.' It's caught on a lot since January of 1933. Gustaf Gründgens wed Marianne Hoppe largely for appearances. Otherwise he was liable to end up like Hans Brausewetter or Bruno Balz if he hadn't saved his skin."

"It was Käthe Haack who interceded in that Brausewetter case, wasn't it?" My reactions to his statements belied the fact that I had concrete know-

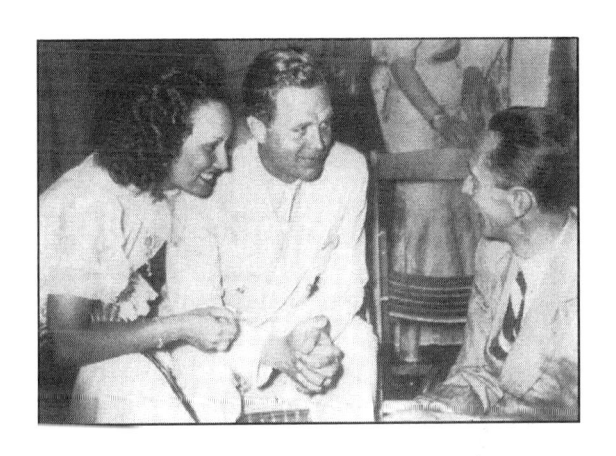

(above) Lida Baarova, Gustav Fröhlich and Dr. Joseph Goebbels in conversation
(below l.) Lida Baarova (r.) Dr. and Magda Goebbels with three of their children

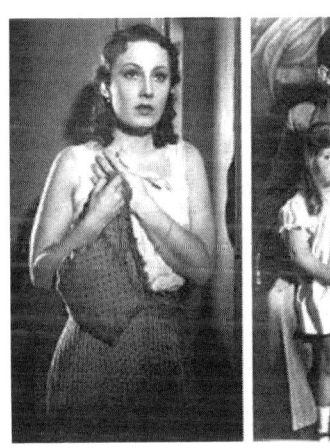

# FILM COMPOSERS/LYRICISTS DURING THE THIRD REICH

**Franz Grothe**

**Bruno Balz**

**Michael Jary**

**Theo Mackeben**

ledge of the hurdles these celebrities had to jump over in order to not only keep their careers intact, but life itself. Someone else had told me how composer Michael Jary convinced the Nazi authorities to waive lyricist Bruno Balz's conviction and sentence to hard labor in a concentration camp for violating Paragraph 175, insisting that the man's usefulness in bolstering wartime patriotism through his brilliant messages was at stake.

"You have people like Haack and Jary who lay their own lives and reputations on the line for a friend and associate," I exclaimed, adding, "On the flip side of the coin one sees the cowardly actions of a Hans Albers, for instance, who renounces his Jewish wife and kicks her out. That's plain wrong!"

"My friend, there are inconsistencies all over the place," Kai reassured me. "Don't you think it's ironic how we rave about 'degenerate' art and music, even mounting up exhibitions and performances so that we can *see* and *hear* just how degenerate they are? Believe me, they are cultural milestones which draw bigger crowds than any ordinary exhibition or mundane concert ever did!"

I shrugged. "Oh yeah, degenerate music. Sure!" I snickered bitterly. "Even Evelyn Künneke's been called on the carpet by the authorities on account of her renditions of »*Es hat keinen Zweck mit der Liebe*« (There's no purpose for love) and »*Haben Sie schon mal im Dunkel geküsst*«? (Have you ever kissed in the dark?) Dr. Goebbels upbraided her for sounding too

American. I guess she does have a pretty daring style of phrasing a lyric and making it sound suggestive."

Kai flinched and said, "But Marika and Rosita both have gotten away with inserting scat lyrics and other racy little flourishes in some of their songs. And Lutz Templin's orchestra still belts out »*Immer wieder tanzen*« (Keep on dancing), though Fud Candrix and the «*U-Bahn Fox/Metro Stomp*» is strictly taboo and carries the 'Nigger Jazz' designation, courtesy of the Reich Minister."

**"Degenerate Music" during the Nazi regime**

Germany declared war on Poland at the beginning of September 1939 after alleged territorial violations and atrocities perpetrated at the Gleiwitz radio station on the Polish-German border. The mood in Germany was not jubilant. My folks had always talked about the excitement when the Kaiser's war had broken out back in 1914. Everyone was in a frenzy to go off and fight. Not so much this time, and I sensed that older people were perplexed about another war occurring within their lifetime.

Guys who had been in the Labor Service were automatically called up and had to participate in the *Blitzkrieg* which raged throughout the great plains of the ancient and proud Polish nation. Since I had completed my service long before the existing regulations went into effect, I did not have to go unless enlistment was in the offing. Blessedly, the fighting in Poland was over in a matter of weeks and immediately the Führer set his sights on the west: Holland, Belgium and France.

Simultaneous to these events, the German film industry switched into high gear and produced movies which were not only entertaining, but also contained the subtlest overtones of patriotic fervor, courage on the home front and the unflinching deeds of our fighting men. There was little, if any outright propaganda. It was more important for Dr. Goebbels to allow the viewer to draw his or her own conclusions based on the weight of several factors. That's where our work on the *Prüfstelle* provided the censorship board with all the right elements for the consideration of what should be included in a particular feature film.

Our technical advice in downplaying the overt danger of horrendous events such as air bombardments by enemy aircraft (a practically daily occurrence) and softening the blow of a soldier's heroic death made blockbuster films like *Wunschkonzert* (Request Concert for the Armed Forces) and *Die große Liebe* (The Great Love) palpable for the German public to digest. By including songs like »*Ich weiß, es wird einmal ein Wunder geschehen*« (I Know that a Miracle Will Happen Someday) and »*Davon geht die Welt nicht unter*« (The World Won't Go Under), we fostered a belief in false hope.

Very little real wartime footage was included in our feature films. That sort of thing was reserved for the weekly »*Tonwoche*« newsreels. The Supreme Command of the Armed Forces made official commentary in realistic enough terminology. If one were to view our film output for wartime twenty years hence, he or she would conclude that there was no conflict. Peacetime conditions and story line were always reflected in the movie scripts. Anything else was automatically labeled "defeatist" and marked for extinction. Exceptions to the rule included *Heimkehr* (Homecoming) with the highly-charged, controversial soliloquy by Paula Wessely which haunted her years afterward, and the 1943

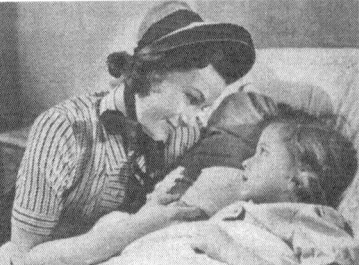

HANS LEIBELT, EGON MÜLLER-FRANKEN, ILSE WERNER, GISELA SCHOLZ in „Fräulein"

ROSITA SERRANO
in
„Die kluge Schwiegermutter"
(bish. Titel: „Schmidt und Schmidtchen")

## ROSITA SERRANO:
# Eine Stimme wird sichtbar

---

Movie magazine feature with the latest news about Ilse Werner and an extensive article about Rosita Serrano, "The Chilean Nightingale"

version of *Titanic* (never released, although the story was accurate down to the smallest detail).

Silly references to being "effeminate" or 'different" were permitted such as the case of the eunuch in *Münchhausen*, but the sexual proclivities of a personage like Bruno Balz remained a guarded secret. The other great composers of the day worked closely with him and never seemed to mind. Chorus boys in the lavish dance numbers were always "butched up" as much as possible, and the results were electrifying. Our films kept pace with the best and brightest coming out of Hollywood which we ordinary Germans no longer enjoyed the privilege of viewing.

My role with the *Prüfstelle* expanded to such a degree that I served in a technical advisor capacity in several UFA, Tobis and Terra productions. I adored seeing the way in which the directors and choreographers put together extended music and dance numbers like »*In der Nacht ist der Mensch nicht gern alleine*« (No one likes to be alone in the night) with its bold *apache danse*, and »*Ich warte auf dich*« (I wait for you) with its unique storytelling quality.

German influence in Europe was triumphant with the fall of France, Belgium, Holland and Norway, stagnant with the unsuccessful attempt to bring Great Britain to her knees by means of aerial bombing, and downright depressing with the defeat at Stalingrad and the massive losses of manpower as well as matériel on the Eastern Front. The entry of the Americans after their Pearl Harbor was brutally bombed by the Japanese gave the conflict an entirely different dimension and a new, even more fiercely hated enemy. Our cinematic industry reflected none of this shift in Germany's wartime fate. The newsreels trumpeted the few victories that remained, and the frequent playing of a recorded version of Beethoven's Symphony No. 3 ("*Eroica*") over the radio signaled another bitter defeat for our troops somewhere.

"I heard you went to Barrandov to watch them film *Große Freiheit Nr. 7* (Grand Freedom Number 7)," Kai commented when I showed up at his place right after a nighttime air attack by British bombers. Minor damage to some of the outlying boroughs occurred, and the S-Bahn tracks were broken up in several places, making the trip arduous from one side of the city to the other.

"That's right," I responded brightly. "I bring back greetings from Hradschin Castle and the entire gang in Prague," a reference to a personal joke about some cronies he'd worked with in the capital of the "Protectorate," as Bohemia and Moravia were now called. "It was a relief to be in a nice, undisturbed part of the Continent for a spell."

"I'll bet," Kai put in. "Everybody's on edge here in Berlin because we never know when the next raid'll be. My nerves are about shot."

I nodded vaguely and put my hand on his shoulder. "I guess I would be also if I had to hang around here so much," I said. "Fortunately the *Prüfstelle* has me bopping between Prague, Marienfelde and Hamburg. In fact, I'm headed there late this afternoon."

»*Nach Hamburg?*« he asked quizzically, almost the same way that Ilse Werner did with Hans Albers in the scene before Gisa Häuptlein leaves her mother's house and goes away with Hannes Kröger. "I thought all the filming was completed at Barrandov."

I slapped his shoulder in a hail-fellow-well-met manner and declared, "Just about, my dear friend. They're taking a half dozen of us to scout out locales for a few extra pickup shots. They figure the moviegoers will like the film better if they see some realism such as actual shots of St. Pauli and Blankenese."

"Ah," Kai said breathlessly. "Be careful over there. Don't let your heart get taken by the horny sailors or any of those loose characters on the Reeperbahn."

Grunting, I quipped, "Fat chance of that happening. From what I've heard it's all tits and pussy, which is safer nowadays anyway, more so than prowling around for the 'other' thing."

Rubbing his chin for a second, Kai blurted out, "I'll wager that if you ask around, sooner or later somebody will point you in the right direction. After all, its wartime."

Promotional poster for *Grand Freedom Number 7*

I looked at him in amazement. "So what does that have to do with anything?" I cried. "That special division of the Gestapo is lurking everywhere, not least of all around the studios and studio personnel where they're certain to find unscrupulous activity at every turn. It's too damn risky."

Kai waved away my concern. "You're making a mountain out of a molehill," he moaned. "The Gestapo is too busy with wartime intrigue and worrying about making sure that Lale Andersen doesn't sing »*Lili Marleen*« during any of her concert appearances anymore. They're also probably wondering if Rosita is a spy for some clandestine renegade organization."

I nodded vaguely. "Yeah, I was sad to hear that she went to Sweden for a guest concert and didn't come back. I wonder if Zarah helped her in any way. She always seemed to favor the underdog. Rumor has it that she was able to save a Jewish boy whom she managed to get to Stockholm. She's a good egg."

I was caught up in thinking about the fate of Germany's divas that I had lost my train of thought. "But you're playing with fire, Kai."

"Nonsense," he bragged. "I've been carrying on a hot little affair with Werner, one of the chorus boys from *Karneval der Liebe*. He told me that Heesters even tried to grab his crotch one time during a rehearsal of one of the big dance numbers."

I grinned. "I believe it. He's such a priss anyway, probably swings both ways. I overheard the asshole mention to Missy, the Countess Wassiltschikow, that he met Hitler once. In his heavy Dutch accent he told her in English, '*Ach*, he voss a very nice maahhn.' It's a miracle that a firebrand like Marika has been able to stand working with a character like that so many times."

"*Tja*, Werner admits that he's kinda creepy, too."

"But seriously, Kai," I insisted, "aren't you afraid that somebody's gonna get wise to your fooling around with little Werner?" It suddenly occurred to me to which hunky guy he was referring. My dick started getting hard in my pants.

Shaking his head and unfazed by my protest, Kai replied, "Not a chance. We're very discreet. Besides, it's like I told you: the Gestapo's got work up to their eyeballs with all the bullshit of war raging about. They don't have time for a bunch of faggots like us anymore. Ever since Goebbels hatched his "total war" extravaganza, the Wehrmacht, Luftwaffe, SS and reserves don't bother with small potatoes. It's strictly boom-boom-boom until this blasted war is over and won."

I was dead sure he was wrong. The Penal Code hadn't changed, so I imagined that people were still being arrested, thrown in jail or languishing in concentration camps without letup. On the other hand, I knew that Hamburg had just endured several severe bombing raids. A good portion of the suburban area had been laid to waste and huge fire storms hampered the cleanup effort. I supposed that the poor souls who counted among the survivors were preoccupied with trying to put their lives back together. Their misfortune could result in my good fortune.

I hadn't had a good shag in ages. And all that talk about Kai and Werner had made me extremely horny. Maybe it was a chance to have a fling with a total stranger in a town with a reputation for saltiness and free love. If I kept my eyes open I would certainly find somebody to get my rocks off with. I was ready to hit Hamburg with a splash.

**Wartime issue of the Tobis studio magazine**

## Chapter Twenty      GRAND FREEDOM NO MORE

The day of my hearing finally arrives. After eating a larger than usual breakfast, I and half a dozen other prisoners go for an earlier than usual exercise period in the yard located in the midst of the massive four-storey jail building. We are allowed to run, jump, do knee bends and even jostle with one another longer than usual. I begin to wonder why everything is suddenly larger, earlier and longer on this otherwise typical day in prison.

"You need the extra food so that your energy won't flag," the jailer explains. "Since you'll be sitting for a long period, you'll be grateful for the additional time spent bopping around in the yard early in the day."

"How long do you think the hearing will last?" I ask him as I finish running in place.

Rubbing his chin, he replies, "Typically three hours, although some go longer. Since you choose to not have an attorney present, I predict that you're in for a long haul." My heart sinks, but I am glad to be rid of Herr Biedermeyer nonetheless.

I try to relax back in my cell, but it is fruitless. Pacing back and forth and feeling my body tighten, the door is abruptly unlocked and two fresh-faced MP's escort me down the corridor to a hearing room. It seems like we've walked a few kilometers, even though I know it can't be that far. All I can think of is how each step brings me closer to freedom.

What awaits me on the outside is still a mystery. I have no one to go to. Based on inquiries I made through the relief organization (whose personnel were hesitant to release information to a prisoner), I found out that Lothar and Gusti both perished in one of the final air raids by Allied bombers over Berlin. Kai and Werner were arrested simultaneously in the closing weeks of the war. The chorus boy was able to evade prosecution under Paragraph 175 due to the intervention of an unnamed director at UFA. Kai, on the other hand, wasn't so lucky. He was sentenced immediately and taken to Sachsenhausen, the infamous camp located just 20 kilometers north of Berlin. He died there during an outbreak of typhus.

My father, the Kaiser's warrior from the first war, was called up for duty in the *Volkssturm*, the ragtag bunch of young whippersnappers and grisly old men whom Hitler and Goebbels had organized into a makeshift home guard during the final months of the war which was as good as lost. How they convinced my dad to serve in spite of his injury almost twenty years earlier astounds me, unless he was forced at gunpoint.

I shall never know the reason he enlisted nor the date and place he was killed, for my mom refuses to talk to me. The two letters I wrote to her after my incarceration have both been returned, unopened. Upon learning of my conviction and sentencing under Paragraph 175, she disowned me. I cannot even imagine the disillusionment she must be going through, having lost a husband in battle and a son to a despicable, criminal lifestyle, not to mention a Fatherland to which she swore allegiance and a Führer whom she idolized. I feel so sorry for her.

The hearing room resembles my cell in many ways, though it is larger and the furniture is arranged differently. The drabness of the place, however, is accentuated here even more inside this room. At a long table three uniformed American officers and a stenographer are seated. Placards with their names have been placed on the front edge. The one sitting on the far left, LIEUTENANT HARVEY JONCQUIL, shows no emotion as I enter and am told to sit down by one of the MP's. His bristly moustache and the five o'clock shadow which dominates his chin and cheeks give him a severe look: a sharp contrast to the fresh, clean-shaven appearance of the other two.

The boyish officer seated on the right, PFC DYLAN SINCLAIR, smiles faintly. His eyes are gray and steely nonetheless. The larger-than-life man in the center is the one who interests me the most. There is nothing outstanding about his face or physique. Though he wears a uniform, he doesn't seem to have a specific rank. His is a definite presence in the room, though. It is obvious that he is in control of the proceedings, surpassing even the authoritarian mien of the lieutenant. His name also inspires confidence: LUCAS FEYERABEND. I feel as if he is almost a kindred spirit. Apparently he is also the only German speaker of the three, for he immediately asks me, "Is it true that you have found your legal representation unsuitable and see fit to excuse him from this hearing?"

Clearing my throat and being alarmed at the sound of my own voice (for in jail we rarely speak day after day), I reply, "Yes, it is true. I do not wish to have an attorney who is unsympathetic to my plight and unsupportive of me."

Officer Feyerabend's eyes open wide as he looks up from some paperwork spread before him. "You do realize," he volunteers, "that not having appropriate legal counsel may jeopardize your chances for all the pertinent facts to be presented for this panel's consideration."

I sigh and retort, "I am aware, but I trust that you three gentlemen will put the questions to me with fairness. I promise to answer in the most thorough and honest way possible. I place my entire confidence in you that the right decision will be made."

Feyerabend seems impressed with my presentation, but dashes my hopes with his next sentence. "I must remind you that our decision hinges solely on the existing German laws," he states grimly. "The Occupation Forces in all four zones of Germany have promulgated authority to the federal court of this nation to either carry out or commute the sentences handed down in conformity with the Penal Code. Our decisions must abide by those laws and statutes."

I process what he is telling me and shudder to

think that my goose may already be cooked. I am not sorry, however, that I told Herr Biedermeyer to go jump in the lake. His presence at this hearing would only exacerbate an already hopeless situation. He'd be enthusiastically nodding and agreeing with the panel every step of the way.

Still having an ace or two up my sleeve due to some of the finer points of the law which I have had the chance to study since my incarceration (imagine, being able to requisition law books from the prison library without limit --- the convict's dream!), I decide to hit hard and drive home a point about semantics. "Some of us were charged with bona fide crimes (*Verbrecher*) and infractions," I begin, "while others were jailed as asocial elements (*asoziale*) for things like work shirking (*Arbeitsscheue*), vagrancy, gambling, illegal profiteering or procurement." Taking a deep breath, I add, "But others, including myself, have been singled out for punishment because of who or what we are: Jews, Romani-Sinti, Jehovah's Witnesses or »*Schwule*« (I employ the German colloquial term instead of "homosexual" in order to find out how extensive Officer Feyerabend's knowledge of our culture really is). Do you understand the difference, gentlemen?"

Feyerabend shifts nervously in his seat. "You bring up some valid points," he asserts. "It's true that several groups have been singled out by the NSDAP ideologues because of religious affiliation and national origin mainly due to the racial and hygienic provisions contained in the Nuremberg Laws of 1935. There is no denying that persons belonging to these unfortunate groups have suffered unspeakable persecution, exile and, in many cases, mass annihilation."

*The Eternal Jew*, a "documentary" film which fomented hate and revulsion among Germans

Knowingly nodding my head, I proclaim, "I am well aware of their suffering and extinction. I spent time in prison as well as in camp with such individuals. I watched how human beings could sink to the level of animals. I experienced the total depravity of that place and witnessed the specter of death on a constant basis."

Officer Feyerabend translates for Lt. Joncquil and Officer Sinclair as rapidly as I spit the words out. At one point it sounds as if Joncquil protests the way the hearing is being carried out. Feyerabend turns to the stenographer and asks, "Fräulein Zorn, have you been taking down every word?" to which she replies in the affirmative. "Very well, gentlemen," he continues, grinning, "I believe that we can dispense with the usual formalities and any longwinded speeches which nobody listens to anyway." I like this man's style and savor his sharp wit. He almost makes the entire proceedings a pleasant experience, although I don't ever lose sight of the serious nature of the hearing.

"Be that as it may," he resumes, "we have been discussing the arrest, detention, long-range persecution and genocide perpetuated by the NSDAP regime on citizens of Germany as well as in the occupied countries. In fitting that into the framework of the existing laws, we conclude that the draft of 1935 in Nuremberg put forth a series of vicious and unjust statutes which did great harm and caused untold misery to entire communities."

He flips through a small stack of papers which I assume pertain to my file. Coming upon a sheet which looks like it had been photostated from a law book, he frowns. "The bad news is that Paragraph 175 of the Penal Code has been in force since 1871, that is, from the time of Bismarck. Efforts to repeal it over the decades, most notably through campaigns encouraged by Dr. Magnus Hirschfeld, have failed. A softening of the law was formulated during the final years of the Weimar Republic, but its chances fizzled as the NSDAP came to power and consolidated its political influence over all aspects of German life." My eyes want to roll to the back of my head because he recites history I already know from having lived through it. Out of respect, I listen attentively and do not wish to take my eyes off him.

"On the whole," Feyerabend explains, "Paragraph 175's original provisions were not changed or modified. The intent of the NSDAP was only to broaden the interpretation and intensify the statutes. They accomplished this not precisely via the court system, but by intimidation and terror. This panel is aware of the special division formed within the Gestapo organization which worked toward the goal of eradicating the homosexual from the society inside the Third Reich."

Joncquil interrupts and asks in a high-pitched nasal tone, "I see from the record that you are registered as a resident of Berlin, but at the time of your arrest and sentencing, you were in Hamburg.

Could you clarify this discrepancy for the panel?"

I launch into a brief description of my duties on the *Prüfstelle* and as technical advisor for Terra Films at the time I went to Hamburg. Feyerabend and Sinclair perk up and seem fascinated, while Lt. Joncquil merely shows his boredom with the subject and his obvious distaste for me.

"And what specifically led to your arrest and subsequent sentencing under Paragraph 175?" Sinclair asks with a sympathetic demeanor.

The line of questioning stuns me. It makes me wonder how little or how much they've read of my testimony to the Gestapo interrogator. I'm not as embarrassed to talk about it as I was, say, a year ago or even eight or nine months prior to this hearing. "I made a foolish mistake in an hour of weakness and paid for it by being arrested, detained, sentenced under a subsection of the expanded umbrella of Paragraph 175 edicts and sent to a concentration camp. What more is there to tell?" Blank stares.

"Within the capacity of my work," I continue, "and being active on the cinematic board of three different studios, I often travelled. Early last year I was transferred to a long-term project at Barrandov Studios in Prague where Terra Films was shooting a feature film entitled *Große Freiheit Nr.7* about a mythical dance hall located on one of the infamous streets which intersects the Reeperbahn in St. Pauli, Hamburg's notorious red-light district."

Scratching his head as he listens to Feyerabend's

translation of my words, Lt. Joncquil snorts, "Why in heaven's name were they shooting the film in Prague and not on the real 'Grand Freedom Street' in Hamburg?"

I grin and reply, "The city had just undergone several separate bombing incidents. The director, Helmut Käutner, as well as just about everyone else at Terra felt it would be safer to shoot the bulk of the film in the Protectorate where the situation was calmer. I, along with a group from the *Prüfstelle*, had travelled to Hamburg at the behest of Terra to scout out pickup shots they intended to use in the film's final print to add to the storyline's realism. I suppose that the director didn't want his film to come off like a fantasy along the lines of *Münchhausen*."

The lieutenant sniffs disapprovingly while Feyerabend and Sinclair both smile. "It must have been a daunting task to accomplish what you set out to do amid the rubble of a city that wasn't back on its feet yet," the latter exclaims.

Shrugging, I respond, "Most German cities took terrible hits from the British and U.S. warplanes. The borough where I lived in Berlin was bombed twice within a year. My aunt and her husband (I cringe at having to refer to Lothar that way!) perished in one the later raids, so I'm told. I was still in camp at the time."

The thought races through my mind just how much these Americans know what it is like to see an

Hans Albers, Leo Slezak and Ilse Werner in the epic
*Münchhausen*, produced for UFA Studios' twenty-
fifth anniversary in glorious AGFA color

Herbertstraße, St. Pauli district, (Hamburg)
where the "working girls" display their "goods"

entire city laid to waste. I know they had their own terrible civil war. It was vividly depicted in the movie, *Gone With The Wind*. I recall scenes of the massive burning of Atlanta, wherever that is, but realize that the event took place generations before anybody I am facing here was born. They have nothing with which to compare the devastation of our country. I'm certain that wherever Atlanta is located on God's green earth, it has most likely recovered and been rebuilt into a thriving city.

"Luckily the portions of Hamburg we were most concerned with, including the harbor and the area around Blankenese, were left untouched by the initial bombing," I reply. "We managed to obtain all the footage we needed and had some free time on our final night."

How easy it is now to think back on all the could-haves, would-haves and should-haves. What might have been my fate had I not done the unthinkable on that final night? What would have happened if I hadn't gone to Hamburg at all? Of course it's useless to think that way because there's no turning back the hands of time --- what's done is done. Kai had convinced me to throw caution to the wind. Much to my detriment I followed his advice and landed in a concentration camp. My life had been anchored in a safe harbor for most of the years of the Third Reich, but it all unraveled when I dared to ask one stupid question.

As I suspected, Grand Freedom Street was strictly

about picking up girls and all sorts of other activity that were much too heterosexual for my tastes. People talked about all the bawdy goings-on inside "Allotria," "Tanzpalast Trichter" and "Liliput 2." I was even miffed to see a club named "Eldorado," a cheap blow to the infamous transvestite hangout in Berlin that the NSDAP closed down shortly after Hitler came to power.

I was dead certain that I could find a willing sailor on shore leave who'd at least settle for a good blowjob after striking out with the broads or not being able to scrape together enough dough to pay a hooker. I even stalked a fresh-faced kid for several blocks through the brightly illuminated streets of Altona. The blond, blue-eyed stunner ended up slipping through the barrier at Herbertstraße to ogle the "picture window girls" whose wares were on display for all comers and whose sexual favors could be enjoyed for the right price. Frustrated, I struck up a conversation with one of the friendlier ladies of the night, an attractive redhead at number 4.

»*Verzeihung*,« I muttered at one point, "but where can one go to partake of, you know,...the 'other' thing?" I queried.

"Ah," she said, not exceedingly surprised or concerned, "I understand. I know what you're referring to. Try St. Georg, especially around Lange Reihe and Pulverteich. It's about two kilometers from here, beyond the big garden park called '*Planten un Blomen*.' And good luck, *Liebling*!"

In the Third Reich a mere inquiry such as that could have aroused enough suspicion. I thanked my lucky stars that I'd supposedly found a hooker with a heart of gold who was pleased to lend a helping hand to a lonely little »*schwuler Mensch*«. I walked for blocks and blocks in the cool evening air and encountered no cop on the beat, no special units from the criminal police (*Kripo*) and certainly none from the secret police (*Gestapo*).

Reaching St. Georg and making my way to Lange Reihe, I was sorely disappointed. "Shit," I chided myself, "my dogs are aching from having to walk all this way for nothing. The fucking streets are empty." I was about ready to turn and walk off when practically out of thin air an exceedingly gorgeous tanned sailor with coal black eyes approached me. Running his hand up and down his crotch in unmistakable provocation (my eyes were popping out of my head at the sight of a massive boner he was sporting inside his trousers), he surely commanded my full attention.

"I am Salvatore," he cooed, and I detected a strong Mediterranean accent. "You wanna suck me dry, baby?" Nodding fervently and feeling as if all control of my senses had evaporated, I followed him into a dark corridor which led to a narrow and even darker passageway. I felt a sharp blow from behind and the force of a boulder made my body collapse to the ground. I vaguely recall being roughed up a bit, similar to my encounter many years earlier with the SA Brown Shirt cocksuckers, but shortly after I must have lost consciousness.

Kai was dead wrong. Not only did wartime not impede the activities of the Gestapo's special department to rope in the "vile homosexual filth" which still plagued German soil: it had stepped up the process vehemently. I had absolutely no defense against the Gestapo interrogators. To my concern about Salvatore and what ill might befall him, the officer in Hamburg laughed in my face. "Don't worry your perverted little brain about him," he hissed. "Salvatore is one of us, a brilliant *agent provocateur*, don't you think? Luise, the 'working girl' you spoke to on Herbertstraße, tipped off him *and* us with a mere phone call." I gnashed my teeth in despair.

Snapping his fingers as if to shake me out of my dream state (nightmare would be more apt, for every time I even thought about the crazy events leading up to my arrest, I went into a catatonic fit), Lieutenant Joncquil barks, "After the interrogation, where were you held and how long?"

I pride myself on always being able to keep track of time. During the months that followed the initial interrogation, the issuance of a formal report that I was to be classified "an unrepentant and incurable homosexual" and sentenced under subsections of Paragraph 175, I lost knowledge of my whereabouts half the time. Due to wartime restrictions, shortages and bureaucratic bungling, I was held in half a dozen jails. Some were bombed out in the nonstop air raids which plagued many German cities. Our jailers evacuated us to the cellars where the rest of the inhabitants scrambled each time, and then we were ceremoniously returned to our cells after the danger passed.

Transport to my supposedly final destination, a subcamp of Dachau called Neckargerach-Rosenholm, came only months afterward. Just reaching that part of Germany proved to be ruinous. The grueling trip seemed to take forever. A portion of it was completed in regular railway compartments with Waffen-SS guards to accompany us, and another part was carried out in open box cars where one was totally exposed, unprotected from the harsh winter cold. Barbed wire strewn on the siding of the cars prevented any of us from escaping. Bombing raids frequently impeded our journey farther south and the trains were evacuated on a regular basis. Several of the more feeble prisoners died en route and corpses were often thrown out of the boxcars along the side of the rails to be hastily buried in mass graves dug by other prisoners.

I dispensed with these trivial details and got right to meat of the lieutenant's inquiry. "I do not recall the exact date," I began slowly, "but it was sometime in mid-January of this year. The train carrying about three hundred prisoners who had survived the transport pulled into the complex at Dachau and we were processed there. I underwent a medical exam

**(left)
"Work Sets You Free"
at entry gates of most concentration camps**

**(below) Camp barracks**

by the SS doctor, and my hair was shorn by the camp barber. I was bathed in cold water without soap and sprinkled liberally with delousing powder, with special attention paid to my armpits, crotch and backside. They assigned me a number (39105) which was sewn onto the left breast area and left pant leg of my striped camp-issued uniform, along with a small inverted pink triangle. I was photographed from various angles and assume that these pictures were added to my camp file. I noticed later than many inmates wore number tattoos on their wrists, but I was informed that they no longer had the facility to continue the process."

Sinclair looks up from scribbling copious notes and asks, "Were you the only one wearing the pink triangle on your uniform?"

I shake my head. "No, I wasn't. I saw about half a dozen other inmates, mostly older and male, who displayed the accursed symbol. Not all prisoners were issued a striped uniform either. Many wore clothing they were in at the time of their arrest. The Jewish prisoners had the regulation five-point star with the word *JUDE* superimposed. Somebody explained to me that a shortage of uniforms necessitated this allowance and that, in all likelihood, the Jews would undergo 'special handling' anyway, meaning transport to a death camp, so why bother?

"Otherwise we all looked alike in our zebra stripes. Some of the newer uniforms like mine had been washed clean and appeared light blue. Most, however, were so dirty and had been parched by the sun that the original blue turned dark purple or even grayish-black. Their shirts, trousers and caps were flea bitten and infested with lice. I tried to avoid those prisoners as much as possible."

Feyerabend blinks and asks, "But how could you do that when you basically had no choice in which barracks to reside or what type of work you'd be assigned and with whom?"

"Your point is well taken, Herr Feyerabend," I reply condescendingly. I know in my heart that he tries to comprehend the prisoners' plight, but he has no idea of the sort of duress that occurs in and

(right) Identification symbols for inmates, from a manual for the commanders of concentration camps

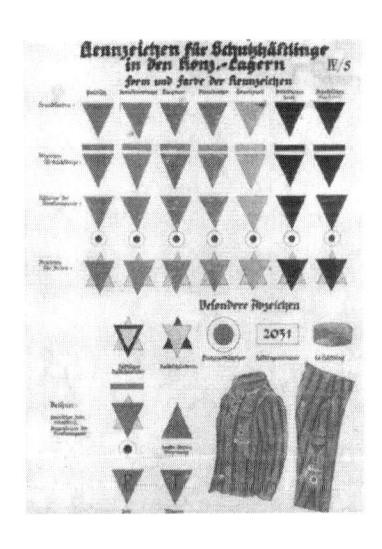

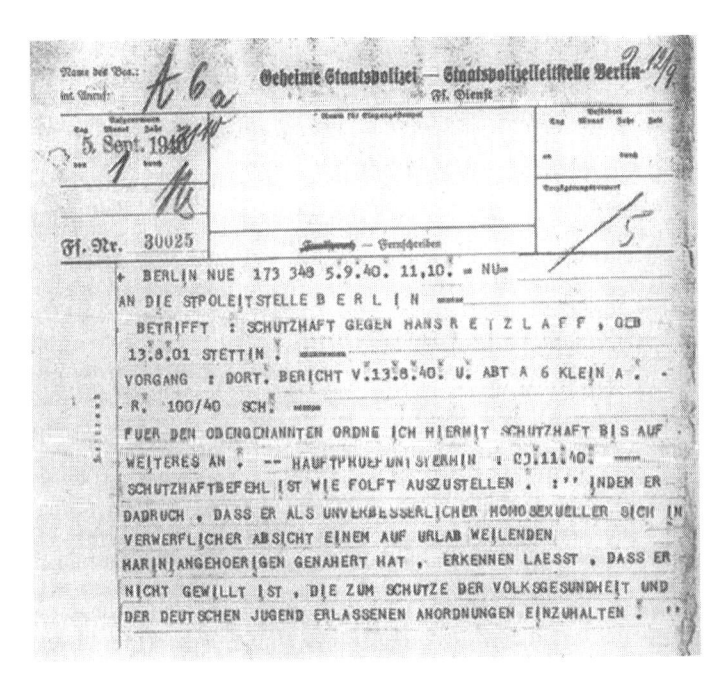

(below) Telex from the Gestapo bureau with recommendations for an "incurable homosexual" detainee

around a concentration camp. I want to educate him and Sinclair (I give up on the unsympathetic Joncquil early on) much in the same way I had to quickly learn the ins and outs of camp existence in order to survive each new day.

"I soon discovered that avoidance was no longer a problem for me," I say boldly. "Apparently the Jewish, Slavic *Ost-Arbeiter*, asocial and criminal elements of the camps wanted little to do with me. I say 'camps,' because I was in three of them, not including the brief time when I was being processed at Dachau." Taking a deep breath, I continue. "I heard verbal threats all the time from individual prisoners, but never from a collective. I learned that the best way for an inmate, any inmate, to survive in camp was to trust nobody and accumulate as little information about individuals as you were able. That's not to say that I didn't keep my eyes and ears open."

"For what purpose?" Sinclair inquires. I perceive that he is even more boyish than I give him credit for and doesn't understand captivity at all.

"Clues to a puzzle," I reply in the only way I know how to pinpoint the concept. "During the times when the Waffen-SS guarded us on the worksite or when Wehrmacht soldiers went off to lunch while we prisoners were idle, I overheard lots of conversations. I am German and we speak the same language, so perhaps I had more of an advantage over a Pole, a Frenchman or other nationalities who numbered among the camp's detainees. Some of the brave, he-men Waffen-SS and Wehrmacht soldiers worried out loud about how close the Americans might be, what would happen if the inmates rioted and how they were going to protect their wives and children from the hated Allies or the beastly Bolshevik hordes. I learned to take cues from body language and facial abnormalities like twitching hands, shifty eyes or a nervous tic. And I, along with many other more seasoned camp veterans, learned to spot the signs of death on a fellow prisoner's face, in his body movements or how he or she responded to beatings and humiliation by the guards. Even worse were the *Kapo* trusties, the cruel, merciless guardians of the barracks and various platoons of prisoners. They were inmates themselves and tried to survive by pushing others down."

Clearing his throat and eyeing his colleagues on the panel, Feyerabend handles the next question. "What was a typical day in camp like? In what type of work were you engaged? What about meals and rest periods?"

I want to laugh out loud at this sophomoric line of inquiry. "Prisoners were roused out of their bunks at four-thirty every morning," I respond, all the while plagued with vivid imagery of the scenes I am describing. "Those who lingered were pulled out of the bunks and beaten with wooden sticks or rubber truncheons. Sometimes corpses remained, the prisoners having died overnight. The *Kapos* ordered one or two of the captives to drag the bodies of these unfortunates out of the bunks before rollcall. I was forced into doing that detail on several occasions.

"Depending on the whim of the camp commandant, Corporal Heintzel, rollcall could take a matter of minutes or be dragged out for as much as two hours of standing and waiting in the freezing cold of the early morning. Prisoners were required to remove their caps (»*Mützen ab!*«) in the presence of any camp official regardless of rank or standing. Failure to do so was punished by extra beatings. Heads not covered by caps during the prolonged rollcall in the dead of winter or the glare of the summer sun made the whole ordeal even worse for the prisoners, wearing down their resistance even further. The aim was to dehumanize the inmates.

"Prior to marching out to our worksite, which changed constantly and was usually several kilometers away, we received a breakfast consisting of *Ersatz* coffee, anywhere from 300 to 600 grams of black bread and a small can of meat or fish that tasted as if it had been rejected by the sanitation inspector. We ate no lunch. In fact, all work stopped and we inmates stood around, watched by unflinching eyes of the Waffen-SS while the remaining guards went to the *Kaserne* to eat for an hour. Work went on for thirteen or fourteen hours, six days a week. We marched back to camp and received our dinner ration shortly before turning in for the night: the same portion of black bread, a pat of rancid margarine and some watery broth into which unpeeled potatoes and an occasional carrot stub or turnip were tossed. Keeping our tins bowls on us at all times was essential if you wished to eat or use it as a hard pillow to plop your head upon during the short night on your bunk. Incessant groaning, sounds of bitter crying and the frequent bickering of prisoners hardly promoted sound sleep. Most inmates spent Sunday, the one day off, to catch up on some badly needed rest."

Feyerabend puts the fingertips of his hands together, stares at them briefly, and then looks up at me, startled. "Were you engaged in the same type of work all the time? Did the camp administration ever line up any leisure activities for the prisoners --- ways of blowing off steam?"

His naïveté strikes me an unfathomable. Does he think I was in the Labor Service or some type of summer excursion in the woods? "We paved roads without the help of heavy machinery or the proper tools, (just 'fart power,' as one of the German-speaking inmates quipped). We repaired portions of railroad tracks destroyed by Allied bombing raids (and escaped by the skin of our teeth during one of them, cursing those who were supposed to be liberating us while they fired at us above our heads!) We moved boulders, uprooted tree stumps, cleared away debris and kept the lines of transport and communication open for the German nation in the wake of two hostile fronts converging on us..."

"During the perilous times when air raids occurred," he interrupts, "did you see a window of escape open up?"

I chuckle dryly. "It's funny that you should mention it. During the raid on the day that tracks were being repaired, a few dozen prisoners scattered in different directions. Some were shot immediately by the Waffen-SS or Wehrmacht soldiers. Others fled but were discovered later, led back to camp and either brutally beaten within an inch of their lives or shot outright. Others returned voluntarily and slipped back into the squadrons, undetected."

Lt. Joncquil slams his fist and shakes the whole table. "Nonsense!" he shouts, and blood rushes to his face. "Why in heaven's name would an escaped concentration camp prisoner want to come back if he made it out safely?"

The man thinks too logically. Of course, under normal circumstances, even with a war raging, a prisoner could conceivably run away, prowl around for food, score a change of clothes and curl up in a warm hiding place. If he ended up blending in with the local population, he could stand a chance of surviving. What the lieutenant fails to understand is that this is Germany. The people who live in these small towns and villages are among the most rabid believers in the Führer and the NSDAP leadership. They are well-versed on "the enemies of the Reich." Necessarily, this includes the "zebra-stripes" and the ones with the five-point star sewn on their lapels. In no way are they to be pitied, but feared and reviled. All the ideological balderdash spewing forth from the »*Volksempfänger*« and the »*Ton-Woche*« newsreels have confirmed these "truths" to the German people. Being out in "freedom," old men from the *Volkssturm* or fanatics among the Hitler Youth could pick you off with a rifle. An irate farmer or crazed villager shooting at you pointblank as you poach in a barnyard for something to eat is a far more dangerous proposition than the predictability of camp.

"You would have to ask the ones who still have any life left in them, Lieutenant," I reply sarcastically. "Or if they are dead, walk among their graves and ask them. For myself, I always remained obediently in camp and did what I was ordered to, even at the expense of my own dignity and well-being."

Lt. Joncquil looks daggers at me. "What the hell are you talking about, man?" he snaps. I reflect on how scintillating it would be for me to describe Corporal Heitzel's sadistic pleasure in shoving broomsticks up my behind until I passed out. How I wished I could do likewise to this smug, self-absorbed lieutenant right now, but conclude that he'd probably relish it. His stuck-up attitude is most likely camouflage for repressed sexual proclivities. I don't see that demeanor in Officers Feyerabend or Sinclair and decide to temper my remarks a little more than originally planned.

"What I am speaking of," I continue, looking away from Joncquil and devoting all my attention to the pair of officers, "is with regard to leisure activities for the inmates. You coyly asked me about that earlier. Camp was hardly a resort, but the guards and *Kapos* devised many grueling exercises for us captives. This was designed to alleviate *their* boredom and enhance *their* amusement. 'Leap Frog' was a mainstay and one that the prisoners dreaded. When you have men who are exhausted from laboring for thirteen hours a day, malnourished from the rotten camp food and humiliated at every turn, the last thing they want is to be forced into hunkering down in long rows to leap over one another in succession while the senior camp officials roar with laughter and the *Kapos* beat you to move faster, faster, faster..." I

**Concentration camp "Leap Frog"**

run out of breath as I imagine myself right back in the midst of one of those horrible contests.

Feyerabend wipes away something from his eye and skims one of the pages in front of him. "We have reports here," he says, "about prisoners being subjected to medical experiments in the camp's sick bay. Were you ever singled out for something like that?"

I shake my head. "At Rosenholm, Corporal Heintzel lectured me and some of the other 'pink triangles' about God fouling up with us, how the merciful NSDAP had allowed us to remain alive and how we were going to be 'purified' and live normal lives, just like every other good German. I heard tell that it was against racial and hygienic policy to do anything medically to Aryans. The catastrophic hormone injections into the testicles of a healthy male were reserved only for Poles, Czechs or Hungarian inmates. I learned that Russian and Jewish prisoners were routinely murdered outright, no questions asked, in some of the more gruesome medical experiments that had questionable value. For me and a female detainee they devised a special activity which almost got both of us killed."

Dead silence reigns over the panel. Even Fräulein Zorn's stenographic pen is poised until I begin speaking again. "A bunch of *Kapos*, Waffen-SS, doctors, orderlies and free employees working at the camp gathered in a small examination room next to the clinic. Inmate Number 57112, whose name was

Irmgard Vogelsang, was brought in and seated on a chaise longue. She was a political prisoner. She had been transferred from the Ravensbrück women's camp after being pulled in during the wave of arrests that followed Claus von Stauffenberg's unsuccessful assassination attempt on the Führer. I was brought in at rifle point and we were both told to remove our prison garb. I noticed that she had a pink triangle crisscrossing her designation as a "political" sewn into her blouse and trousers.

"Corporal Heintzel stepped forward and proudly announced something to the effect that SS doctors and scientists were going to prove conclusively that two otherwise healthy, exemplary Aryan subjects who just happened to "erroneously profess homosexuality" could copulate and produce a healthy offspring for the glory of the Fatherland."

I feel as if I am back in that horrible room with the overpowering antiseptic smell, the dozens of pairs of eyes looking at me skeptically, the helplessness on Irmgard's face and my awkward movements. I believe even now that she was grateful for my clumsiness and failure to get an erection. I have no way of knowing if she survived the war. Heintzel was so angry at the outcome of his folly that he recommended both of us to be shipped off to Mauthausen where death surely awaited us. It was only thanks to the rapid advance of Allied troops that we were spared, in spite of the ordeal of being shuffled by the Waffen-SS from one camp to another

"Total War, Shortest War" campaign

*Volkssturm* squadrons

Claus von Stauffenberg

during the final months before our liberation.

"Late in February, I think it was," my voice starts to tremble and Fräulein Zorn asks me to speak louder, "the transfer to Mauthausen was suddenly cancelled. I was ordered to gather my belongings and get ready to go up the road to Kochendorf, another subcamp of the Dachau complex. I was still in fairly good physical shape and scheduled to work in the abandoned salt mines where a group of Hungarian Jews were developing advanced jet aircraft engines for the Luftwaffe. I suppose they were part of the 'new miracle weapons' that the Führer and Reich Minister Goebbels had bragged about as part of the stupid 'Total War, Shortest War' campaign they'd launched after our miserable defeat at Stalingrad. I recall working at Kochendorf for nearly a month. It was tough, backbreaking labor without any safety measures in place. Prisoners were severely injured and dropped like flies from exhaustion and hunger around me every day. Somehow the will to live just overpowered me to keep pushing onward to stay alive until the Allies gained more ground and would blessedly storm our gates one day soon."

Feyerabend flips a page over and places his index finger about halfway up the paper. "It states here that our troops liberated you in Allach," he says, unsmiling. "Is that the final camp you were in?"

"Yes," I proclaim. "Pandemonium swept over the Kochendorf subcamp when Allied troops were reported to be within thirty kilometers of Dachau.

We were marched out hastily as the entire installation was set on fire by the guards so that none of the technology would fall into enemy hands. I heard one of the Waffen-SS guards frantically explain that the sick and injured prisoners were going to be left to burn alive because there was no time to move them. Most of the Wehrmacht soldiers had already fled and the Waffen-SS were right on their heels, leaving only Hitler Youth brigades and *Volkssturm* squadrons to preside over us when we reached Allach. Both groups consisted of extremely frightened looking old men and boys. Supplies had been cut off, most rail traffic was halted and communication was sporadic and unreliable. Even more of the 'zebra stripes' attempted to walk away, but were intercepted and shot right on the spot by the trigger-happy Hitler Youth and alarmed civilians. I survived, but was rearrested by your armed forces when my conviction under Paragraph 175 surfaced in the files that were requisitioned from the camp."

I breathe a sigh of relief. The hearing is almost over. Two hours have flown by. Fräulein Zorn's hand has been most dexterous. She is the only one who smiles faintly at me as the panel stands and excuses itself to deliberate. "You shall remain here until we return with our decision and recommendations to the German court," Feyerabend shouts as he is halfway out the door, flanked by a scowling Joncquil and a pie-eyed Sinclair. I look at the MP's who remain guarding me and ask in broken English if I am allowed to visit the toilet. Neither of them responds, and I sit in agony for nearly half an hour.

"Hmmph," I mutter, "still being treated like the enemy even though I rejoiced when you guys drove triumphantly through the gates at Allach, Kochendorf Rosenholm and Dachau. You are my liberators and I would do anything for you to show my gratitude." Still no reaction. I give up and cross my legs defiantly.

The door swings open again, and this time only Officers Feyerabend and Sinclair enter. "What did you do to Lieutenant Joncquil?" I ask, tongue in cheek. Feyerabend translates for Sinclair, and both burst out laughing. Sitting down without the benefit of Fräulein Zorn's transcribing talents, the laughter subsides as their faces assume serious expressions.

"Lieutenant Joncquil's opinions are so radical," Feyerabend says diplomatically, "that we two jurists feel that he is unsuited to pass fair judgment." I take this to mean that the lieutenant is so homophobic that he would string me up on the highest lamppost and watch me hang. "Unfortunately our decision conforms to what the military and occupation forces are required to delegate to the German federal courts. Officer Sinclair and I are not at liberty to express our personal distaste for this process. The idea of resentencing an individual who suffered harsh imprisonment and tortuous conditions is repugnant to us. That is why I have asked the stenographer to stay out of the hearing room until we were able to tell you these things, strictly off the record, of course. I will, however, call her back for several quick questions I still have to ask you."

I feel a mixture of comfort and uneasiness at his words. "Before Fräulein Zorn's return," I say with urgency, "may I ask you for clarification? Can my case be appealed on the grounds that during my years of living in the Third Reich I never produced a single offspring for the Fatherland? Surely that could be taken into consideration in what you recommend to the court."

Feyerabend thinks for a second, and then rubs his chin. "While it is quite commendable from an anti-Nazi standpoint, we are not dealing with statutes and laws that were specifically formulated at the behest of the NSDAP regime. It goes back to a law passed well before the concept of a Third Reich was ever on the scene. It is retroactive in every sense of the word, so the law still stands even in its most watered-down form."

It is time to pull an ace out of my sleeve. "What about the fact that my work on the *Prüfstelle* never resulted in outright propaganda pieces being produced or promoted?" I wait patiently for Sinclair to hear the translation. This time, it is he who answers and speaks in eloquent terms, almost to the point that I wish to believe him if it didn't go against me personally in this damn legal process.

"My fellow jurist and I are in the process of putting together a dissenting argument which will be submitted to the German court." He looks almost lovingly at Feyerabend who does not see the twinkle in the other man's eye. "Our opinion of your involvement in the film industry and technical advice you gave not only did not contribute to the propagandistic nature of the medium, but in a certain measure you subverted it by encouraging realistic scenes and situations to appear on the screen in movie houses all over Greater Germany as well as in the occupied countries. You allowed minds to be diverted from the machinations of the Nazi leadership and depict truth to the German people. Just your work alone on *Große Freiheit Nr. 7*," he struggles with the pronunciation of the German words, "is proof of your willingness to seek the truth. The additional agony you suffered as a result of suppressing your own physical needs for so many years and to be caught up in an evil web of betrayal is also cause for concern in our dissent."

I am flabbergasted. I have people who are on my side, but they haven't told me much about my prospects of being set free. "Do you think there is any chance for my release?" I ask sheepishly.

Feyerabend steps in and replies, "It depends on how the German federal court reacts to our dissenting argument and how willing the judges are to look away from an antiquated law passed seventy-four years ago and view your case from an entirely different perspective." He pulls out my file again and fishes out a sheet. "As a footnote," he adds, "you"ll be interested in knowing that *Große Freiheit Nr. 7*, the film in question, has not been released to theatres in Greater Germany to date. Only moviegoers living in Prague, Pilsen, Olomütz, Brünn and other cities throughout the Protectorate of Bohemia and Moravia were able to catch the film. Word has it that there will be a general release in Germany and Austria by late September or early October. I guess whatever was in that film enraged Herr Goebbels so much that he held it back."

I smile and am pleased with myself on a job well done, even though the final phase of it threw me into this cesspool of internment. And my joy evaporates within a month when I am standing in a German federal court and listening to the justice order me to serve out the remaining nine years and eight months of my ten-year sentence "for violations of statutes and subsections of Paragraph 175 of the German Penal Code."

**Epilog   DIFFERENT FROM YOU AND ME**

Years in prison can either drag or fly by. Since I always organize some sort of activity, whether it is cleaning and rearranging my belongings in the cell, devouring every book in the prison library and putting in requests for extras, or working in the laundry and bakery for a modest stipend, time passes quickly and I barely notice the rustle of its wings. My behavior here is exemplary. After all, the torturous time I spent in camp and the uncertainty I faced with my postwar imprisonment and resentencing makes this seem like child's play.

Being locked away in warmth for winter and coolness in summer, having my meals, leisure time facilities, medical and dental care all provided to me at state expense, I am spared many of the harsh growing pains Germans endure from day to day. I don't have to dig out of rubble, locate lost loved ones, scrounge for food or dicker with black marketers. The calamity of postwar instability, the threat of communism and the dilemma of currency reform do not affect me. Behind bars I experience none of the privations and discomforts suffered by ordinary Germans. Prison is a refuge, a haven of rest!

Roughly six months after I land in Sternmorgen, a huge walled complex on the southwest tip of our country's borders with Austria and Switzerland, I receive a thin airmail envelope with a San Francisco return address. Lucas Feyerabend writes me the first of what will be frequent correspondence for the length of my term. He confesses that he left no stone unturned in order to discover which conclusions the German court reached in my case and where I would be serving out the remainder of my sentence. Ostensibly he wants to stay in touch and I verify that having an American pen pal suits me fine. Secretly, I am thrilled that he contacted me. By the time my sentence is up, Lucas Feyerabend will become the most important man in my life.

The letters start off innocently enough. He tells me how fascinated he was with the description of work on the *Prüfstelle*. He simply had no idea how vibrant the movie industry was during Nazi times. "*What did you expect, hordes of us sitting around watching* Triumph des Willens *and screaming* »Sieg Heil!« *nonstop?*" I counter him in my reply. "*We Germans are made of flesh, blood and bone like the rest of humanity and enjoy a lavish musical, a great adventure story or a brilliant comedy as much as the next guy.*"

In subsequent letters he apologizes incessantly for the injustice that was committed in allowing me to be resentenced under Paragraph 175 and asks me to forgive him. I tell him that I have nothing to forgive him for because he put his best foot forward and wrote the dissenting argument which the German court hadn't even bothered to take into consideration. He reports to me that a lot of research on the Holocaust is being done, with more to follow

**Allied troops supervise former concentration camp guards in burying victims of the Holocaust**

in coming years. Gradually the severity of the concentration camp system and the horrendous atrocities are being revealed worldwide. He performs a particular inquiry for me which has personal significance, and I am saddened to learn about the outcome. Mohamed Husen, the prolific black cinematic extra, had in fact been arrested for "race defilement" with an Aryan woman. Both were sentenced to the Sachsenhausen camp where they perished separately. I write to him about Kai Fleischner's detainment in the same camp and what I know about his demise, but never include any details about my association with him in the »*schwul*« sense.

After a while I begin to read between his lines. Lucas mentions a great deal about his mom and dad, but never refers to a Mrs. Feyerabend or any little Feyerabends. He asks me if I remember his fellow jurist, Dylan Sinclair, and launches into a tale about the boyish-looking man with whom he has remained friends as they both excel in their respective careers in jurisprudence. Lucas comments about the long conversations he has with Dylan and how the younger man fondly thinks back on my hearing and is amazed how I managed to live by my wits in the various camps. He expresses sadness to think that a homosexual, admittedly already a conflicted individual, would be forced to suffer degradation and separation from society. *"Often I am not sure whether he is referring to your situation and others who wore the 'pink triangle,'"* Lucas exclaims in writing, *"or speaking about himself and his own struggle. I cannot get him to open up and offer anything deeper."*

I have to laugh about the way Lucas beats around the bush with regard to his own sexual needs and wants. I suppose that the little I've heard about the childish way American handle sex is true. Lucas is a faithful correspondent, though, and I await his letters with anticipation. We never run out of things to write about, so I know it is only a matter of time when we'll approach "the subject."

About a year after he tells me the finer points about Dylan, I receive a letter shortly before the

Christmas holidays that makes a crash landing in my psyche. Lucas relates what happened the last time he saw Dylan. The youthful attorney had often complained to him that his parents were putting pressure on him to find a suitable girl to marry and produce some offspring so that they could savor the joy of grandchildren in their old age. At one point Dylan showed up at a function Lucas was attending with other law professionals. He had an extremely attractive young woman in tow.

*"I couldn't help noticing how ill at ease Dylan looked and what a mismatch this sort of woman was for him --- much too brash and showy, without an ounce of intellect or charm. When he told me hesitantly that he was engaged to her and that she had insisted they elope by year's end, you could have knocked me over with a feather, I was so stunned."*

Lucas pens many other observations about Dylan which makes me sense that he really desires him and wants him for his own. The "kicker" comes at the close of his letter: *"Ten days ago Dylan's body was found in a clearing near Redwood City. He had taken a .45 caliber pistol and shot himself in the mouth. The coroner claimed that he died instantly."* I sit on my bunk and cry for nearly an hour after reading the letter. So much needless pain and suffering because we are different from the others....

I take advantage of "Movie Nights" in prison and am largely disappointed with the abominable trash they come out with in Germany nowadays. One film does stand out, and Lucas even mentions having seen it in a San Francisco arthouse theatre: *Die Mörder sind unter uns* (The Murderers Are Among Us). It is intriguing for me to watch, tucked away behind the walls of Sternmorgen, because it depicts a postwar nation in which I have absolutely no involvement. Such bliss in capitivity!

One weekend I did get to see the long awaited *Große Freiheit Nr. 7*, which some of the inmates pooh-poohed. I, on the other hand, enjoyed it immensely and let on to no one in the jug that I had anything to do with some of the technical aspects of the final product. Not for nothing did I discover why the film was so objectionable to the sensitive Dr. Goebbels that he withdrew it from circulation to theatres in Greater Germany. The depiction of perpetually drunk sailors and the wiles of loose women did not square with the portrait of *Volksgemeinschaft* and *Gleichschaltung* which the Nazi leaders wanted the German people to see. Even some of our prisoners were aghast when "Little Goody-Two-Shoes" Ilse Werner's character, Gisa Häuptlein, allegedly spends a night in the arms of Willem, the other love interest in the film. The level of prudishness even behind bars cracks me up.

Between films, work in the laundry and kitchen and chatting up a few of the other inmates who express interest in me physically (I politely decline and have no fear of reprisals, for serving time in

Germany is not as harrowing as it evidently is in other countries), I enroll in a couple of correspondence courses. I throw English language lessons into the mix and begin learning enough that I can pick out a word or two when we watch American films with subtitles. I'm allowed to have a radio and tune into Armed Forces broadcasts from Munich as often as they are on the air. I adore the American accent (schools in Germany are notorious for emphasizing only British pronunciation) and I manage to understand whole sentences in no time.

Soon I begin writing in English to Lucas, and he is stunned at how rapidly I am learning his language. I'm overjoyed when he sends me a parcel filled with books by American authors like Theodore Dreiser, John Steinbeck and William Saroyan, as well as translations of German authors like Erich Maria Remarque and Franz Kafka. I had read their works prior to the NSDAP ban on such "degenerate" literature that was tossed into the bonfires. Kafka's short pieces sound even more ominous in English. His description of justice and the nightmarish hell of doubt and separation describe perfectly the way I feel about having been sentenced under Paragraph 175.

Lucas breaks down over a period of time and writes about personal issues. I learn to love and cherish everything about the guy. He is so different from Lothar and Kai, and I explain the difference to him quite openly in my letters. I also tell him about

(left) Hildegard Knef
in *The Murderers are Among Us*
(right) Postwar poster for *Grand Freedom #7*

Gay demonstrations in the late 50's & early 60's

growing up in the village with strapping country boys and my run-in with the Brown Shirts. *"Your wealth of experience only raises you in my esteem,"* Lucas gushes in a missive shortly before my term is up. *"And besides, you're so appealing, how could any of us help ourselves? I won't conceal from you the way I felt the first time you walked into the hearing room. I wished to God that the others in the room would have disappeared so that I could have laid you across the table and ravaged you right then and there!"*

I am blown away when I read it. All I can reply, tongue in cheek, is, *"Gee, Lucas, you're so romantic!"*

In another letter he is excited about the first flickers of a movement designed to intensify the struggle for homosexual men and lesbians to attain fair treatment in his country. "Gay liberation" is being spoken about in dribs and drabs in San Francisco, and the Mattachine Society has a fairly high profile in the city. Some demonstrations and a few well-organized boycotts take place. I am thunderstruck at the way the winds of time shift. It makes me love the United States of America and Lucas even more.

My release from Sternmorgen in 1955 occurs right around the same time that Chancellor Konrad Adenauer visits Moscow and negotiates a deal with the Soviet Union for the repatriation of German prisoners of war. Joyous scenes at airports throughout the Federal Republic push Adenauer's approval ratings to soaring heights. Also on the up-

and-up are my own prospects as I enter life on the outside for the first time since May 1945. I exit the gate at Sternmorgen with a document in hand that enables me to obtain an efficiency apartment in Munich and the promise of a job with training based on my correspondence course completions. I thank my lucky stars that I had the foresight to not fritter away my time needlessly while in captivity.

The mere idea of a spark igniting in what is known as "the gay community" (a term which turns out to be the best transliteration of Dr. Magnus Hirschfeld's original concept of a »*Schwulengemeinschaft*«) amazes me. In freedom I notice that we Germans are too busy enjoying the »*Wirtschaftswunder*« (economic miracle), brought to us through the courtesy of the Marshall Plan, to give a passing thought to anything remotely connected to a gay rights movement. I suppose it is the United States of America which must be the reason for this and so many other good things happening in the postwar period. We feel safer against a Bolshevik onslaught now than we ever did under Hitler. And we're no longer picking fights with other countries and puffing ourselves up like we used to. Specious demands for "living space" and lofty claims of "Aryan superiority" were all stuff and nonsense, and fall by the wayside.

Unlike most Germans, I spend the first decade after the war in a cosseted environment, living vicariously in a country which doesn't see fit to allow me to roam among liberated people, but which takes care of all my needs. Now that I have freedom, I am saddened by the materialistic, superficial striving with which most people in West Germany carry out their lives. The sense of community we once had, the habit of always "pulling together," especially in wartime, has all but vanished. The chasm between poor and rich also widens and becomes more intense with the arrival of scores of refugees from the Communist-dominated East. They flee from austerity and want, and the glitter of capitalism on a grand scale hits them like a bullseye. That is, until reality sets in: it is attainable only at a price.

Culture suffers the most from this backlash. Whereas it used to be electrifying to see a performance of Carl Orff's *Carmina Burana* to the point of being totally swept away, the silly nonsense that passes for wholesome entertainment boggles the mind and insults the intelligence of levelheaded people. Does Peter Kraus really love Conny Froboess? Might Conny not really fall easily for Gus Backus? Are Peter and Gus belting out songs like "Hands Off Beautiful Girls!" due to some sinister agenda? Besides, when "Rex Alexander" is suddenly transformed into "Sexy Rexy Gildo," not much room is left over for true art anyway. Even the contributions from veterans like Albers, Rühmann and Rökk pale in comparison to their earlier work. They are getting old, just like the rest of us!

What caps it for me is the nasty way the newspapers write about the returning diva, Rosita

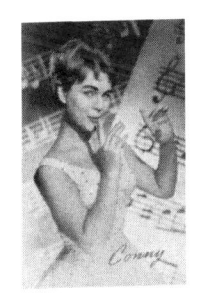

Postwar German teen idols: (l. to r.) Peter Kraus, Conny Froboess and Alexander "Rex" Gildo

Two additional photos of Rosita Serrano: with her beloved dachshunds (l.) and a publicity still from the 1950's, taken around the time of her return to perform in Germany

Serrano, even though audiences receive her warmly, by and large. "*The Nazi Nightingale Screeches Again*" is an example of the cruel manner in which journalists whip up the boos and jeers she has to contend with at a performance during "The Night of Prominents" at Berlin's Sportpalast. Certainly a person of Rosita's talent, elegance and class doesn't have to return to a country where Reichsführer Heinrich Himmler once issued her arrest warrant on charges of espionage. She does it out of love for the German public, even if that public appreciates her less than it did in her heyday before the war. Secretly, I like to think that the espionage charge sticks and imagine Rosita as a latter-day Mata Hari!

I ponder that idea at the same time as Lucas writes me about how he can pull some strings with U.S. immigration, prepare a dossier of legal mumbo jumbo and pave the way for me to emigrate to America and live with him. He is prepared for the long haul, and he convinces me to do the same. I figure that if I have to make concessions to materialism and superficiality, the United States is as good a place as any. The opportunities to pull myself out of a rut are also there, or so Lucas tells me. I am prepared to burn all my bridges behind me, leave them smoldering in Germany and make my way to the New World.

And it comes off brilliantly. I like the country from the moment I set foot in it. One can easily see that it is a highly energized place, full of all sorts of great possibilities for everyone, especially a wide-eyed immigrant. My love for Lucas, the one who pulls it off so perfectly, grows stronger every day. I live with him in San Francisco in a cramped second-storey flat for which he pays a fortune. As beautiful as "The City By The Bay" is with its wonderful museums, vibrant cultural and social scene, fine dining and the charms of such variegated districts as Fisherman's Wharf, North Beach, Nob Hill, the Tenderloin and Twin Peaks, it unwittingly promotes a feeling of claustrophobia which neither of us desires at this stage in our lives. We're crotchety old men both approaching the half-century mark!

After a year or two of living across the Bay in Berkeley and even a stint in Sacramento, during which time Lucas builds up a formidable bevy of contacts and associates in private practice (I play "housewife" and do a bang-up job of it, if I do say so myself!), we come to the conclusion that the place for us is Southern California. A friend of ours who fancies himself a poet quips, "Oh, so you two are gonna trade 'chill and fog' for 'heat and smog?'"

I put out feelers for a job in one of the studios and already have a few interesting prospects within days. Loads of German expats who fled the Nazis to start a new life in the States are impressed with my technical knowledge and have a few advisory positions in mind.

Lucas is much encouraged due to my success in landing a job and starts representing a lot of famous celebrities who need the services and expertise of a topnotch attorney. We hobnob with all the Hollywood notables, and our gorgeous home off Moraga Drive is the scene of many a formal dinner, upscale soirée or colorful bash where all the stops are pulled out. It all depends who is in attendance.

Since we are both highly successful and leading charmed lives, Lucas insists that we surround ourselves with the best of everything. This extends to every morsel of food that comes into the house, whether it is a regular delivery from the Bel Air Shop-Easy Market, Gelson's or "care packages" shipped airmail from Harrods (Scottish shortbread cookies, Yorkshire chutney) or Fauchon (caviar, *pâté de foie gras)*. I am reminded how Liz Taylor demands that Chasen's signature *chili con carne* be flown to her "on location" anywhere in the world. Lucas and I are just pikers: we have packets of O.L. Jardine's "Chili Fixins" sent to us via one of his Dallas associates.

I do, however, draw the line whenever I get a hankering for some genuine fare from the Old Country --- Lucas likes to dub it my "Kraut food." I make my way to several butcher shops and sausage kitchens around town, but inevitably end up in the South Bay area at a place called Alpine Village. It's the kitschy idea that Americans have of what a central European town must be like. The market is actually fairly good for all the imported items they usually have in stock. I park the car, go in and linger for about an hour, sometimes two, comparing prices and sampling everything from slices of *Zungenwurst*, little hunks of Swiss and Emmenthal cheese with tiny toothpicks stuck in them, rum-filled and brandied-cherry stuffed candies plus spoonsful of cold pickled red cabbage and warm potato salad with bacon. I also delight in speaking German with the employees and some of the customers because I don't have much of chance of using the language anymore. Not much else interests me in the area, though, so I drive off after each "Kraut food" shopping spree and hit the northbound onramp of the Harbor Freeway as quickly as possible.

I take a peek at some of the German magazines like *Bunte Illustrierte* and *Der Spiegel* to stay abreast of current news and views. I feel detached from Germany with each new year that passes in my adopted country, so even these glossy weeklies can't help me regain what is irretrievably lost. My quest has turned to the fulfillment of the American Dream.

I look for hints of a blowup much like what occurred in the States with the Stonewall riots in New York City, the first Christopher Street parades on both coasts and the emerging gay rights movement. Lucas and I are hardly "joiners" and watch everything going on around us with detached amusement. The level of promiscuity on both continents is a cause for concern. We are grateful to be in a monogamous relationship, even though we are tempted on all sides within the boundaries of our professions. Younger guys treat us kindly because they're prowling around either for a sugar daddy or a sucker. I always make it clear to them that I've never had to pay for it and am not going to start now.

More and more, formerly straight guys seem to be "coming out," and the level of experimentation and curiosity is at an all-time high. From what I can gather, the old adage still applies: Americans have a childish obsession with sex, whereas in Germany and the rest of Europe, it is considered merely a way of life.

Somebody becomes aware of my stack of German magazines and decides to enroll me in a subscription to a local paper, *Die California Staatszeitung*. In addition to roundups of local and national news from German communities high and low, advertising for lots of German-owned shops and businesses fill its columns. I notice that the Alpine Village movie theatre, of which I am vaguely aware, promotes its weekly double bill.

One Friday afternoon I skim through its pages and the words *Anders als du und ich* (Different From You and Me) hit me like a brick. Looking closer, I see a small «§175» printed alongside the title. Can it possibly be a recreation of the 1919 landmark film *Anders als die Anderen*, the one Lothar had seen featuring Conrad Veidt and Dr. Magnus Hirschfeld? I doubt that the Alpine Village movie house would show a classic film, since it seems more a bastion for the "Connie Loves Peter" genre.

"I'm stunned," I remark to Lucas over dinner. "I

looked the film up in my German cinema lexicon and discovered that it was released in 1957. And please hold on to your chair --- it is directed by none other than Veit Harlan."

Lucas drops his fork and stares at me. "You mean the asshole of *Jud Süß* fame?" he cries. "What is he trying to do, atone for sins and omissions of the past by putting together a gay-themed flick with a positive message?"

Knitting my brow, I respond, "You Americans naturally assume it is something positive. My guess is that the film has a homophobic bent, knowing the inner workings of the *Prüfstelle* and the heavy hand of the German censor."

Lucas's face lights up. "Well," he asks campily, "why don't we find out for ourselves? What prevents you and me from taking a little trip this weekend to Alpine Village? You have things to pick up at the market anyway, right?"

Flinching, I shake my head and reply, "Oh, I think not. That place'll probably be packed to the gills with old biddy grandmothers and their wrinkled, belching oompah-pah husbands. Unless you really have your heart set on going, I'd just as soon stay away."

Lucas shoots me an acid grin and says, "You forget that we're both in our sixties now and hardly spring chickens either." Pointing his finger menacingly at me, he adds, "And what's this bullshit about 'you Americans?' You're just as apple-pie American now as I am, so don't get your dander up!"

It's a stormy afternoon with nonstop rain when we head over to Alpine Village for our "movie date." We have time to kill before the features start, so I head over to the market to stock up on a few nonperishables. Lucas says he wants to browse around some of the shops. I warn him that all he's likely to see is overpriced Lederhosen and useless imported tchotchkes made in China. He balks and tells me, "I'll take my chances and meet you in front of the theatre in half an hour."

I push my cart and haven't even gone completely up and down the first aisle when Lucas storms in and searches frantically for me, alarming the other shoppers. He's as pale as a ghost and I wonder if I should ask someone to call for an ambulance. He grips my arm and pleads, "Drop what you're doing and come with me. You won't believe what I just saw."

Marching me briskly over to the imported gift store ("Ouch, Lucas, take it easy!"), he leads me toward the back and points to an exhibit. I see books and pamphlets arranged around a three-sided display board plastered with swastikas, iron crosses, inscriptions like »*Blut und Ehre*« (Blood and Honor) and »*Führer, befiehl, wir folgen dir*!« which I always equated with the expression, "Your wish is our command." There is a plaque with the crazy "glow in the dark" buttons like the old man back in Dahlem showed to Lothar and me. *Mein Kampf*, the Hitlerian bible, is available in several languages as are reprints of speeches by Hitler, Göring, Goebbels and Julius Streicher, the Jew baiting publisher of *Der Stürmer,* a virulent anti-Semitic newspaper.

The blood rushes to my head and I am filled with rage, but I learn to control my temper in these types of circumstances. I pat Lucas on the back and grin in a way he recognizes as my voiceless admonition of "Don't worry, leave it to me. I'll take care of this."

A gnarled old woman wearing a blue taffeta dress covered with a gray smock and sturdy orthopedic Oxfords comes behind us and flashes a toothy smile. "Can I help you two gentlemen with something?" she asks in a crackly voice with a pronounced German accent. "We have lots of nice people who come in and are immediately attracted by that display. It just goes to show you that there is still only one man who

"The Only Glowing Example for Every German is Our Führer, Adolf Hitler" (glow in the dark buttons)

can solve our problems and one party which can save the world from total ruin."

I don't want to let on to this bitch what my personal involvement with the Führer's blueprint for New Order in Europe entailed. I'll have a little fun with her before I lower the boom. "*That* guy?" I quip, pointing to Hitler's portrait and smirking. "Oh, his ideas are so passé."

Gray-smocked Brunhilde evidently girds her loins for battle and her lower lip trembles in a little pout. "That is not true, sir," she protests. "What Germany needs nowadays is another Hitler."

I do a double take, and I see Lucas seething. I tap him gently on the arm, his cue to hit the door. He walks away slowly and deliberately so that he can still eavesdrop. "*Another* Hitler?" I ask incredulously. "You mean exactly like the one who told us Germans that we weren't worthy of winning the war and bailed out on us?"

Brunhilde's eyes brighten with a combination of delight and confusion. She switches to German and asks, "Why do you say this? Do you not appreciate how the Führer remained in Berlin and died a hero's death?"

I take a step forward and get right into her face. She takes two steps back, perhaps out of fear or maybe to give us more breathing space. "I really don't give a shit what happened to Hitler, Goebbels or any of those other bastards," I hiss. "I spent the final days of the war in a concentration camp."

Her eyes narrow and she looks me up and down. "A good German like you in a KZ?" she declares. "I refuse to believe it. Why, they only threw Jews, Gypsies, criminals and other mongrels in there. What would they want with a fine, strong, upstanding Aryan?"

Feeling playful, I brush back my hair with the campy movement of my left hand, open my eyes wide and purse my lips. "I was a pink triangle," I lisp.

Brunhilde looks like a deer in headlights for about five seconds, and then a light bulb must be going off in her brain. »*Ach, rosa?*« she stammers. »*Das ist aber Kennzeichen für homosexuell...*« She chokes slightly, and I hear a pitiful gurgle well up in her throat. Her face contorts with an unmistakable look of hatred and revulsion as she screams, "Get out of my shop right this minute!" Reminiscent of Corporal Heintzel bellowing at us in camp, she adds, »*Raus!*«

Lucas eyes me as I emerge from the shop. "I suppose we should just scrap the movie and go straight home," he moans. "She's a really ugly customer, huh?"

I am constantly shocked that Lucas, the nearest and dearest person to me in the whole world, underestimates my ability to see humor in the direst of situations. "Were you scared?" I ask sarcastically. "She doesn't faze me at all. I think she is utterly charming and I thoroughly enjoyed our lovely little talk about old times. C'mon, let's go see the movie!"

We miscalculate and come into the darkened

**Zarah Leander and Christian Wolff in *Der blaue Nachtfalter* (The Blue Moth) 1959**

theatre about halfway into the second feature on the double bill. It turns out to be Zarah Leander's final screen appearance in a full length film. In 1959 she already looks old and worn out, and no amount of makeup or lighting can hide the glaring truth. She costars with Christian Wolff in *Die blaue Nachtfalter* (The Blue Moth). He also ends up having a starring role in the main feature, so this is like a mini Christian Wolff film festival. He's very handsome and plays his role solidly and convincingly. There is obvious chemistry between him and Zarah to the point that I perceive she does not mind playing his mother in the film.

When *Nachtfalter* ends, Lucas and I sit in our well-worn, lumpy seats, staring at the screen which bears a huge rip starting from the bottom edge and continuing halfway up. It has been repaired with some sort of glue which leaves a foamy green streak along the ripped edge. There is a strong smell of urine and an equally strong aroma of disinfectant. This visit to the Alpine Village movie house is not so much a tribute to late 50's German cinema as it is an assault to the visual and olfactory senses.

"That guy is cute," Lucas gushes in reference to the film. "It'll be intriguing to see how he plays a gay guy in the next feature. His acting is sensitive and touching alongside Zarah Leander's portrayal as the "wronged" woman, don't you think?"

I shrug and reply, "I suppose so. American movies are so superior to their German counterparts. I thought so even when I lived back in the days when the guy with the moustache was in charge. They could have thrown me into a camp on account of those seditious opinions alone."

Soon the opening titles of *Anders als du und ich* are flickering across the screen. The theatre had been two-thirds full for *Nachtfalter*, but scarcely ten people stay for this film. For the next hour and some odd minutes we watch, and I am largely appalled. Lucas looks over at me every so often and knows my moods like the back of his hand. When the word »Ende« appears and the lights come up, he turns and asks, "Do you wanna go somewhere to grab a drink and we can talk about it?"

The rain lets up and we have a pleasant drive

*Different From You and Me*, the 1957 film allegedly dealing with Paragraph 175, directed by Veit Harlan

Two scenes from *Anders als du und ich:*
(above) Klaus confronts his father
(below) Boris tries to seduce Klaus

along the cliffs in Palos Verdes. The moon shines brightly as we come upon a small upscale roadhouse with a patio. The tables and chairs are still wet with rain, but we sit down anyway and order some highballs. No one else is around. We settle into our drinks and I stare at the ocean. The gentle flapping of the waves calms me as I think back on the movie and want to get mad all over again.

"I'll tell you one thing, Lucas," I begin. "Based on my technical knowledge of film, that thing was censored to the point of a total hatchet job. I hope somebody comes up with some production notes one day. I'd like to see which scenes were cut out or altered to make the idea of being gay seem so revolting."

Lucas nods knowingly. "The supposedly gay characters were portrayed as limp-wristed pansies and slimy criminals," he opines. "The character of Manfred could have been more sympathetic, but he came off as a maladjusted little twerp. The scene in the turnabout club with the drag queen singing was actually very good, but it was presented like a freak show to be reviled by 'decent folk.' And the adult characters were all so incredibly ignorant and in denial, it was almost laughable if it hadn't been so pathetic."

"Did you notice," I put in, "that in addition to their unredeemable qualities, the writer assigned foreign names like Boris, Marcel, Francesco and Achim to all the gay guys, alluding to the concept of a small-scale invasion by foreigners? My God, we weren't even that xenophobic when the Nazis were in power."

Shaking his head, Lucas confesses, "I cringed when Christian Wolff's character, Klaus, was seduced by the maid, Gerda. It's just assumed that he suddenly becomes straight and his flirtation with the gay boys was just a silly phase he was going through. What a waste!"

I chuckle. "Magnus Hirschfeld is probably spinning in his grave," I exclaim. "Harlan even had the nerve to include a brief reference to the good doctor when Frau Teichmann looked up the definition of 'the third sex' in the encyclopedia. The director could have done so much with a story like that if given half the chance to make a positive statement. The resulting film just makes people feel worse about themselves."

Lucas knows all my gentle moods and soft spots. He also can tell when I feel harder than nails. He has only approached the subject of my captivity once or twice during the entire time we've been together. Even though he is a brilliant jurist and a fairly smart guy all around, he astounds me with his views on certain matters.

"Look on the bright side," he chirps after I tell him about a documentary on Jews persecuted by the Nazis which I evaluated for an independent film producer. "You survived. You weren't starved to death or worked until you dropped from exhaustion. You weren't shoved into a delousing chamber in the guise of a shower room with Zyklon-B crystals poured into the ventilation system to gas you. So count your blessings."

Resisting the urge to slap him, I buck up and proclaim, "Getting thrown back into prison to serve out my sentence was not exactly the bright side."

"But you know," Lucas protests, "that I did everything within my power to try to get you sprung. If it had been up to me and Dylan Sinclair, you'd have been free to go your merry way. The law, however, required us to remain impartial. And we had motherfuckers like Lt. Joncquil to contend with. I fear that he represented the prevailing opinion. Ignorance and just plain intolerance reigned at the time, whether it was integration of the armed forces, equal rights for women and minorities or loathsome attitudes toward homosexuality and any lifestyle that deviated from the norm."

I want to burst forth with a whole string of thoughts and ideas like he does, because they well up in me for ages. "It kind of irks me to see how much attention is paid to the Jews who were the victims of the Nazis' whims. The film they released about Eichmann and that TV miniseries, *QB VII*, emphasized it. And another multi-part TV special entitled *Holocaust* is scheduled to air over NBC next year. That's gonna drive the point home ever further. By and large, people act as if no other groups except Jews were singled out for persecution or eventual extinction."

Knowing that he can only ask questions when we are deep into a topic as intense as this, Lucas chimes in, "Didn't you mention once to me that nobody in Germany wants to talk about this aspect of the NSDAP years?"

Smirking, I reply, "It's easier to get a dentist to pull teeth than it is for German's to say anything about history as recent as World War II. They'll joke about it, of course, with silly declarations like, '*In 1945 we shouted*, »Nie wieder Krieg!« (Never again war!) *In 1955 it was*, »Ohne uns!« (Without us!) *And in 1965 it became* »Nie wieder Krieg ohne uns!« (Never again war without us!) *That's the way it goes,*' they'll tell you, but getting them to acknowledge that gay people were imprisoned, tortured and sometimes brutally killed never comes up in discussion."

"How did people react when you told them about your own time in the KZ and, subsequently, more prison time after the war?"

"I was rarely asked," I reply wistfully. "The few times I tried to recount my own experiences, I watched people's eyes glaze over with boredom or disgust. One of my coworkers in Munich exploded with laughter and said, "You goddamn faggots deserve everything you get!"

"Didn't you run into a former camp mate who had also worn the pink triangle?"

The incident Lucas refers to is perhaps the most heartbreaking of all. A fellow inmate whom I only knew as Gustav was at a newsstand near Sendlinger Tor when I recognized him. I was glad to see him because I'd heard erroneous reports that he'd perished attempting to escape from Kochendorf before everything burnt up. Gustav was clearly not pleased about running into me.

"I invited him to have a beer or two with me to talk over old times and what we'd been busy doing," I remark, steadying my eyes on the moonlight's reflection on the water. "He politely declined and I proposed an alternate day and time. He nervously made some excuse that he wasn't available. When I pushed him further and asked when it would be convenient, he admitted that he really didn't desire to open any old wounds by bringing up the past. My guess was that he'd also served out his sentence under Paragraph 175 and wanted it to remain hush-hush because it had stigmatized him so."

Lucas nods vaguely. "I'm beginning to see how destructive Paragraph 175 is to a person's whole life and to an entire culture," he murmurs. "We're really no different in this country. The American Medical Association no longer classifies homosexuality as a mental disorder, but that happened only a few years back. The gay rights movement is picking up steam, but folks like Anita Bryant are kicking up a fuss. I wonder if it ever gets better."

Shaking my head, I retort, "Not until they repeal stupid, out-of-date laws like the morals charge accusations still used to rake people in throughout the United States as well as broader sections of the Penal Code like Paragraph 175. Do you know that the slime-ass Commies in East Germany actually threw the law out in 1969? What the hell is the West German government waiting for, some kind of fuckin' reunification with the Soviet sector?"

We exhaust that topic and move on to current triumphs and woes. I let Lucas in on a rumor I heard that they are thinking of producing a blockbuster disco movie starring none other than John Travolta. Lucas tells me about his latest case and how the opposing counsel is trying to settle a multimillion dollar suit out of court. A deal is evidently on the table and hasn't been rejected yet. The moon is silvery as we order a third round of drinks, and my backside begins to quiver from the cold, damp air, sending a chill through me. My ass never fully recovered from the "workouts" of the past and I'm still sensitive to extreme heat or cold.

Even though our lives intersect with luminaries of

stage, cinema, the fine arts, music and business, Lucas and I belong to our own mutual admiration society and never run out of things to say to one another or ways of expressing our undying love and affection. As we curl up in bed tonight, something occurs to me before I switch off the light. "You know, I could write a much better story than what was shown in that asinine movie."

"And so you have, my dear," Lucas purrs, holding me close and kissing me tenderly, "so you have."

**THE END**

**Memorial to gay and lesbian victims of Nazi persecution**

# If you enjoyed this book, you might also like:

Order from Amazon.com or amazon.co.uk

NOW AVAILABLE In KINDLE FORMAT!

See all available titles from this author:

http://crowbird52.wix.com/rodionrebenyar

## ABOUT THE AUTHOR

**RODION REBENYAR** is the pseudonym of a Sacramento-based author and poet. He published his first collection entitled ***BOYS ON PURPOSE: A Collection of Poems, Prose and Short Stories with Decidedly Gay Overtones*** in 2011.

This was followed by a full length novel, **THE CHOICES WE MADE: Story of Gay Friendship, Love and Tragedy** in 2014. Later that year, he published **FELLOW TRAVELLER: Whimsical Poems, Prose and Short Stories about a Gay Man's Adventures**.

At the beginning of 2015 **FIGHTING FOR LUCHO: A Gay Man's Struggle Begins**, the first book of a trilogy appeared. In July of the same year he released **WILLIAM GERHARDT: A Story Largely Untold,** Books Two and Three of the trilogy should be available no later than the end of 2017.

He is currently working on **KENJI WANTS OUT** and **MALE BRIEFS: Short Stories with a Homoerotic Bent.**

For more on this author (or to "Like" on Facebook):

**http://crowbird52.wix.com/rodionrebenyar**

Made in the USA
Columbia, SC
13 March 2022